WHERE SECRETS LIE

SECRETS: BOOK THREE

LEANNE WOOD

Book 3: Secrets Trilogy

Secrets

CHAPTER ONE

Justice Thomas Jacob Carmichael of the New South Wales Supreme Court had witnessed a great deal since being sworn in as a judge. His contribution to the legal profession was extensive and he possessed a wealth of knowledge and experience; an in depth knowledge attained over many decades. During his time at the Supreme Court he had presided over many prominent cases, yet no case had ever presented such drastic and shocking evidence as that now before him.

Wearing a scarlet robe and hood, trimmed with silk together with an accompanying bench wig that concealed his hair and extended over his shoulders, he looked over the courtroom with a discerning eye. His appearance signified the seriousness of the court proceedings. The traditional garb imbuing a sense of solemnity, respect and dignity of the law. Inhaling deeply, he cleared his throat before addressing the court.

It was the final day of the sentencing hearing and I just wanted for it to be over.

Standing in the dock dressed in a black suit and tie the defendant remained closemouthed. His head tilted forward, eyes facing the floor.

Crown prosecutor Chester Ryan was the first to speak. He told the court the murder of one victim was premeditated, while the other murder was simply a case of the victim being in the wrong place at the wrong time. Stating the defendant should be given life imprisonment and referring to police interviews with the prisoner it was revealed the attack on the third victim, was also intentional. A deliberate attempt to cover up the previous murders. Had police not arrived at the scene when they did, circumstances would have been very different. A psychiatrist called by the Crown, Dr. Zavian Cooper said the defendant suffered from no more than mild depression and given his predicament that was to be expected. In terms of mental impairment, he did not believe there were any other diagnosable disorders.

The court then heard from Detective Superintendent Beau Bailey, a seasoned member of the Major Crimes Squad who confessed he was personally troubled by the circumstances surrounding the murders.

In a bizarre twist as many of the horrific details of the crime emerged, he revealed the discovery of a confession police located at the crime scene. A hand written note, linking two of the victims to a cold case that had baffled police for over six decades. This case involving the disappearance of a husband and wife, Reginald and Eleanor Rumming. The pair had vanished without a trace on Christmas Eve in 1939 and despite the best efforts by authorities, the case had remained unsolved. The prosecution believed it was this ghastly declaration of guilt that ultimately led to the death of both victims, who they claimed sought to expose the truth. Detective Superintendent Bailey said he thought nothing would really surprise him after being in the Major Crimes Squad for such a long time, but this had. It was an explosive finding.

In graphic detail, he described how when police arrived at the scene they had been confronted by the accused brandishing a small sabina sword, its blade dripping with blood. The accused was covered in blood and repeatedly screamed out, "I am the gatekeeper!" Police were able to apprehend him without incident and he was taken into custody where he gave a chilling confession, which included the final tragic moments of the victims' lives. Listening to the detail I felt as though I would be sick. I just wanted it all to be over.

As the only surviving victim of this violent crime I had the chance to express to the court and to the offender how the crime had affected me. I knew taking the stand would be extremely difficult, but I also knew victim impact statements would be considered during sentencing. *Sometimes we must face our demons so that we can move forward*, I thought.

It was imperative my statement touch on the physical and emotional effects of the defendant's actions; the impact on my daily life and the pain I had suffered. Putting everything in writing was crucial as I wanted him condemned to spend the rest of his days behind bars. To never see the light of day. In my mind he was nothing more than a measly parasite, who should have been squashed out of existence.

The prosecutor signalled. I would soon be called to take the stand. Sitting still I began to feel nauseated and dizzy. Looking downwards to the papers clutched between my fingers, I noticed my palms had become sweaty. I became concerned at my ability to read my words.

Swallowing hard, I focused on the thought; tomorrow would be the first day of the rest of my life. But first I would have to survive today. I would survive today. I would take the stand and read my victim statement.

My time had come. Sitting up before everyone I looked nervously over the courtroom, momentarily gazing at the defendant. He appeared lost in the proceedings. For a second I felt great pity. He called himself, "the gatekeeper" and I had survived my harrowing ordeal. I knew I was far greater than he could ever dream. I knew he would never beat me. I cleared my throat. I began to read.

"Nobody can truly understand how I feel. The trauma I have suffered…"

Hesitating for a moment I gasped for air. Unsure if I could go on. I could feel the warmth of a tear in the corner of my eye. A wave of nausea. I inhaled deeply. A twinge tickled my nostrils. Pushing myself back in the chair I felt its cold and hard surface; it reminded me why I was there. I was there to do a job. I was not sitting there to recite a warm and fuzzy tale. This was no gathering of friends. I had a duty to perform. I continued. "I first came in contact with the defendant when I was upstairs in the house with one of the victims. Hearing a noise we went to investigate and that was when the defendant lunged out of the darkness and struck his first victim knocking him to the floor. The defendant was screaming, 'I am the gatekeeper!' as he attacked furiously. Repeatedly kicking the victim again and again, while he was lying on the floor. Frozen, I tried to yell but couldn't. I stumbled back. In the darkness. I watched on in horror. The defendant slammed the door to the room behind him. He held us hostage. I was terrified. He just kept yelling. 'I am the gatekeeper! I am the gatekeeper!'He looked possessed. We were trapped. Trapped in the same room with him. He kept pacing back and forth. Thrusting a sword in front of my face. I pleaded with him to let us go. That was when I heard someone call from downstairs. I heard footsteps coming up the stairs. The defendant threw the door open. He charged out with his sword in hand. Again screaming, 'I am the gatekeeper!' He must have hit the other victim with extreme force. I heard a huge thud. I crawled out of the room. I peeked downstairs. Blood. I saw so much blood. It pooled at the base of the stairs. A body covered in blood. The defendant was standing over the body. He was holding the sword. It was covered in blood. He turned his attention towards me. I feared I would be next. I scampered back to the room. The defendant said nothing as he approached. He just pulled the door closed locking the two of us inside. Footsteps indicated he had headed back downstairs. I tried in vain to render first aid to the first victim. I believed the two of us may have been able to over power this madman. But, he was unresponsive. Seconds later, I heard a whacking noise. Like the resounding blows you hear when a butcher is cutting up a side of beef. I was petrified. I tried to escape through the window. But it was sealed closed. All was hopeless."

Breaking down I stammered and stuttered as I struggled with my words. Clenching my fist I tried to pull myself together. Nothing could stop my cascading tears as I described how prior to my attack I had witnessed the defendant murder two others. His actions seemingly unprovoked.

Pulling myself together I continued to describe my version of events and the fear the defendant had instilled. I revealed the weeping scar on my torso. A scar I would carry for the rest of my life. Describing how in the final stages on that day, I had been attacked by the defendant who wielded a sword. The sharp pain I felt in my side. How when I looked down, I could see blood was beginning to soak my shirt. I felt the pain intensify.

I described my inability to sleep. The fear of closing my eyes. How every time I closed my eyes I could see them lying there. Their bodies covered in blood. Hearing the sirens and in a desperate attempt to escape I knocked the defendant to the ground, before fleeing out of the front door where I was met by police. The defendant charging out of the same door moments later. The sword in his hands.

Overcome by emotion I broke down into tears. My internal trembling had escaped. I had become visibly shaken. My hands trembling. I retrieved a tissue to wipe my tear soaked eyes and running nose. My sobbing echoed around the silent courtroom. Taking a deep breath I felt as though a plastic bag had been placed over my head, which forced me to gasp for air.

"E-e-e-ev-ev-er-every   m-m-m-mor-mor-morn-ing when I w-w-w-wake, I have to r-r-r-re-remind m-m-m-m-my-my-my-my-myself I am s-s-s-sa-sa-sa-sa-safe."

Releasing a loud sigh I became paralysed by the tragic feeling of isolation. Overwhelmed by emotion. My struggles were endless. I tripped up and over words. Words were no longer being read from my statement. For written words lacked the emotion I was so desperate to convey. They could not express what my heart felt. The undeniable loathing. Pen strokes on paper were simply small black lines that formed words. My writing, commenced with oversized capitals. I hung onto all curvy letters giving my g's extra long hooks that terminated in great tails. My statement was cursive and print all mixed together, it was big and small. Messy and jagged. Disjointed sentences and random thoughts could never come close to summing up my sense of pain. I wanted to yell, to scream, to release every profanity that came to mind. He was an oxygen thief, a waste of skin and space, a low life scum sucker, a maggot who deserved nothing more than to be squashed beneath the sole of a shoe. How could the court be offended if I let fly with a few profanities? My motivation in voicing these words would not be to insult or incite hatred but to express what I strongly believed and felt. I wanted the defendant to feel the lowest of the low.

Lowering my head I again looked down at my papers. My words appearednothing more than a blurry horrible mess, scribblesthat resembled those of a three year old. Placing my papers onto my lap I stared towards the Judge wondering how the court could expect me to comply with restraint, to withhold expressing my anger. How could hurt and pain be communicated without it's accompanying blame.

I could feel the tension in my forehead, the raising of my eyebrows. A sharp pain ached from the inside of my lower right lip, which I inadvertently bit while floundering like a fish out of water. Justice Carmichael looked upon me with gentle eyes. I could hear my breath, it had become rapid and I feared I would hyperventilate and faint as I experienced a tingling sensation in my hands, accompanied by dizziness and chest pain.

"Take your time," he urged.

I nodded. *Oh my god, I need a bag! Someone get me a paper bag!* I thought in a panic. My eyes darted around the courtroom looking for assistance. But there was no paper bag and no assistance. Just silence and staring eyes. Cupping my hand over my nose and mouth I sounded like puffing Billy, the steam train chugging around the mountain. Panting, huffing and puffing. Would this feeling of dread never end?

Picking up the glass of water I took a sip. I was not thirsty but needed to wash away the metallic taste of blood that filled my mouth, before I could continue. Eventually, I regained my composure and was able to go on. "I so desperately want my life back. I no longer live. I simply exist. I fear. My life is fear. Not the kind of fear one feels when they see a spider. This is all consuming. It attacks furiously. It is unrelenting.It's a fear that invades my every thought. Affects my every action. Restricting. Smothering. It's a fear that has extinguished any glimmer of hope for happiness, any sense of being able to breathe without restriction, to live as I once thought possible."

My appeal was emotional. My eyes glazed over by tears. The court remained deadly silent to my quivering voice. Within a matter of seconds I was again floundering with emotion. I closed my eyes only to be greeted by the haunting images I prayed would disappear. Tears escaped my eyes. The cascading warmth reminded me of the warmth of blood. I existed in an inescapable nightmare. For my boogeyman had a name. He had a face and if one was game enough, they could even touch him. I could not escape the images that were burnt so deeply within my mind by simply opening my eyes.

"My fear is real. I fear for my life should the defendant be given anything other than life behind bars!" I blurted, pausing for a moment shocked by the strength and loudness of my voice.My words were clear and forceful. Beads of sweat decorated my forehead and upper lip. My chest felt as though it would burst.

"I know it is nearly impossible for you all to fathom what has transpired over recent months. The personal loss I have endured. Witnessing two brutal murders has had a devastating effect. Deep down, I am still hurting. I am not sure I will ever recover. I have lost those I love. I want them back. The thing I miss most is not being able to talk to them. As humans we are creatures of habit. I want to do things as I had done them before. I keep forgetting we can no longer talk. When I pick up the telephone I expect to hear their voice. When I open the door to my home I expect I will see them standing before me. I don't want them to be gone. I want them back. But, it was not possible.All of my days are now filled with gloom, hopelessness, anger, depression and tears. Please....I beg of you…this parasite deserves to be locked away for the rest of his life, please!"

With those last words my time on the stand was over. These proceedings simply meant someone was finally being brought to justice. That alone, would not ease my pain. Sentencing would not erase the memories of my trauma. The vivid images of blood over everything that I could see clearly in my mind. I would continue to be haunted by flashbacks. My anxiety would not disappear. Nor would my concentration improve.

Police and autopsy findings supported my story. Blood was spattered and smeared throughout the house. A pool of blood at the base of the stairs was not fully congealed. It had only dried at the edges. The dismembered remains of one victim were found under the house. The second victim, also discovered under the house had wounds consistent with a series of blunt force trauma injuries to the jaw and back of the skull. These findings suggested he had been struck several times and stomped on whilst on the ground. Broken bones in his hands and bruising to his knuckles, suggested the victim struggled for a period of time. Several defensive wounds indicated he did not die without a fight. Numerous broken bones would have rendered him immobilised. The final blow being a stab wound to the chest. Both victims suffered horrific deaths.

After a short recess the defence counsel, Elliott McGitten presented what he believed were mitigating circumstances. It was his belief the defendant suffered from a substantial impairment by abnormality of mind or diminished responsibility. The expression, 'abnormality of mind' covered the mind's activities in all its aspects, not only the perception of physical acts and matters and the ability to form rational judgment, whether an act is right or wrong. It also covered the ability of an individual to exercise will power and to control physical acts in accordance with rational judgment. Listening to this defence made me feel sick. If this legal argument were believed, the defendant would be acquitted of murder and found guilty of manslaughter. Manslaughter carried a far more lenient sentence; it was not something I wanted to hear. The question was not whether the defendant did not resist the impulse but whether the defendant could not resist the impulse. He also insisted the defendant showed signs of remorse stating, "he knows the pain he has caused, his guilty plea is a sign of remorse." The defence psychiatrist, Dr. Olivia Mitchell diagnosed the defendant with aspergers and severe depression, making it difficult for him to foresee the consequences of his actions. Explaining individuals with aspergers appear to be indifferent to others. They are unable to read social cues, appear to lack empathy and avoid eye contact under pressure. She claimed these were all visible symptoms. The defendant also lacked the ability to distinguish the difference between literal and metaphorical speech, struggled to hold a two-way conversation, had poor listening skills and was honest to the extent of bluntness. This honesty was reflected in his admission to the crimes, as was his extreme anxiety and his obsessive behaviour.

I felt like jumping up from where I sat and screaming out, it was all bullshit but thankfully I was able to contain my emotions and finally they shut up.

The Judge called for another recess. I was fuming. I stormed out of the court. I paced back and forth. I watched the time. Waiting to be called back inside. My nerves mounting. My nausea returned. I was sweating. I could feel the perspiration seeping from my underarm, running down my torso. The court room door thrust open. The judge was returning. A sentence would be determined. I dashed back inside.

Inhaling deeply, the Judge cleared his throat before addressing the court.

"Will the defendant please stand."

Watching intently as he followed instructions I wondered if he would display any sense of remorse. Besides entering a guilty plea he had remained silent, expressionless. Swallowing hard, I released a loud sigh and found myself crossing my fingers while I prayed for a harsh sentence. The Judge continued.

"You have pleaded guilty and been convicted of two counts of murder and one count of grievous bodily harm with intent to murder. In sentencing you I have weighed up several things. Having heard what the medical witnesses have said and knowing what you did and what you said from the evidence before me certain questions must be answered. One question is whether the court accepts you lacked the ability to exercise will power to control what you did. Not whether you did not resist the impulse, but whether you could not resist the impulse. Having heard your confession, one can only describe the severity of your crimes as totally reprehensible and amongst the most brutal, heinous and barbaric. When taking into account your mental state at the time of your crimes, I can not accept the mitigating circumstances presented."

Hearing those words I clenched both fists and released a whispered cheer, "Yes." This murdering bastard was going to get what he deserved. Closing my eyes I prayed, I begged for God to listen, "Please, please, please." Opening my eyes I focussed on every word. I watched Justice Thomas Jacob Carmichael's mouth as he spoke. This man was a smart man. A stupid person did not become a Judge. He had to get it right. Surely he would get it right. A huge lump entered my throat. I swallowed hard. Doubt entered my mind. Legal arguments had worked for other offenders. Legal loop holes had seen many repeat offenders return to the streets. Australia's track record in keeping perpetrators of crimes off the streets was not so great. Convicted murderers roamed our streets. Convicted paedophiles who ruined the innocent lives of young children were out and about in a couple of years. Our legal system was a joke. Nothing was guaranteed until the final sentence was read. The courtroom was silent. People sat straight backed on their chairs. In the rear of the court reporters gathered taking notes. A sketch artist glanced furiously back and forth between the defendant and his clip board. It may have been possible for him to depict a likeness but no drawing would encapsulate the immense pain and tension experienced. Clenching my fists I could feel my fingernails as they embedded into my sweaty palms.

My focus intense. My eyes on the Judge. His lips pressed firmly together as he paused to take breath. He appeared in slow motion. Everything and everyone around him became a darkened blur. Again, I begged for God to listen, "Please, please, please." I leaned forward. I held my breath. Heat. I was burning up. I could no longer feel the hard wooden chair beneath my body. Just heat. It was as if time was standing still. Everything suspended. Would he say the words I longed to hear? His eyes were staring. His forehead furrowed. His nose twitched. His cheeks slightly blushed. Were they a reflection of the courtroom heating turned up or the inner burning rage he felt towards this low life? At last he spoke again.

"I accept the Crown has proven you acted with the intention to kill and with a reckless indifference to human life. Meaning you foresaw the probability that death would result from your act. In sentencing I must take into consideration the high risk you represent to society. Having done this, it is not possible to grant you any discount for pleading guilty. It is the belief of the court, this early plea and cooperation with police was purely because you knew the evidence was overwhelming. Therefore, in respect of these crimes and after taking into account submissions made and having regard for the current law, I sentence you to imprisonment for life without possibility of parole."

Members of the courtroom could be heard cheering, sobbing and whispering, "Yes," as the life sentence was handed down. Shaking uncontrollably I burst into tears. The killings had stunned Sydney residents. This bastard had got what he deserved.

Rocking back and forth he showed no emotion as his sentence was read out and finally he was led away.

The gentle clinking noise from his handcuffs fading as he disappeared from the courtroom.

Justice Carmichael's words signified the end of a gruelling two weeks in which the court heard details of the sequence of events that led to the murders.

Unable to contain my emotions, I wept and clapped as the defendant was led away. The sentence was like music to my ears. While it would never erase my pain, it signified the culmination of about six months of heartache and agony. Another chapter of my life was closing; I would be able to move forward hindrance free.

CHAPTER TWO

For nights after Claire passed away, Ben would wander out to the backyard and gaze up at the stars talking to her. He wanted for her to give him a sign, any sign to indicate she was still near. His grandmother had left instructions. Claire, his mother had gone leaving him nothing. It was a time of great turmoil. He wondered if she was reunited with his grandmother, Queenie. Everything appeared ruined. He was furious and needed someone to blame. This wasn't supposed to happen. Unable to completely come to terms with recently losing his grandmother, now he was supposed to accept his mother, his Princess was gone. Someone needed to be held accountable. Accidents just didn't happen. His father was supposed to protect them. He had failed in his duty. No wonder his grandmother cautioned him about his father.

It was he who had broken the news. He claimed she had been involved in a car accident. He had failed to be by her side. Ben wondered if his father was hiding something. Had he played a part in her demise? Since his grandmother's death only months ago he had witnessed increasing tension between his parents, which made him wonder if it was the underlying work from the evil forces his grandmother had warned him about.

For years she had educated Ben about Lord Antony the evil warrior, who was so convincingly disguised as his father. Had Lord Antony picked this as a time of weakness? Was this the time in which he would make his move to destroy the royal lineage his grandmother had spoke of? His grandmother had been his protector; she had been his mother's protector. He had held her secrets close to his chest and their loving bond close to his heart. Ben was not prepared to let this all slip away.

It all happened late on a Thursday afternoon. Walking through the front door Ben had no idea of the tragic news he would soon struggle to comprehend. Hearing a sobbing noise emanating from the lounge room, he discovered his father hunched over sitting on the lounge. A blubbering mess. Immediately he went to his side to find out what was going on. His mother was nowhere to be seen; he hadn't seen her for days.

"What's happened?" Ben questioned.

"It's your mother, it was a car accident."

"How, how did she have a car accident, where is she?"

"I don't know, I wasn't there?"

"Why, why weren't you there?" Ben asked raising his voice.

"Why are you interrogating me? I told you I don't know," Anthony replied abruptly, shaking his head.

"Where is she? Where is mum?"

"She has gone…" Anthony burst into tears as the words escaped his lips.

"Where, where has she gone?" Ben yelled grabbing him by the shoulder. "What do you mean gone?"

Anthony raised his head. His look told Ben something devastating had happened. He watched his father's lips quiver as he delivered the news.

"She's…dead!" he howled in agony.

"You're wrong, it can't be! You should have been there! Why weren't you there? It's your fault! You drove her away! You and your arguing drove her away!" Ben screamed.

Staring with mournful eyes Anthony sobbed into his handkerchief.Reaching out he tried to embrace Ben. His words made his son sick and so Ben stepped back shaking his head.

"No! No! No!" he stammered, "it's not true, I don't believe you!"

But it was true. Ben's mother was no longer and he couldn't bear to look at his father. Anthony and Ben were like salt and pepper, they may have belonged on the same table but they were nothing alike. It was Claire who had held their family together. Filled with rage Ben turned his back and retreated to his bedroom.

Lying on his bed he buried his face into his pillow as he wailed with pain. Someone needed to be held accountable. He blamed his father. He blamed God. He blamed everybody and everything. Someone needed to pay. There was no clear pattern to his thoughts and feelings. Disbelief, denial, anger, heartache and despair followed by resignation and a calm acceptance. If his mother's death were the result of evil forces then he would not let them destroy any further. His grandmother used to tell him it was important to keep your friends close, but your enemy closer; he had no reason to doubt her words. He believed in his grandmother and everything she told him. There was no logical reason for him to think she would lie, her words were gospel.

After all, Queenie knew best; it was vital for Ben to maintain his show of strength. To display weakness would make him vulnerable. He needed to return to his father. Heneeded to assess the situation. Only once this was done, would he be in a position to take control. He needed to take control.

It was imperative he maintained his faith in Queenie's words.

Finding his father a blubbering mess, Ben wondered if he was acting. Did he really feel pain and loss? If it were a facade, then Ben would have to go along with it. Nothing would take away his devastation but no one; not even his father would destroy his right to rule. It was his destiny to rule, after all he was Lord Benami. His Queen had spoken.

Sitting together they embraced. Ben could sense his father's pain and believed it to be true. Maybe, he did love his mother as he claimed. But if that were the case, why would his grandmother say he was at the ready to destroy? It was crucial he remain on guard. He could not doubt the words his grandmother spoke, yet he could not abandon the one person who remained by his side. They had suffered a great loss, a devastating loss; both experienced an emptiness that would be hard if not impossible to fill.

Claire's death did not come after a long and suffering illness. It was not anticipated. There had been no time to prepare or gradually absorb the realism of a dramatically changed world. Overwhelmed by a sense of bewilderment, Ben began to feel anger boil from inside. Life wasn't fair; she had done no wrong. His mum was loving and kind and caring. She was healthy and in the prime of her life, but sometimes life wasn't fair. Life was life and it could be gone at any moment. For any reason. Bursting into tears Ben wrapped his arms around his father recalling the happier times they had shared. Their recent holiday on the Hawkesbury River, the joking and laughter. A roller coaster of emotions were experienced by themboth, laughing about things they used to do and moments later breaking into tears. Sitting next to his father Ben realised it was the closest they had been in a long time. He did care about his father. Family was extremely important. His grandmother had always stressed the importance of protecting your family and the family name at all costs.

Ben believed losing his mother, in many ways was like falling over when running. Initially, he experienced shock and required time to acknowledge his pain. But eventually, he knew he may pick himself up.Like with some falls, it may take awhile before he was ready to get back up again. There was no time limit for healing and acceptance. Ben also knew, how important it was to seek out support if required. With time, he would start walking again. Eventually, he would return to full speed running. Life would always continue to move forward. Taking each moment as it came was the only way.

Confusion would eventually be replaced by calm. Time would heal all his wounds. His memories would never disappear.

CHAPTER THREE

Separating his fingers Ben felt the soft string release from his grasp. Looking skyward, he watched as his bright purple balloon joined the others gently drifting upwards. Floating away, dancing in the breeze towards the heavens where his mother and beloved Queenie lay waiting.

They had specifically selected brightly coloured balloons, to represent Claire's vibrant life and personality. They were sure she would have loved their choices. Canary yellow was chosen as it was the colour of the first car Claire had owned. Golden orange resembled the sunsets she deeply admired. Scarlet red represented the love and passion she possessed, along with the lipstick she wore. Deep cobalt blue matched the ocean she adored swimming in. Emerald green for the grass they would picnic on as a family. And of course bright amethyst purple; her favourite colour.

Anthony stood next to Ben, head tilted back with his hands firmly placed on his hips. He too was looking upwards, watching intently. Returning his focus to the sky Ben watched as the balloons appeared smaller and smaller. Floating, further and further off into the distance. The only thought that infiltrated his mind was his wondering where the balloons' journey would end. Would they continue to climb so they may be touched by an angel before falling back to earth? Time appeared to stand still, not a sound could be heard. It didn't seem long before their colours became unrecognisable. Soon after, they resembled black dots. Gradually, they became smaller and smaller until finally without even a blink of the eye, they were gone.

It was a clear day; the warmth of the sun cloaked Ben's body in a soothing embrace. The powder blue sky with only a few cotton ball clouds scattered on the horizon provided an amazing backdrop for their emotional release. Anthony was a wreck, tears danced on his cheeks glistening in the sun. His sadness flowing down his face. He told Ben Claire's funeral gave them all the chance to say goodbye, I love you, I will always remember you and I am sorry. He said he knew Claire would be up in heaven waiting to hear his words. He insisted the day was about celebrating Claire. Her existence in this world. The time they spent together. Sharing recollections of fun times and times they had that were funny and memorable. It was a time of reflection. Ben didn't share his father's views about saying goodbye. He believed saying good bye was reserved for those occasions when you clearly knew you would not see the person again. Ben was confident he would see his mother again, that she, Queenie and he would be reunited. He did not say goodbye.

Rebecca, their next door neighbour was present. It was a small funeral and she was undeniably shaken by Claire's death. Claire and Rebecca had shared a close friendship for many years. Both were caring individuals and so Rebecca assured both Anthony and Ben that everything would be okay. She had promised Claire she would look after the men in her life should anything ever happen to her.

"Your mother's love will live on in your memories even though she has gone, her love will remain forever," she said. Her words offered comfort. Yet still, Ben waited for his own sign to be delivered. He was sure she would send a sign. She had to send a sign. How could he accept that she would not?

Placing his arm around Anthony's shoulder Ben gave him a half smile, "It's going to be okay dad, we will get through this…"

"Yep, yep," he murmured.

"We will dad, you will see…" he paused.

Anthony looked lost, his blank expression left Ben feeling his father's actions could be somewhat unpredictable.

"In time things will be as intended," Ben said.

Ben wasn't sure how things were meant to be; he didn't know why he had said they would be as intended. The only thing he knew was he had to remain close to his father; the person who was responsible for placing food on his table. Without his father, there was no moving forward.

With all the formalities of the funeral over, it was a relatively quiet trip home. Rebecca drove while Anthony maintained his silence sitting in the front passenger seat. Ben sat in the back just as he had only months prior when they had attended Queenie's funeral. Looking out of the window everything appeared so surreal. Rebecca's words appeared muffled. She was reminiscing about moments she had shared with Claire. Chuckling every now and again she continued with her story telling. It was evident she missed her friend. Her stories conveyed the love and affection she held towards Claire.

"Do you remember the night we all went out on Sydney Harbour for New Years Eve? I think it would have been about three years ago. Oh the fireworks were spectacular, so much better than when you see them on TV." She paused as a smile danced across her face. She chuckled and continued.

"Remember that bloody gust of wind. Claire's hat flew straight off her head and into the water. She was screaming and jumping up and down like a mad woman. Screeching at the top of her lungs. Flapping her arms furiously. Demanding you jump in and save it."

Full bellied laughter replaced her chuckled words as Rebecca rocked back and forth in the driver's seat. Slapping one hand on her thigh. Reaching over she tapped Anthony on the leg and began to laugh like a confused hyena cross bred with a chicken on steroids. Anthony blushed. He moved his hand to where she had just touched his leg. He nodded but remained silent. He recalled the evening. With a split second of silence and stillness she was off again.

"Oh my god the look on your face!" she laughed hysterically. Tears ran down her face. Her voice a mixture of high pitch screeching combined with cackles and snorts, increasing in loudness.

"I thought you were going to end up in the drink!"

Suddenly her resonance lessened as she released a sigh. The seriousness in her voice reappeared as she looked towards Anthony.

"You were her hero, you know...her knight in shining armour. I didn't think you would have been able to retrieve her hat. But you did and she was so thankful and proud. She loved you so much, she loved the two of you with all her heart."

Rebecca's laughter was contagious. For those few moments all three joined in with the smiling and laughter as her story offered an emotional escape. Temporarily unburdening them from their sadness. Claire's memory would continue to live on within their hearts.

Ben returned to his gazing out the window as they passed shops. He watched as people strolled along the footpath. Everything looked so different. The people appeared smaller than they had previously. Squeezing his eyes shut he blinked several times. A strange sense overwhelmed his body. It was as if his eyes were playing tricks on him.

"Are they smaller?" he questioned.

Rebecca and Anthony asked what he was talking about.

"Everyone is small..." he chuckled.

"No they aren't, I think you need to rest your eyes are playing tricks on you," Anthony chuckled not realising the significance in Ben's words. There was no way anyone could have possibly predicted what was about to happen. For this was just the beginning.

CHAPTER FOUR

Anthony needed to keep busy. Distracted. Talking about Claire was too difficult, too upsetting. His one true love had been stolen, his world destroyed. He contemplated sorting through her things but it was all too hard, too soon, too painful. Their bedroom contained a floor to ceiling wardrobe. Anthony's clothes were squashed into a small section closest to the bedroom window. Claire's clothes were hung in accordance with colour and style throughout the remainder of the space. Over the years her section had grown. His section reduced to a small area of hanging space, three drawers and two shelves. Sliding the doors open Claire's clothes appeared well organised, perfectly ironed and ready to be worn again. It was all too hard, too soon, too painful. He slid the wardrobe doors closed. He collapsed on their bed. He burst into tears. Why had his wife been stolen? Where had she been coming from when she had been killed? Did it matter? The fact was nothing would change, she would never return.

Reaching across he pulled opened her bedside drawer. Slipping his hand inside he retrieved one of her nightshirts. Soft and silky to touch, pink and infused with the familiar scent of her favourite Calvin Klein, Euphoria perfume. Anthony held it to his face and began to sob. He inhaled her scent; he recalled her gentle touch, her soft lips, and her warm body. The nightshirt had the word *Paradise* across it with a colourful parrot and some hibiscus. Anthony had joked when she first wore it, stating Claire had been so much more than his piece of paradise. She was his world, his everything. And now his paradise was lost, gone forever. His world in chaos. The last few weeks had been a nightmare. Hunched up in a ball he began to shake and shiver. Uncontrollable wailing. Crying hysterically. He needed to keep busy but how? Without Claire he lacked direction and motivation. *Where had she been coming from when she had been killed?* He thought as he closed his eyes. Hugging her nightshirt he began stroking it as if it were her hair. Her soft, silky, gorgeous sandy brown wavy hair that sat just below her shoulders. In his minds eye, he could see her once again. He could see her beautiful hazel eyes. He longed for her touch, her gentle and loving touch. To feel her warmth. To embrace her. To tell her he loved her with all his heart and more, forever and a day plus more.

For Ben everything was so messed up and confusing. Lying on his bed he wanted for nothing more than to go back in time. Closing his eyes he transcended to a happier moment. Sitting next to the pond, he was listening intently as Queenie spoke. Watching her lips gently press together as she paused between her words. Each word invoked, created and shaped so many characters and events. She was an amazing storyteller, who at times left him mesmerised. He could listen to her for hours. Her words and the passion in which she spoke were like a marriage made in heaven.

His earliest recollections of their time together involved the telling of stories. Initially, this was with her reading words from books, pointing to pictures. Later, these books were discarded; Queenie needed no reference, for she could recite the most amazing stories. And Ben was lucky enough to not only be granted the privilege of listening to these stories but also prompted to shape and build on them. Guided by her gentle persuasions. Her stories became their stories; her adventures and crusades, became their deeply guarded secrets.

For Ben his grandmother was no ordinary grandmother; she was far from it. For she was in fact, a powerful Queen. It was imperative for his Queen to educate him in all facets that would enable him to protect her and all she represented. One basic fundamental his grandmother taught him from an early age was that everyone had a place in life. He lived in a world that possessed a tiered society structure. Just as in Feudal Japan his ancient culture had four basic levels. In fact, Queenie explained their secret society was far older than the Japanese were, for it had existed since the beginning of time when tracerteps ruled. Tracerteps were great warriors similar to the Samurai. They were powerful men who were revered. Acts of disobedience and boldness against them were punishable by death. Just as with the Samurai, members of lower class were required to bow and show respect to the tracerteps. If respect was refused, the tracerteps were legally entitled to chop off the recalcitrant person's head. Tracerteps ensured laws were upheld and different classes were maintained. According to his grandmother, Ben belonged to the highest class of all; The Golden Circle, this was reserved for very few, those destined for greatness.Below him was The Upper Class. Then there came, The Inhabitants. With the lowest level in status being, The Parasites. It was crucial everyone carried out the role they had been born to play. A member of the Golden Circle could not socialise with an Inhabitant. No more was it accepted that Upper Class members breed with a Parasite. Hidden within this tiering were evil warriors. They took on various forms, inconspicuously blending into everyday life. They were intent on destroying his Queen and all who served beneath her. Loyal servants of the Queen accepted dying to protect her name as a privilege and great honour. Offering your life to the Gods guaranteed you would be destined to return with far greater status in the next life. People were willing to do anything to obtain power. Sacrifices were essential.

Ben's grandmother carried a huge responsibility. Essentially by being Queen she was the pinnacle of society. She was the most powerful for she ran the show, the ruler of the world, enforcer of the laws and punisher of those who failed to obey. She had been born with great powers and an even greater obligation to ensure everything was as the almighty Gods commanded. It was imperative he held her secrets guarded. For he too was a chosen one, in fact according to his grandmother Ben was the powerful Lord Benami, son of the people. One day it would rest on his shoulders to be the protector of all, for the Gods had spoken, it was Benami who would carry on her amazing work.

Queenie told Ben how the Gods spoke to her regularly. The Gods had teased her with the brief sign of a successor years ago. But evil had banefully taken him from her. The Gods then decided to skip a generation declaring his mother, Princess Clara too weak. They knew they had to be patient. They knew he would appear with all the strength and tenacity required to fulfil such an important role. Secrecy was paramount, for weakness would open the paths to great evil transformations.

Ben's role was to protect the weak Princess Clara and the powerful yet aging Queen. His duty was to serve those above him and not to succumb to the ever-tempting cries from the evil forces. Queenie declared his father, whose name within the earthly realm was Anthony was really Lord Antony. It was imperative for Ben to be ever watchful and vigilant around Lord Antony, for he was a dark knight who possessed the ability to bounce between the role of protector and evil warrior. The evil forces had their claw securely embedded in Lord Antony and he could not be trusted.

Lord Antony had been born into the Upper Class and as such he was equal in status to Ben's mother Princess Clara. Queenie explained how she had been forced to lay with Edward, the grandfather he knew little about. This decision was made in an attempt to preserve the Golden Circle lineage. As the Queen, she was bound by an unwritten obligation to do anything and everything possible to protect her people. Unfortunately their laying together produced Claire with her endless shortcomings, a result of Edward's inferior breed. Queenie had hoped by limiting Edward's access to Princess Clara, the Princess's powers would improve over time and she would be granted access to the Golden Circle but that was not the case. It was only when Queenie began to age, she also realised keeping Princess Clara close to her further increased the chances of the evil warriors infiltrating the barriers she had so diligently constructed and maintained.This was when she granted permission for Lord Antony to marry Princess Clara, hoping with all her heart they would produce a Lord worthy of carrying on where she would one day leave off.

"My little Lord Benami," she would say with great delight holding Ben close to her chest, "I promise to always protect you and you must promise to always protect me."

"I will, I will!" he would reply, nodding his head. She had given him so much and so he would be forever in her debt.

Her stories left him with a feeling of greatness for he was the unblemished chosen one. His mother, while he looked up to her and showed her the respect she deserved, had been denied access to their inner circle of strength. Allowing her entry could render them defenceless. Exposing her vulnerability could destroy everything. Queenie explained how their magical world ran parallel to the life they encountered everyday on earth. Only a handful of souls were privileged enough to know the truth behind all.

Queenie's words were clear; she had proven her powers. There was no doubting her warnings and stated ramifications. The future of their existence depended on Ben.

Sunlight danced across the pond. Dragonflies hovered above the water surface and as he closed his eyes while listening to her every word, he was transformed into yet another magical moment in time.

The rays from the sun were penetrating his clothes, warming his body. Everything was so still and peaceful. Her voice was mesmerising. The closeness he felt towards her offered great comfort and support. Lying on the grass he nuzzled his cheek onto her lap. His neck cradled by her thigh as she sat propped up against the tall gum tree, stroking his hair. Soft and gentle strokes started along his hairline, massaging his scalp. Her fingers absorbing all his worries, gently twirling through his hair.

"I have a castle that has a secret garden," she whispered.

"But hush, like I have told you before, you must

promise this remains our secret or the dragons will not let me continue."

Opening his eyes in an instant, he frowned fearing she would stop.

Pointing to the dragonflies she waited for his response.

Eagerly, he nodded his head in agreement. Queenie had previously warned him how dragonflies were really dragons in disguise. If invoked by anger they would transform into their true giant form. Lashing out and destroying all who dared to go against the greater good of all. His belief being his grandmother represented the greater good of all. He knew and feared the repercussions of what would happen even if he dared whisper what she had so gallantly decided to share. The dragonflies were watching and evil forces surrounded them, they took on various forms.

"Look around you. Look at the dragonflies. Always remember the dragons. For they can see far better than any other. Study them as they study you."

Holding out her hand palm facing upward, Queenie instructed Ben to maintain stillness and to watch closely. He was amazed as she beckoned what appeared as an innocent dragonfly. She was silent, he was silent and while she nodded her head he maintained stillness as instructed. Hovering close to the water edge the dragonfly immediately changed the way it faced, turning its attention towards them. Queenie nodded again and without delay the dragonfly commenced what Ben could only describe as a spectacular aerial display, initially hovering proceeded by sudden upward and downward manoeuvres, flying backwards and even upside down, before it swooped to her welcoming palm.

"Wow!" he whispered with a huge smile on his face.

"Hush," she scolded, "his name is Darius. He is a dragon guard. Look at his eyes. Take note how his head consists almost entirely of his two huge compound eyes. See how they wrap around his head like an astronaut's helmet, giving him a 360-degree view. Remember my child, the dragons can see all. They can see flying towards you and they can see while flying away."

Ben could feel his eyes widening as he watched and wondered what would happen next.

"Thank you Darius my loyal servant, you may now go," she said with a smile.

In an instant, he was gone and Ben was left marvelling at the magical performance he had had the honour and privilege of witnessing.

Returning her glance towards him she continued with her instruction.

"You should never completely believe what you are told. To hold an element of doubt means you maintain your guard. To believe everything means you have dropped your guard. This can lead to an attack from the evil warriors."

Ben nodded acknowledging her words of warning. How could he disbelieve or disregard such an influential and commanding Queen, one who possessed great powers? She had dragonflies dancing to her commands. Her loyal servants surrounded them and he was sure they would report any suspicious activity. Evil warriors had the ability to watch their every move; they were at the ready.

"Now, what was I saying?" she asked with a puzzled look.

"You were telling me about your castle, it has a secret garden," he whispered.

She smiled as if she had just asked a rhetorical question. Her words merely a test of his listening abilities.

"Ah yes my castle. It's a magical place no one knows about, not even your mother," she said, cautiously glancing over her shoulder towards her house.

"Can you take me there?"

"Yes, I will take you there. But only if you promise never to tell anyone and I mean anyone, no matter what."

"I promise, I promise! Look, Look! I will even do a pinkie promise!"

Holding out his hand Ben offered his little finger as a sign he could be trusted.

"My little Lord Benami, how you make me smile!" Chuckling at his response, she wrapped her little finger around his. It was promise.

Flopping backwards his head found rest once again upon her thigh and she resumed stroking and playing with his hair. He was at peace and so he closed his eyes, knowing nothing could harm him even with the dragons hovering above. His Queen was his ultimate protector.

Ben carried so many wonderful memories of his grandmother. She was the best and he would never be able to completely encapsulate the appreciation, admiration, love and respect he felt towards her. He felt privileged to have her in his life. He considered it an honour to do as she requested. Even in his younger years she never treated him as a mere child. Both shared so much more than he could disclose, for they were amongst the elite few; the Gods had hand-picked them.

Opening his eyes, Ben released a loud sigh before stretching and yawning. So many wonderful memories filled his heart. Memories that would remain with him forever. Climbing off his bed he knelt down facing it before looking over his shoulder towards his closed door. Hearing no sound he slowly lifted his mattress, feeling around with his right hand while maintaining a close watch on his door. He was searching for the envelope Queenie had left. It was imperative their secrets remain guarded. Reading her words he felt great closeness. No one understood Queenie like he did.

My Dear Lord Benami,

I am so sorry I had to leave. Please know I love you with all my heart and one day we will be reunited. Until that day, I will miss you and I know you will make me proud. Be assured, I am never far away and I will always look over you.

This is your time now, your time to stand strong and to shine. The continued and unbroken existence of our Royal lineage is paramount. The future is in your hands. Do not be afraid, your power and destiny will surpass all challenges that may confront you. The dragon warriors will protect you andkeep me informed of all that transpires.

Recall all of my teachings. Listen for my voice and you will hear my instruction.

I know full well you will attain the greatness we spoke of, for greatness is your destiny.

Never forget our beliefs and values, your rite of passage to higher realms, for you are the one and only, the powerful Lord Benami. Your purpose is to serve our golden circle lineage that has survived since the tracerteps. It can not be destroyed. Serve us well and you will be rewarded with greatness.

Always remember what happens in the family stays in the family.

Until we meet again, stay strong and know I am always watching over you.

Love and hugs

Queenie

The envelope contained two extremely important letters. This letter. Her letter to him provided the reassurance Ben desperately needed. Since his mother handed it to him he would have read the words nearly one hundred times. Queenie's words offered hope for the future. Holding this letter to his chest Ben wanted for nothing more than to make his grandmother and mother proud. Queenie's secrets were safe, returning her letter to its hiding place he was confident he would do her words justice.

CHAPTER FIVE

Standing in the kitchen Anthony released a god almighty cry. In his hand he held a bundle of papers. Papers he had discovered on the day he found out his loving wife Moo had been killed in an accident.

"Secret life, fuck your secret life!" he yelled.

Looking at the papers there was no doubt in his mind that the pages would reveal some form of sinister content. Shirley Rumming had been his mother-in-law, a woman he had at times considered a thorn in his side and a manipulator. He despised the fact his son seemingly placed her up on a pedestal referring to her as Queenie. In Anthony's mind she was nowhere near resembling royalty, maybe the queen of deception, but that was as far as it went. She was a woman who preyed on the naive. And what worried him most of all was the impact this bitch of a woman had had on his son.

Calling Ben into the room he knew he had to confront him with his discovery.

"Have you seen this?" he asked.

Ben shook his head, "Nope!"

"Ben we need to be able to talk. I know you are hurting but I am your father and I am here for you. I didn't drive your mother away. This is what drove her away, your grandmother."

Clenching the papers within his hands there was no denying his burning rage.

"This is where it all stops, here with me. I am going to read this crap, I am going to see what the old bitch wanted people to know and I am going to make sure everyone knows her secrets. Secrets consume, they are burdens that weigh people down, dragging them down with every breath and they destroy. I look at this crap and I know in my heart this is in someway responsible for your mother's death. I am telling you Ben, your grandmother had a hand in your mother's death."

Ben stood silent. Listening to his father he knew it was no time to make comment. Accepting his father's words with a nod of his head would enable him to maintain peace without sacrificing his loyalty to his grandmother.

"Your grandmother is gone. Your mother has gone. It's just you and me now. We must stick together…" he paused, "are you listening to me?"

Nodding his head Ben again acknowledged his father's words. The love he felt towards his grandmother was powerful, his father's derogatory remarks cutting. Ben had been broken by the loss of his grandmother and more recently after his mother's death, he felt defeated. His energy drained, his deadpan eyes and stolid look reflected the heaviness in his heart.

"Is that all?" he asked in a monotone voice, "can I go now?"

"Yes, yes you can go, but I am telling you…this is not the last you are going to hear about this. I am going to get to the truth even if it kills me. Your mother's death will not be in vain!"

Looking towards his father he knew he meant what he had said. Turning around he stomped out of the room and down the hallway where he slammed his bedroom door. Cocooned inside, he wondered how far his father was really prepared to go. *Even if it kills me*, he thought. Was his father prepared to give up his own life in order to expose a secret? Maybe his grandmother was right. Maybe his father couldn't be trusted.

Ben's bedroom insulated him from the real world. Since Claire's death Anthony hadn't ventured anywhere near it. He wasn't aware its state reflected the turmoil his son was experiencing. Had he taken five seconds to see, he would have realised force was required to even pry the door open. The cause of resistance a mountain of dirty laundry stuffed up against it. Dirty socks, underwear, shirts and shorts all mixed in with an array of smelly sneakers and various other shoes. His unmade messed up bed had become home to scattered schoolbooks, an abandoned model of the solar system, an empty pencil case, pens, pencils and a pencil sharper along with discarded shavings.

It was a pigsty.

His once spotless desk, that stood on the opposite wall to his bed was overflowing with papers that had been written or scribbled on. Rulers, pens, markers, a broken blue stapler, two empty sticky tape dispensers, liquid paper and scissors accompanied these papers. Half-empty chip packets, apple cores and banana peels, together with dumped cans of soft drink and the remains of a cheese and Vegemite sandwich decorated in mould created a rotten stench capable of assaulting one's nostrils, while sending out a welcome invitation for vermin. This mayhem overflowed onto the floor and spread like a wild virus extending under his bed. Yet, for Ben this state of disarray was not viewed as vexatious or oppressive. His room was a place he could escape to.Comforted by the familiar humming sound of his fish tank filter, he had no pressing need to feed his fish or clean the green brown algae covering the tank walls. As his fish were gone. He had flushed them down the toilet.

Clambering over the clutter and mess he retrieved the sword his grandmother had wanted him to own. The sword was one thing he cared about as it reminded him of how important he was. Taking it in his hands he could feel the power. Closing his eyes while wielding it in the air he could not only hear the swoosh noise as its blade cut through the air but also his grandmother's voice. *Protect and serve!*

With Anthony immersed in his own grief and now fixated on finding out the truth behind Shirley's words, Ben had an open run on what he chose to do. Withdrawing from friends, building a world of seclusion in which he could fantasise about the stories he had been told was an easy option.

"I am Lord Benami!" he would declare, "the powerful Lord Benami!" Slashing the blade through the air his tirade would continue while the belief in his grandmother's stories strengthened.

"Mess with me and you will pay the ultimate price!"

Minutes and hours passed by. Both were deeply engrossed within their own worlds. Consumed by grief and anger at the events that had transpired. Their lives no longer fixed on the living, but transcending into thoughts about the departed.Conversation became limited and crossing paths generally occurred only at meal time.

Dishing up the evening meals Ben accused Anthony that the food placed in front of him tasted funny. Even prior to launching his accusations Anthony could sense something was wrong by the look on his son's face, after taking his first mouthful.

"What's wrong?" Anthony questioned studying Ben's face.

"This tastes weird!"

"Why?... Its spaghetti bolognaise."

"What did you put in it?...You put something in it?"

"What do you mean, I put something in it?... Of course I put something in it...I put many things in it, mince meat, tomatoes, capsicum, onion, mushroom, garlic... I made it like I normally do."

Screwing up his face Ben pushed the plate forward. "Yuck!"

"There is nothing wrong with it, it's nice," Anthony said in a raised voice, defending his cooking ability.

"It tastes funny!"

"Here have mine, mine is fine."

Shaking his head Ben glared at his father, believing something had been placed in his food.

Maybe it's poison, he thought.

"I know what you are doing!" his voice raised as his eyes stared.

"What are you talking about, you like spaghetti... here have mine and I will have yours!"

Pushing his plate forward Anthony grabbed Ben's plate and took a mouthful.

"There is nothing wrong with it, see!"

"I am not eating it! You eat it! I know what you are doing!"

Shoving his chair back he rose to his feet and placed his hands on his hips, standing firm in his defiance.

"I am not eating it and you can't make me eat it!"

Without another word he turned away from the table and stormed down the hallway towards his room.

"Ben, Ben come back here...there is nothing wrong with it, come back here!"

But Ben was gone. There was no use in talking for in his mind he was sure his father, the evil Lord Antony had placed some form of poison in his meal. Maybe his worst fears were coming true. Maybe Queenie was right. Anthony sat shaking his head. After a short moment of silence he resumed eating his dinner. Chasing after Ben he thought would get him nowhere, besides to him his dinner tasted nice and Ben's antics were not worth worrying about.

In his room Ben's paranoia continued. He was convinced his father had placed some form of poison in his dinner and no denying would change his mind. Reaching into his wardrobe he grabbed out some food he had hidden earlier. Tonight he would munch and crunch on salt and vinegar chips. Pulling at the top of the packet the seal released and out came the pungent waft of salty sourness. Salt and vinegar chips were among his favourite. Inhaling the spicy tang he admired the crinkle cut slithers of potato moreishness. Reaching in he grabbed one and placed it in his mouth. Suspended on his tongue with his mouth open just enough to allow in a small amount of air, he inhaled deeply sucking in the acetic fumes causing himself to cough and splutter. A smile came to his face as he bit down. Closing his eyes he listened, feeling it crunch between his teeth. Gently moving his tongue to direct its firm surface. His grinding action continued until such time the crunch noises disappeared. The pungent flavour vanished. His chip now soft and warm. Ingested to make room for the next. The combination of salt, sugar and fat made eating them alluring; they were addictive. The momentum in which he retrieved them increased, as did the number he placed in his mouth at one time. Munching, crunching, followed by a meltiness of potato mash until all that remained were crumbs in the bottom of the packet. Crumbs, that would be polished off by placing the packet to his mouth and up-ending it. This was the most successful means in ensuring every last morsel was gone. Licking his fingers his emotions turned to one of sadness. His mother loved salt and vinegar chips and he missed her more than ever.

Laying on his bed he could hear the gentle tapping of rain against his bedroom window. Weather reports had predicted severe storms to the north of Sydney. It was dark outside yet every so often the evening sky was lit up by lightning bolts and the house shook from the noise of rumbling thunder. Maybe the reports were wrong. Maybe they were going to be in for a wild night. An ominous bank of blackened storm clouds overshadowed Sydney, they were much closer than predicted.

CHAPTER SIX

A blood-curdling yell interrupts the suspended silence and resonates over the hilly surrounds. Down the grassy slopes, colliding with unseasonable thunder. A flash of lightning illuminates the night sky. More lightning follows. Lightning bolts streak across the sky. Their jagged lines resembling the violent actions of a mad man. Like beacons, they reveal the macabre results of an earlier happening.

The figure of an unknown person emerges from amongst the dark shadows of the trees and approaches the playground equipment in the gully. And as the wind increases in intensity, the merry-go-round begins to turn. Squeaking with each rotary motion. The gentle breeze has rapidly gained fury. Swings in the park react swaying back and forth, their changing movements resembling those of a conductor's arm motioning an increase in tempo. Another clap of thunder invites pelting rain. However, this does not deter the unknown person from their journey to the play equipment. Like someone possessed; they are on a mission. At the merry-go-round he watches as it spins before him, a lifeless mangled ball of soaked fur. Eyes and mouth agape as if releasing a silent howling scream.

"I told you I didn't like cats, but you didn't listen when I warned you to stay away!"

He continues speaking as it passes him by, carried by the momentum of the driving wind and rain.

"Why didn't you listen?"

Finally, he extends his arm bringing the merry-go-round to a sudden halt. Bending over he retrieves the ball of fur. Picking it up and pulling it towards his chest. He sits on the wooden planks, his feet on the ground anchoring all movement. The merry-go-round is still, its squeaking silenced.

The soft tortoise shell fur matted with blood.

Again he questions, "Why did you not heed my warnings?" His words sound remorseful. Yet, his actions are to the contrary. Releasing his hold he clutches the lifeless body between his hands extending his arms upward to the sky, as if performing a ritual. The lightning beckoning him to act.

In his hands he feels a mixture of warmth and coolness. Warmth from the flowing blood, that seeps from the lifeless cat. Coolness from the soaking rain. The liquids merge within his palms and flow down his arms. Their journey ends along his rain soaked body at the curve of his elbow. Falling to the ground they splatter between a mixture of mud and rubber mulch. He shows no regard for the life he so ruthlessly extinguished or concern for the consequences should he be found. For his mission is to appease the Gods. His act fundamentally about reinforcing the alliance between himself and his Queen.

"I am the gatekeeper, the powerful gatekeeper!" he yells.

Standing up, he again extends his arms holding the cat high as if offering it as a gift. An eerie stillness descends, a momentary silence. The rain stops.

"I am the gatekeeper, the powerful gatekeeper!"

His voice loud, forceful and assertive, collides with the distant sound of thunder, like a herd of wild horses stampeding through the next gully. The wind begins to gust initially in short waves. Each gust becomes more intense, wild and blustery. Erratic and squally, one-minute in his face the next pressing from behind. Leaning into the wind he struggles to see through the impenetrable curtain of water. A deluge has begun. A crash of thunder sends his heart pounding; the smell of wet rubber surrounding the swings lingers in his nostrils.

"I am the gatekeeper, the powerful gatekeeper!"

CHAPTER SEVEN

Ben woke in a lather of sweat. His body was trembling, his head pounding and heart racing. He had an inexplicable feeling something was terribly wrong. The dishevelled state of his doona and sheets indicated he had had a rough night. Throwing the bed covers to the floor he staggered over the piles of discarded clothes and junk stacked around his room and opened the blinds. The sunlight beamed through like a halogen torch being held centimetres from his face temporarily blinding him. Recoiling back he rubbed his eyes and tried to gain focus. Fine grains of sleep fell from the corner of his eyes as he yawned rubbing his face. He refocussed and looked again. Peering out of the window the street appeared desolate and quiet. His father's car was not in the drive, which left him believing he had gone to work. It was a Saturday morning. Something was dreadfully wrong, but he could not put his finger on it.

The bureau of meteorology had issued a severe weather warning for the night before. North of Sydney could expect to be hit by sustained gale force winds, heavy rain that could lead to flash flooding and unusually large surf waves were expected to cause dangerous conditions on the coast. The State Emergency Service advised people should move vehicles under cover or away from trees, secure loose items around property, stay indoors and away from windows while the conditions were severe. Individuals were also reminded they should never attempt to walk, ride or drive through flood water andthey should always keep clear of storm drains and creeks.

It was only in the light of the day that the damage was evident, the storm had travelled further south than expected. Ferocious winds had swept through leaving a path of destruction; broken limbs, splintered branches and scattered debris. Howling wind and rain battering against his window had woken Ben just after midnight. Flashes of lightning lit up the night sky, the cracking sound of thunder surrounded him. The gods were sending a message; something had angered them. His grandmother Queenie had always told him thunderstorms were a warning sign of things to come while driving rain pelted the earth in an attempt to cleanse infected souls.

Gazing up at the sky he noticed the absence of clouds. The heavens offered a clear powder blue canvas backdrop to what appeared a nice day. The tops of the trees swayed gently, indicating a slight breeze yet it looked hot. Over recent months the grass had changed from a deep rich green to tinged brown with scattered flecks of light green and ever increasing patches of dirt. The dryness of the grass delivered a crackling sound under foot.

Images of what he had been thinking moments before he woke flashed through his mind. He placed his left hand gently over his left ear. It felt hot and radiated a throbbing ache. When he opened and closed his jaw a burning sensation shot into his throat like a hot poker. A sharp pain accompanied his swallowing. He began to wonder had his experience just been a thought or was his discomfort the result of what he feared? Glancing back towards the sky his mind became full of suspicion. In his mind he believed evil forces had abducted him. They had implanted a tracking device inside his head, that would monitor all of his movements and feed off his vibrational responses. Immediately he became panicked. His breath became rapid. Frantically he stuck his finger in his ear. Twisting and turning it. Wiggling it back and forth. The coolness of his fingertip temporarily easing the biting heat from within. The evil warriors were his enemy, as was his fear. Fear had the ability to strike savage blows. It could feed off his paranoia, restrict his movements, strangle all hope and suffocate all sense of normality. Overwhelmed by apprehension he began to question the logic behind his haunting thoughts. They were preposterous. Completely contrary to what was considered common sense. Evil forces did not exist. People were evil, but evil forces? Shaking his head he began to argue with his thoughts. He stopped. Frozen. Staring. His heart racing. His eyes darting around the room. All was still. All was silent until…

"They are watching you."

A soft whisper entered his ears. Paralysed by panic he began to tremble. His feet anchored to the floor, his head turning in all directions trying to determine who had spoken. However no one was there. He was alone. The burning within his ear persisted. Shaking his head he continued to reassure himself he was alone and he had heard nothing. How could he hear someone, if no one was there? Placing his cool palms against his ears he closed his eyes and contemplated going back to bed. If he closed his eyes then maybe his ears would not play tricks on him. Besides there was no need to get up. He had no pressing engagement. The burning feeling was simply an ear infection.

"They are watching you," the hushed voice echoed.

Ben's eyes sprung open. Swallowing hard, his eyes

darted around the room. Still, no one was there. Shaking his head an unsettling feeling began to well from inside. Yet he could not tell what it was. Stumbling towards his bedroom door he glanced at his open wardrobe. Everything was hung as he remembered. No gaps or dark hidey-holes were evident in which someone could be concealed. It had to be his mind. Half asleep he had been hit by the blinding sun, shocked by the damage outside then struck by hundreds of tiny needles in his forehead. His head continued to pound. Headache tablets and food were crucial. The strange voices were just his mind playing tricks on him. Pulling his bedroom door open he moseyed out and along the quiet hallway running his fingers along the wall. His eyes following the tip of his index finger, his mind questioning whether the wall was flat and smooth or crooked and textured. Things did not seem right though he could not work out what. A sense of dread lurked in the shadows and followed him into the kitchen.

Reaching the kitchen he swung the door of the fridge open and peered in. A variety of condiments occupied the top shelf; vegemite, peanut butter, strawberry and raspberry jam, marmalade, cheese spread and honey. His decision was made, he had not had peanut butter and honey together for years. When he was younger he would buy half a bread roll with peanut butter and honey for morning tea at school. Always, it had to be the top of the roll and invariably he would have to reassure the canteen lady he wanted both together. Peanut butter and honey was a comfort food. The crunch of the nuts along with the sweetness of the honey would tantalise his taste buds. They were perfect together; alone honey was too sweet and peanut butter was far too pasty but together they were magic. Grabbing two slices of bread he placed them in the toaster, poured himself a fresh orange juice, fetched and swallowed a couple of headache tablets and then sat and waited for his toast to pop up. Closing his eyes his thoughts returned to his unsettled feeling and the weird events of the morning. All was still. All was silent. Even the air appeared neutral; it added neither warmth nor coolness to his body. A soft cracking sound radiated from the toaster as the mixed grains in his bread exploded in the heat. The ticking sound of the stained glass clock that hung on the kitchen wall above the window outshone the popping grains. Focusing on the ticking made him feel calm, it reminded him of his grandmother's house. She had owned a grandfather clock, that stood in her lounge room. Ben had spent so much time with his grandmother, the ticking of the clock brought back soothing tranquillity. Within minutes a gentle waft of golden brown toast crept into his nose. During one of his science classes Ben had learnt 216 seconds was the exact amount of time required to produce the perfect level of crispness; the ultimate balance of external crunch and internal softness to his toast. He had adjusted the controls on the toaster to achieve perfection and his father had been instructed not to play with the controls. Releasing a loud sigh he hoped his headache would ease and his breakfast would help to calm his concern. Maybe all he needed was food.

However, eating his breakfast only added to the sense of heaviness he felt. Apprehension and concern lingered, increasing his level of anxiety. It rolled in and over him like frightening, unstable and never-ending waves in the ocean. A sense that he was drowning in a dark and scary sea of fear made him close his eyes tightly as he prayed for peace and calm. What made him think of bizarre things? Why was he hearing voices? How was it his eyes saw weird things? Everything appeared so different, so strange, so overwhelming.

Returning to bed Ben felt so sad and so distressed. The juice, toast and pain killers had done nothing for his headache. The distraction of food did not stop his puzzling thoughts. Tears ran down his cheeks. His mind felt so twisted and confused. His heart started to pound and he became scared and paranoid. The voices he had heard were terrifying. Lying on the bed he stared towards the ceiling. Suddenly, he felt pressure on the top of his head. With his eyes open and staring he found himself in total darkness. Frantically he began blinking. Desperately rubbing his eyes. Terror and confusion, bizarre images and thoughts an individual experienced in nightmares invaded his mind. It was as if his mind was falling apart. He screamed aloud, "Help! Stop! Leave me alone." However no one heard and no one came.

Suddenly the light returned, he could see his familiar room. He could feel the soft bed below his trembling body. Looking around he wondered what had happened. His thoughts were jumbled; as if he was listening to multiple radio stations all at once that were not tuned properly. Lying still he tried to analyse his thoughts, but they made no sense. Climbing off his bed he returned his focus to the street outside. Peering through the window he became suspicious. Gazing across the street he studied the trees. Everything he looked at appeared in patterns. Every leaf clearly distinguishable but clearly separate from its neighbour. A strange sensation hovered round his head. His body felt light; as if he had the ability to float. Looking at the palms of his hands they appeared not as his own. Turning his hands over he noticed dirt under his fingernails, yet he could not recall how the dirt got there. Closing his eyes a feeling of great peace came over him. He could no longer feel the floor beneath his feet. His body appeared weightless, everything gently spinning around. Euphoric, his body rising, soaring upwards, moving about in a spirit world in addition to within the world in which his bedroom belonged. Simultaneously in a parallel universe, a world that offered great peace disconnected from the real world. He could see himself in a cocoon, safe and secure; one day he would emerge as a butterfly. Maybe not a butterfly but brighter; better than ever before and stronger. He would be untouchable, unstoppable. He had no concept of what was happening, only the notion all would be as it was expected to be. Opening his eyes the ethereal sensation disappeared and he returned his attention to the skies. Evil warriors had tried to infiltrate his mind but they had failed. His aching head began to ease, the heat from within his throbbing ear began to cool. The tracking device implanted inside his head began to dissolve. Queenie and the gods were looking over him. They would protect him. Everything would be fine, he just needed to be mindful of his father. He was sure his father was now two very distinct people. One was good; Anthony his father. The other was bad; the evil Lord Antony who would try to destroy him.

The concerning thoughts persisted even with his eyes open. He needed to be careful, evil could strike at any moment. Gathering some clothes he wandered to the bathroom. He hoped a shower would cleanse his soul, drown his paranoia and wash away his concern. Locking the bathroom door ensured he would be safe from attack.

CHAPTER EIGHT

Life was extremely difficult; Anthony's words rubbed Ben the wrong way. He hated school and despised his teachers. Fearing his actions would be viewed as a failure he worried what his grandmother would say if given the chance. She would never just meander along with the flow of things. She took charge of situations. He was concerned his inaction would displease her and resented the way in which his father claimed his grandmother was nothing more than a deceitful liar and manipulator.

It was time to take control of his destiny and Tynan James the school bully was clearly in his sights. He needed someone to teach him a lesson and that someone was going to be Ben. The school swimming carnival was where he would launch his attack. Tynan James was a parasite who instilled fear in the weak. Ben clearly believed he was the ruler of all and it was time he proved his power. His greatest fear was disappointing the gods and his beloved Queenie.

Walking along the side of the pool he noticed Tynan approaching. Smaller students veered out of his way.

"Hey Tynan!" he yelled, looking him up and down in disgust, "I am going to make you wish you were never born!"

Before Tynan had a chance to respond Ben's fist made contact with his ribs. Hunching over he could tell he had knocked the air out of his lungs. He could see the pain on his face as he clutched his belly before collapsing to his knees. Ben's job had only just begun. Glancing over his shoulder he checked to see if the coast was still clear. Several other students had gathered to watch and cheer. With Tynan overpowered and kneeling on the ground he seized the moment and launched his right foot into Tynan's chest propelling him into the pool, like a sack of potatoes. The onlookers cheered and encouraged more action. His fun was only beginning. Tynan hit the water with a loud splash, and Ben watched the bubbles rising to the surface. Floundering in the water Tynan finally came up for air. His tight curls sprung out like tiny springs. His clothes appeared oversized as they swayed in the water. Frantically he looked around trying to find his bearings.

"I am not finished with you!" roared Ben.

Leaping into the pool he grabbed Tynan's clothes and pulled him under, keeping his own head above the cool water. Thrashing about Tynan's arms struggled to reach the surface. His legs kicking furiously. More students gathered at the side of the pool giving high fives, cheering Ben on and rejoicing at Tynan's downfall. Releasing his grasp Ben offered Tynan a slight reprieve. He didn't want to kill him, just show him who had the power. Coughing and spluttering Tynan gasped for breath. His mouth wide open. His eyes blinking frantically. Fear was written all over his face. The taste of victory was Ben's. Taking a mouthful of the acrid smelling chlorine, Ben spat in Tynan's face. Raising his fist he gave a sinister smile, before punching him in the face several times. Tynan's nose exploded like a can of crushed tomatoes being hit by a hammer. Blood poured from his nostrils. Watching the water change colour, Ben felt satisfied he had dealt justice. He was pumped. His anger was raging. His adrenaline levels were so high at that point he could have punched his way through a brick wall.

"Ben White get out of that pool this instant!" Mrs. Claremont, the school counsellor bellowed.

He had been caught but he would have the last say, "Don't ever forget who is in charge!" he scoffed.

Swimming over to the edge he climbed out. He was satisfied. His job had been done. Students cheered as Mrs. Claremont ordered them to disperse. He was a hero. He was the ruler of all. The gods had spoken and Queenie would be proud.

Later that afternoon Anthony met Ben at the Principal's office; he was beyond disappointment or anger. Glaring at him he said nothing. He looked as furious as a raging bull on an anthill. His cheeks flushed, nostrils flared and his jaw tightly clenched.

Mr. Cartwright the school principal had not witnessed the attack on Tynan James. Yet, he spoke as if he had. Ben was sick of looking at him and became extremely enraged by his comments.

How dare he. Who does he think he is, sitting on the other side of the desk dictating to me what was right and what was wrong, he thought.

Mr. Cartwright possessed a look of superiority that infuriated him. Staring across the desk, Ben paid little attention to the words being spoken. Rather, he studied all the annoying physical features his principal possessed. The deep side part in his hair. The heavy framed coke bottle glasses he wore. His stumpy fingers that he tapped on the desk. Not forgetting his pants up to his chest.

All the while thinking about how badly he felt he was being treated, his anger building from within.

He should be thanking me for putting Tynan James in his place. After all, he is the principal; it is his job to control bullies. Everyone knows about Tynan James, kids donate lunches to him, they give him their pocket money and hand over homework without hesitation. Tynan James starts rumours, pushes, shoves, kicks, insults, threatens and embarrasses. His actions result in some kids being scared to go to school. No one dared to speak out about his actions for fear of repercussions. Mr Cartwright had failed in his job.

"You weren't there!" Ben snapped.

Anthony kicked him under the table. Ben was furious. It was impossible for Mr. Cartwright to make accusations as to what happened without witnessing the incident. Ben didn't care if he had spoken to Mrs. Claremont. It was his opinion Mr. Cartwright was making out he had witnessed everything and that was not the case.

"You four eyed duck face!" he screeched looking at his stunned reaction. The finger tapping stopped. "You old bastard you wouldn't know shit, even if you slipped in it!"

"That's enough Ben!" Anthony demanded.

Mr. Cartwright's eyes widened. Through his glasses they appeared like two huge golf balls. His nostrils flared and his lips puckered up like a cats' arse straining to release. His look resembled a mixture of a constipated cat and an angry duck and so Ben laughed.

"You insolent child!" he snapped, "I will not have a student speak in such a manner."

"I will not have a student speak in such a manner," Ben babbled mocking him.

"Ben that is enough!" Anthony demanded.

Rolling his eyes Ben pushed his tongue hard up against the roof of his mouth, clenching both his jaw and fists. His father may have appeared like a raging bull, but by this stage Ben was his red rag. The fiery red colour, a reflection of his inner burning rage. His insolence unwavering without regard of the consequences.

"Mr. White may I have a word in private?" Mr. Cartwright asked calmly not daring to look in Ben's direction. Ben grinned believing Mr. Cartwright feared his power, for he was the chosen one.

Leaving the office he could only imagine what they were saying, but he did not care. Queenie would be proud and that made him happy.

With Ben out of the room Mr. Cartwright breathed a sigh of relief. Being a principal meant he would certainly encounter numerous disobedient and disruptive students, but that didn't mean he could handle situations of hostility. Anthony sat speechless shaking his head; recent events had left him feeling at the end of his tether. A person could only take so much, out of options and close to breaking point. His issue was would he explode or implode?

"Mr. White, firstly I would like to say that I am so sorry to hear of your wife's passing. Please accept my deepest condolences. I can-not begin to imagine how you must feel and what both you and Ben are going through. As you know Ben has been struggling for some months now… however, threatening the safety of other students will not be tolerated nor will disobedience."

Anthony sat listening with tear filled eyes, nodding his head like one of those dogs you see sitting in the back of cars their head suspended by a large spring. He was defeated. As Mr. Cartwright spoke his voice altered from sympathetic to stern, his words were as serious as a heart attack. There was no denying the seriousness of the situation. Anthony was utterly demoralised.

"I am very sorry Mr. White, but Ben's actions have left me with no other choice but to suspend him. I do believe this suspension will be of benefit to everyone… the third term ends in two weeks and therefore a two week suspension will allow time for him to reflect on his behaviour and better come to terms with his recent losses."

Anthony saw no reason to rationalise or defend his son's actions; there was no point in getting mad. Emotionally exhausted he accepted Mr. Cartwright's decision and took receipt of the suspension letter, along with a copy of the Department's suspension procedures. Extending his right hand across the table, thumb up and palm flat he shook Mr. Cartwright's hand.

"Thank you and I am very sorry…"

Leaving the office he could only hope this suspension would afford Ben the time to reflect over his misbehaviour and accept responsibility for changing it. Mr. Cartwright had assured him the school would provide a study program and devise a support plan for when Ben returned. All Anthony could do would be to pray things improved, but only time would tell.

Leaving the school Ben expected to be hit with a barrage of abuse, but instead there was nothing. Walking back to the car Anthony increased his stride, while Ben hurried along behind taking two steps to his fathers one. The sound of students singing and playing percussion instruments from within the music classroom resonated across the main courtyard. His school had an awards' ceremony coming up and so these were a selected group of students who had been excused from participation in the swimming carnival to perfect their performance. Ben wanted to know what had transpired after he had been instructed to leave the principal's office but could tell his father was in no mood for conversation.

"You have been suspended," Anthony snapped as they reached the car.

Lowering his head Ben dared not show his happiness. Being suspended was like music to his ears. At last, the gods were working in his favour.

"Get in the car I am sick of your crap and I don't want to listen to your excuses… you… you disgust me," he barked leaning over the car, his finger jabbing back and forth in Ben's direction.

Slamming his door shut Anthony's next fight was with his seatbelt. Reefing down on it, the belt bit back, its safety feature kicked in. The more he tugged the more it snapped until finally he clicked the buckle into its locking mechanism.

Whilst many believed conflict and confrontation were necessary aspects of healthy communication, Anthony did not. Tough situations generally instigated his shut down, retreat or go silent modes. Today, it was silence. In the car it was as if someone had hit the mute button. Anthony's dead air approach left Ben feeling shunned and rejected. It was as if he didn't matter and didn't belong. His ignoring hurt. Ben felt beyond insignificant. He knew he was the cause of his father's pain. He also felt guilt as he too could have chosen to speak. However he was not sure if he wanted to bother with him. His father was obsessed with what he believed was finding the truth. What truth? Everyone was battling their own internal demons. Sitting in the passenger seat he kept his face forward, while looking out the corner of his eye he studied his father's face. He appeared smaller than he had before and old and worn out. Deep lines ran down the side of his face, they were lines Ben had not noticed in the past. A tuft of hair stuck up on the crown of his head like a cockies peak. Ben began to wonder, is this man really my father? He looks and sounds like him, but then again, he is different.

CHAPTER NINE

Arriving home Ben felt even more confused by his thoughts and so he sought solace within the confines of his bedroom. Gazing into his mirror everything appeared so surreal.

"What? What now? What do you want?" he questioned.

"Is that you?" Rubbing his fingers gently along the side of his face he stared intently.

"Ahhhhh!" he laughed, "it is you, helloooo how are you?"

His words made no sense, yet they sent him into hysterical laughter.

"Pleased to meet you, Lord Benami."

Studying his face he thought it looked different. In his mind he believed the mirror was a portal to the spirit realm. Amazed his reflection moved when he moved. The reflection's mouth opening and closing as he spoke. Looking down at his hands they also appeared changed. Jagged words flew from his lips. His eyes wide. Pupils darting as the intensity in his voice increased. Wild and violent. Moving his face closer to the mirror's surface. He could no longer maintain focus on his own eyes. Instead, he believed the image he saw belonged to another soul who existed in the space behind the mirror. Hearing what sounded like a voice he questioned.

"What do you want? Stop staring at me!"

Balling his fingers to a fist, he drove them into the mirror.

"That will stop you!" he yelled.

The voices stopped. The menacing whispers disappeared. Replaced by an excruciating pain in his hand. His fist was pounding. His emotional pain quickly turned to physical. His actions had been successful in creating a distraction and for that moment, he felt relief.

Overcome by emotion he began to laugh. He laughed so hard his loud, unrestrained bursts could be heard throughout the house. Yet, Anthony did not come to see what was happening. Free flowing tears released from his eyes. His knees buckled taking him to the floor. Kneeling amongst the piles of clothing his situation had stopped being funny. His hand was covered in blood. One larger shard poked out of his skin just above his index finger, like the fang of a vampire and several finer slivers of glass grazed the top of his knuckles. Pulling hard on the shard it released without resistance and blood spurtedover the top of his legs. Grabbing a cloth he wrapped his wound and dashed to the bathroom, soaking it under cool running water. From the bathroom he could hear voices, this time he recognised them as coming from the television and so he presumed his father was being entertained by one of the programs he appeared addicted to.

The next thirty minutes were spent interruption free,removing all the foreign bodies, sterilising, wrapping and bandaging up his wounds to prevent infection. With disaster averted Ben returned to his room and sat on his bed staring into nothingness. His mind was a blank. His eyes, failed to register his surrounds. His ears, failed to hear any noise. His taste buds, were vacant. The air housed no odours. All was numb. Even the pain in his hand had gone and so he sat staring; staring into nothingness. Seconds, then minutes, until finally hours passed.

All was still.

CHAPTER TEN

For Anthony and Ben seclusion from each other was briefly interrupted by heated exchanges until finally arguments became an integral part of their family dynamics. Anthony was totally oblivious to the magnitude of his son's anguish and suffering. Blind to the fact, that deep within Ben's mind confusion was stirring. A mystical character was coming into being. Left undetected there was a great chance he would witness the emergence of a hostile, almost sadistic personality. A person's mind was extremely powerful. Irrational thoughts had the ability to control and destroy. Thoughts are not facts, yet for Ben the delusions and voices were very real. Corrupted thoughts controlled his life.

Walking up to the front door Rebecca could hear raised voices. She had not seen Anthony or Ben since Claire's funeral and was concerned about how they were coping. Although hearing the voices she wondered if she should dare to continue forward. She had promised Claire she would look after her family and in doing so had decided she would prepare them a meal she hoped they would enjoy. Apricot chicken was one of her favourites. A large casserole dish would not only fill their bellies but offer home style cooking she was sure they had both been missing. It was just approaching dinner time and as she got closer to the front door she noticed the absence of any food odours. Feeling the warmth from the dish held firmly between her hands she was sure she would be a welcome guest.

Pressing the doorbell she waited nervously as the yelling stopped. Hearing footsteps from behind the closed door she smiled nervously and hoped with all her heart that her presence would not be rejected. Much to her delight it was Anthony who greeted her. In his voice, there was no resentment as he politely asked her inside.

"Hi, how are you? I hope I am not intruding…I just thought you and Ben may enjoy a nice meal. I have prepared a lovely apricot chicken."

Placing the dish on the sink she turned towards Anthony expecting him to say something. Instead he grabbed her and wrapped his arms around her as if she were a long lost friend he hadn't seen in years.

Embracing Rebecca in his arms Anthony could feel the warmth from her body, the love emanating from her every pore. If only it were Claire in his arms. Inhaling deeply, he could smell her soft scented perfume as his left cheek cradled gently upon her shoulder. Her hair flowing down the right side of his face. And for a moment he was totally lost. Completely mesmerised by the caressing hands of this beautiful woman. What would his beloved Claire think of him, to be in the arms of another woman so soon after she had… a little voice inside his head spoke out *this should not be happening*. Pulling away he looked deeply into Rebecca's eyes wondering how he could feel so close to a woman who he regarded as his wife's best friend and so soon after... How could he betray her love? But were his actions a betrayal?

"I'm…" pausing for a moment Anthony was not sure what he was or what he should say.

"I'm…"

"Shhh…I know," Rebecca replied.

Tears welled in Anthony's eyes as Rebecca pulled

him towards her. Her arms wrapped firmly around his waist. Their embracing was supposed to be one of comfort. For Anthony the feelings attached were very different. Overwhelmed by a deep longing to be held he resisted all temptation to pull away. Up till this time the feelings he had experienced had been reserved for Claire and only Claire.

And while Anthony had initiated the closeness, it was now Rebecca who appeared wanting, her hands rubbing his back in a smooth and uninterrupted circular motion. Leaning forward Anthony decided not to fight what he was feeling. Again his head found rest upon her shoulder. Although this time he turned his face away from her neck and closed his eyes. Listening to her breath he absorbed all the love she had to offer. His body next to hers. Her hands still travelling over his back, extending to just above his behind. Pulling her closer seemed the natural thing to do. Undeterred by the voices Anthony tightened his clasp and pulled Rebecca in while he released a mmmmm sound. In an instant Rebecca's caressing stopped, replaced by patting. Anthony wondered if he had overstepped the mark. Had he totally misread the affection she had imparted? Pulling back gently he feared his actions may result in her withdrawal. Creating a small distance while maintaining body contact at the shoulders he hoped would not lead to her interpreting there was anything more than intentions of comfort and support. Although in that moment, he was unsure of what he had intended. The situation immediately transformed into one of awkwardness. Had he misread Rebecca's intentions? Had Rebecca misread his intentions? But how would she know what his intentions were if he himself did not know? To think something, did not mean he would act.

Ben's thudding footsteps down the hallway interrupted their potential crisis, although as he made his way to the pantry he did not appear to care what they were doing. Retrieving a packet of chicken flavoured chips he flung the pantry door closed, about faced and high tailed it back up the hallway. The familiar sound of his bedroom door slamming signified he had made it back to his seclusion.

"I don't know what has gotten into him," Anthony released a loud sigh. "He has been expelled from school and it doesn't seem to matter what I say."

"He will be okay he is just grieving, we all grieve in our own way."

"Grieving, huh…" Anthony shook his head, "the other night he accused me of putting something in his dinner. I truly do not know what has gotten into him."

Taking Anthony by the hand Rebecca asked if he wanted her to speak with Ben. It was an offer he rejected.

"No thanks, but thank you…I just don't know how much I can take. Since being suspended it seems the only thing he does in the day is sleep, while at night I can hear him constantly pacing back and forth and talking in gibberish. It's like he has his whole world completely arse up."

Rebecca leaned forward and wrapped her arms around Anthony. This time there was no confusion as to the motives. She was there simply as a friend. To offer comfort and support.

"You know you can call on me whenever you need anything, both Ben and yourself. I am here for both of you, please remember that."

"I will and thank you and thank you for the apricot chicken it smells delicious. I really don't know…I don't know how I would cope without friends like yourself."

"Please Anthony there is no need to thank me, I know you appreciate what I do the same way I appreciate you in my life." Pausing for a moment, Rebecca felt somewhat nervous by the closeness of their encounter. Stepping back she took a few steps towards the front door searching for a reason as to why she should leave.

"Well I had better get going I still have some things cooking on the stove. Enjoy the chicken and know I am here for you, for both of you." Her words were slightly stuttered. The word *both* clearly articulated.

Feeling more than just a little perplexed as to what had just transpired Anthony began to question his feelings. Rebecca was a vision of beauty and he could not help but to gaze at her as she wandered back down the front path, before taking a short cut through the hedges that separated their houses. This time unlike so many others, she appeared different. It was as if he were noticing her as a woman for the first time. She walked with confidence. Head held high, posture up, buttocks firm. She moved sexily with a little springiness in each step. Her gentle strides introduced themselves at her well rounded hips. Hips that were smooth and sensual. Her symmetrical body balanced perfectly against her rhythmic and graceful movements. His observations were tantalising. Her legs appeared long and smooth, calf muscles firm but not oversized. Momentarily mesmerised by this new found vision of loveliness he began wondering what she would be like between the sheets. But he didn't just want her between his sheets. Rebecca had more to offer than just a body. She wasn't a piece of meat. Her beauty extended way past midnight, even after her make-up had been removed. Her alluring appeal was something to be cherished. Her friendship could never be taken for granted. And in the end if their friendship evolved, Anthony was sure this would be based on more than just wanting to fuck her. In any case, if anything was to eventuate it probably wouldn't be for some time. His love for Claire had not diminished with her passing. Comfort sex was out of the equation, for he was definitely not a fuck and conquers guy. He was a man who appreciated beauty and understood women deserved respect.

Returning to the kitchen all thoughts of Rebecca between his sheets vanished as he was greeted by the mouth watering aromas of the chicken dish. Lifting the lid he watched as steam released revealing a golden mixture of chicken laced with plump juicy apricots. A soft sweet scent of onions accompanied the mouth watering aromas, along with the sound of his rumbling stomach. Looking up the hallway he listened to hear if there was any noise coming from Ben's room, but there was not. Grabbing a bowl from the drawer he served up a heaped serving and resumed his position on the lounge, watching his scheduled TV programs.

Hours ticked away. Anthony lay asleep. He had enjoyed dinner and some beverages then passed out just after nine o'clock. Slumped over on the lounge like a huge whale shark; his mouth wide open. Occasionally his head would embark on a wild ride around his shoulders, jerking as his chin bobbed up and down striking his chest. His Darth Vader snoring was all too familiar yet, tonight he was excessively loud as tossed into the mix were also sounds that resembled a cat choking on fur balls. Waking up with a kinked neck he wiped his eyes trying to focus on his watch. It was just after midnight and this was certainly not the first time he had fallen asleep on the lounge. Down the hallway he could hear footsteps coming from Ben's room and what sounded like something being dragged along the floor. Rising to his feet he thought it best he investigate these strange noises. Tip toeing down the hallway his curiosity heightened as he heard voices he believed belonged to more than just one person. In fact they sounded like two very distinct people engaged in a conversation. Although he was unable to decipher what was actually being said.

Placing his ear against Ben's door Anthony stood frozen. What he heard made him even more confused. The conversation if that was what he would refer to it as appeared disjointed. The speech fragmented. The topic of discussion rapidly shifted from one thing to the next. Yet nothing made sense. Some words he did not even know. It was as if they had been made up. Then there were what appeared to be uncontrollable outbursts of laughter followed by sounds of moving objects. *Maybe I am just hearing things,* he thought, after all he had downed more than a few bourbons and had been watching a horror movie before he dozed off. Maybe what he thought he was hearing was simply his mind playing tricks on him. His eavesdropping was fruitless. It was time to resolve his curiosity once and for all.

Knocking on the bedroom door everything went silent.

"What?" Came an unexpectedroar that made Anthony jump back with fright.

"Are you alright Ben, is everything alright?"He replied in a startled voice.

"Yes!" The voice snapped.

Not wanting to intrude or aggravate the situation Anthony responded by simply telling Ben he was going to bed and suggested his son did the same.

The next morning Anthony rose to the sound of his alarm. Feeling a little worse for wear he had no recollection of the evening's events. All was silent in Ben's room and so he made himself a much needed cup of coffee, showered, got dressed and left for work. He hadn't really taken on many jobs since Claire had passed away but today he needed to be on site of a housing project he had been lucky enough to win the contract for. Closing the door behind him he could only hope his son would get himself up and start to go through the school work he had been handed to complete while on suspension.

It was a long but successful day. The contract would be extremely profitable. Things were looking up. Arriving home Anthony was pleasantly surprised by Ben. He was in the kitchen and had prepared them a nice dinner, sausages with onion gravy, mashed potato and mixed vegetables. Sitting across the table he studied his son's face. It was time for him to broach the subject of Shirley's secret and his intended action to get to the truth. He knew Ben could become extremely defensive about his grandmother, but he had to be open and honest. His decision to proceed with his investigation was a way in which he would be able to achieve closure.

"Ben I need to talk to you about your grandmother and the book she left."

Turning towards his father Ben glared, his jaw tensed and his eyes bulged.

"I don't want to talk to you about her!" he snapped before turning his back on his father.

Anthony knew it was a delicate subject. He also knew placing his head in the sand and ignoring it would not make it go away. Inaction never got anyone anywhere and sometimes we just had to face those things that scared us the most. He was not prepared to let the secrets of an old bitch destroy any further.

"We need to talk about her, I need to find out the truth. All these secrets are destroying us. Can't you see you have become angry. I am afraid to talk to you without you erupting. It's because of these secrets, your grandmother has created a divide."

His words were enough to provoke Ben to go over the edge. Flinging his head back toward his father a demonic look came over him. Anthony jumped to his feet ready to defend. Ben's breathing became rapid and his lips curled into a hellish snarl. His eyes returned to that bulging appearance Anthony had witnessed only moments ago, however this time his eyebrows deepened.His breath became heavy and loud. Anthony was adamant he would not allow his son's anger to deter his discussion.

"Stop it! Stop it now!" he demanded, his voice growing louder with every second, "you're a teenager and you will listen to me, I am your father!"

His father's words infuriated him. How dare he stand before him and dictate what he should or shouldn't feel. Unleashing his rage Ben picked up the plate of food from in front of him and flung it towards the table where his father stood. His son's rage had escalated to a place beyond predicability. Hitting the table with a loud bang the plate smashed. Mashed potato splattered and a medley of carrots, peas and corn kernels were sent hurtling across floor. Anthony stood stunned. Ben had heard enough. No one, not even his father had the right to bad mouth his grandmother.

"I will not listen to you bad mouthing my Queenie!" he roared.

His explosive outburst was followed by an anger fuelled retreat full of swearing and cursing as he stormed down the hallway that squashed all hope of a father and son discussion. Anthony knew Ben's storming out of the room was his son's only way of trying to calm himself down. He also knew many others may have believed his son was ruling the house, dictating what could and could not be discussed. However following him down the hallway would only escalate the situation. Cleaning up the mess he was left wondering if he would ever be able to have a simple conversation with his son that didn't spiral out of control. He feared what his son would do next. He also began to question his ability to be a parent and what would next set off a volcanic eruption. He knew he had to confront the issue of his behaviour calmly and tell Ben in no uncertain terms his behaviour would not be tolerated. He also knew he had to discuss Ben's grandmother and the book she left that alluded to a secret life. There was also the issue of the other house, the second house in Paddington. It was vital for all the secrets to be exposed, all the questions to be answered.

Anthony was determined, nothing or no-one would alter his plans.

I will get to the truth, I will expose all the secrets, he thought.

CHAPTER ELEVEN

Ben's bedroom became his own little isolation tank and in his solitude he began to hear more voices. He was convinced his father Lord Antony was plotting to conspire against his family. Plotting to destroy what his grandmother Queenie had assured was his for the taking. He was Lord Benami, the chosen one. The voices told him evil Lord Antony would do everything and anything to destroy his powerful Golden lineage.

Barricading the door to his bedroom was a must. Attack he believed was imminent. Pacing back and forth he stomped over the clothes and rubbish that covered his bedroom floor. Kicking those things he found annoying out of the way. It was as if he was on some sort of march of madness. His words poured out in gibberish making no sense. His disorganised thinking had now grown in intensity and was mirrored in his speech. Glancing towards his door he became concerned about the gap at the bottom, between where the door ended and the floor commenced. Retrieving a towel from the end of his bed he shoved it tightly against the floor. Pushing and shoving his fingers to securely block any possible crack.

His inner voices were wild and furious, accusing and angry. They told him how the school and his father had conspired against him. In actual fact, his father's computer was linked to those in Mr. Cartwright's office. They all had information on him. Their aim was to destroy. They plotted against him. It was imperative he remained vigil at all times. Suddenly his pacing stopped.

His blank, vacant facial expressions changed to one of puzzlement. His eyes squinted, his right eyebrow raised and his head tilted to one side.

"What did you say?" his voice contained curiosity laced with a touch of anger. A frown came over his face followed by a gentle nod of his head, as if he were acknowledging someone else. But no-one was there.

"I know, I know!" the tone in his voice highlighted his concern.

Springing over his bed he lunged towards his bedroom window. The curtains were drawn closed, they had been that way for some time. Peering out from the edge he became panicked.

"I can, I can…I know, I know…shhh…they don't know we are in here!"

Grimacing at the corner of his mouth, his eyes of shock darted around the room resembling those laughing clowns you see at amusement parks with their mouths wide open. Only his head was propelling from left to right at an amazing rate, as if searching for something.

"Hide, we need to hide!" he blurted in a terror-stricken whisper.

Hurdling towards the bed he grabbed the covers in both hands and threw them over the top of himself.

All was still. All was silent. Except for his faint panting from beneath the covers.

When Anthony arrived home hours later. Ben was nowhere to be seen. Although it was not long before he graced his father with his presence.

"Hey, how are you Ben what have you been up today…I hope you have started on that school work."

Ben looked at his father shrugging his shoulders and nodding his head.

"Yep, I have started…and I have already had dinner. I was hungry before so I had some noodles."

"Oh…no worries, well as long as you are okay. I could make you something if you like."

"No!" Ben snapped, "I said I was fine. I don't need you to make me anything!"

Retrieving a can of drink from the fridge Ben watched as his father plonked himself down on the lounge.

"Well I am going to do more of that school crap then."

About facing and heading back towards his bedroom Ben's relaxed stroll was interrupted by what his father said next.

"I am going to go to the house tomorrow, you are more than welcome to join me."

Clenching his jaw they were words that angered him. He knew there was no stopping his father's persistence and so tomorrow he would accompany him on his visit to the other house.

CHAPTER TWELVE

Ben was seething his father had woken him up early and all attempts to stop his investigations had failed. Before he knew it he was ushered into the car and they were on their way to the other house. Driving up the street he knew exactly what they would discover. Unbeknown to Anthony this was not the first time he had been to the house. In fact he had been there many times with his grandmother. Looking towards his father he noticed beads of sweat on his forehead along his hairline. Ben's fear as to what would happen next was like a clump in his stomach. Swallowing hard he wondered if his forehead was also covered in sweat. A storm appeared to be brewing there was a cool breeze, yet his body was filled with a distinctive heat. Wiping his brow then his eyes his agitation increased. Leaning forward he gazed out the window watching other teenage students walking along the street. It was a school day. They were wearing his school uniform. The compulsory bright red check patterned shirts made them stand out like large tablecloth beacons in the night. *Suckers,* he thought. At least he didn't have to contend with boring classes.

Years ago school had appeared as a home away from home. It was a place where imagination was welcomed. Ideas were tossed around the classroom and individual participation was encouraged. These days it was more like hell away from home. An institution where young minds were controlled. Independent ideas were frowned upon and if it wasn't in a text book then it shouldn't be considered. Restrictions, regulations and domination, commanded by dictators. If it didn't exist in the syllabus, then it didn't exist. What a stupid name; a syllabus. They were all in the silly bus and it was headed by one major idiot – the school principal, Mr. Cartwright. Teachers, who did they think they were? They didn't spend the majority of their lives standing up in front of a classroom just for the love of it. Unlike the students they were paid to attend. They enjoyed the extended school holidays and many appeared to revel in the power that was albeit lacking in other areas of their lives. Where else would an adult acquire so much uncontested supremacy. For Ben his view on school had certainly changed.

Looking across towards the sports field with the two-storey buff brown-bricked science block in the background Ben spotted 'the beloved.' The self-titled label for the most popular girls in his school. At his school class played an important role as did labels. Everyone had a label, you were either popular, unpopular, a mingler and or an outcast. Even male students were pigeon holed into class. Ben had once been associated with the popular students, now he sat more as an outcast. How could anyone talk to him when his mother had just died in such tragic circumstances? Parents did not die, they were either happily married, suffering years of internal turmoil supported by therapists or struggling with divorce while arguing over the custody of children. The world was a lonely place when you were a teenage outcast.

Members of the beloved were popular and believed they belonged to an elite class; they were selective and exclusive. They viewed the world differently to most. Some were born with a silver spoon in their mouth, while others aspired for greatness. They did not go to friends for barbecues and snacks. They enjoyed dinner parties and refreshments. For members of the beloved, holidays were vacations and psychiatrists or shrinks were personal therapists. It was a powerful group headed by none other than Tristan Rose. Tristan was a born leader, wealthy, very outgoing, naturally pretty, as well as smart. She had long dark brown hair that looked flawless everyday and chocolaty brown eyes. Tristan Rose had the ability to make Ben smile. He had sat next to her for English in his first year of High School. Surprisingly she was actually nice, willing to engage in idle chatter and open enough to share the occasional joke. The only negative quality Ben could identify about Tristan was her ability to get rude and snappy when she was not the centre of attention. Tristan loved being in the limelight. All of the guys loved her and many of the girls aspired to be just like her. Strangely enough she had not had a boyfriend all year and unlike many of her friends she appeared perfectly happy and confident with her single status.

Wherever you saw Tristan you would also spot Bree Kavanagh. She was loud and outgoing and Tristan's best friend. She followed Tristan like a lost puppy. They had known each other since kindergarten. They were inseparable. Their mothers were also best friends who enjoyed a game of hit and giggle at the elite tennis club in Randwick. Spoilt wealthy wives of successful businessmen, they liked to think of themselves as high-end fashion queens. Sadly, they simply appeared as mutton dressed up as lamb especially when they frequented the Royal Randwick Racecourse members' stand. Seeing the girls made Ben think of his own mother, Claire. She had also possessed a love of fashion and enjoyed flying to Melbourne for the occasional shopping spree, however she was always conscious when purchasing her age appropriate clothes. Ben missed his mum. Bree reminded Ben of what his mother would have looked like when she was younger. Her hair was sandy brown, just past her shoulders, her face round and full with a scattering of freckles. Looking at photos of his mother in her teenage years was astonishing for the resemblance between the two was uncanny.

Beatrice Evans was another follower. She was disturbingly skinny and short. She had red hair in big loose curls and brown eyes. Beatrice never ate lunch as she always claimed she was too fat. She was more a wannabe; friends with all of the popular girls, but not quite there. Over time Beatrice had changed herself so much Ben believed she had forgotten who she really was. Beatrice's parents were well off but not wealthy. She could be nice but also snooty. Ben had tried to talk to her earlier in the year as they had shared many classes during primary school, however he soon realised she thought she was God's gift to the world and so he cut the conversation short. It seemed her continued focus on wanting to keep in with the popular girls had destroyed her ability to be a conversationalist. Beatrice was a highly successful member of the school debating team. Publicly she spruiked about equality and the overvalue of money, yet her conversations always revolved around the price and cost of everything from relationships to items purchased at department stores. In Beatrice's world everything was in some way linked to the almighty dollar. Her biggest flaws were she could never keep her mouth shut, she continually mocked people who she thought were below her and she talked about people behind their backs. Beatrice was definitely a back stabber and capable of doing anything in order to get what she wanted.

For Zander Fischer acceptance into the beloved occurred as her popularity skyrocketed. Going out with the most popular guy in school had more than just a few perks, especially when he was Tristan Rose's older brother Jordan. Overnight Zander propelled from the renowned to the acknowledged. She was the total opposite to Bree Kavanagh. In the past Bree had even referred to her as gutter trash. Why was she gutter trash? For years she was notable for being a slut. Flaunting her big boobs she would show them off wearing push-up bras and skin tight tops. Boasting she could have any man she desired. Two years prior rumours went she had had an abortion during school holidays. Now she claimed to be a changed woman, a one-man girl, who appeared obsessive over her appearance. She did not need high-end designer clothes to be noticed. Zander Fischer was also extremely sporty and head of the swim team, she represented the State and when she donned her swimming gear people cheered for more than just a win. She was a show off and muscular but not in a hulking way and she never failed to entertain. Of the entire beloved, Zander Fischer was the only one privileged enough to have a nickname; Nemo.

All four shared a strong, well-suited relationship. Watching them Ben felt disheartened. His friendships no longer existed. They had become brittle and broken, disintegrating until finally lost. The world was a lonely place.

Scanning the schoolyard Ben went ballistic. He had spotted a distant figure up near the main gate.

"Stop the car, stop!" he screamed.

Anthony hit the brakes hard, the tyres screeched and the car came to a sudden halt. Through the scattered gum trees and beyond the cluster of lunch seats stood none other than the frizzy coiled headed bully Tynan James. It appeared his recent bashing had not altered his bullying stand over behaviour. Intimidating the weak was like a game to him. Undeterred and as bold as brass someone needed to stop this repulsive, arrogant, egotistical gorilla. He needed to learn a lesson. Leaping from the car Ben offered his father no explanation. Anthony sat stunned not knowing what was happening. With his head down Ben jumped the fence and increased his pace finding coverage behind the trees. Willing himself to appear insignificant it was vital for his attack to possess an element of surprise. The mere sight of this oversized thug infuriated Ben. Where were the teachers? Why hadn't something been done to stop this bully? What power did he hold over the authorities that made him invincible? He needed to be taught preying on the weak was not tolerated.

Tynan was preoccupied. He was holding the school bag of a smaller student. Riffling through its contents, oblivious to an impending attack. Advancing steadily Ben had seen too much.

"Get away from him you bastard," he yelled.

Tynan spun around quickly. He appeared shocked. He pushed his latest victim to the ground.

"You low life piece of shit…You parasite, I am going to teach you once and for all," Ben bellowed.

Not wanting to get involved students scampered away, while others stopped eager to see a bit of action. Tynan glared towards Ben as he straightened his stance. This time there was no pool. This time he was ready. This time he was determined to win. Drawing closer and closer boiling anger rushed through Ben's body. Tynan cracked his knuckles and clenched his fists.

"Bring it on."

Ben charged forward swinging his fist towards Tynan's head. Tynan ducked. Ben missed his target. With one quick jab Ben slammed into the ground. He could hear faint laughter. A sneering Tynan stood with his hands on his hips. Grinning he scanned his surrounds. His success only proved to reinforce his belief that he held the ultimate power. Ben lay on the footpath. Defeated, he watched other kids scoot by not wanting to get involved. If only they all stood up to this bully, a unified force could overpower and crush him.

"Fuck off you pissant…This is my gate…This is my school…I control what happens here. Why don't you run home to your mummy, oh no you can't do that she's dead. Best you go to your daddy then…go on run along, he is waiting for you in the car."

Crushed by embarrassment Ben opted to say no more. Limping back to the car he was livid. Tynan James may have won that battle, but the war was only beginning.

Opening the door he climbed into the passenger seat not saying a word. Anthony looked at him while shaking his head and asking if he was all right.

"Why did you do that? Who is that guy? Ben you are going to get yourself in serious trouble if you don't learn to control your anger."

Closing his eyes tightly Ben tried to shut out his father's words. Everything was wrong. He wanted to go to bed. He wanted for nothing more than to shut himself off from the world. Locked away in his bedroom he felt safe. He would allow his thoughts to travel to a better time, a happier place. Outside he was exposed. His father insistent on taking him to a place where he knew things would only get worse.

Anthony babbled on about finding the truth behind his grandmother's words, yet the only thing Ben could think about was concealing what his father wanted so desperately to expose.

"I know what you are doing," Anthony continued, as he started the car and accelerated away from the kerb, "you think by causing a commotion I will just turn around and go home…well I won't."

Ben said nothing. Gazing out the window his eyes remained fixed on Tynan James. Who did he think he was to claim that the gate and school belonged to him? The gate and school belonged to all students. Ben laughed, in his mind revenge would be his. It was just a matter of time. Tynan James was a mongrel dog. Ben wondered if he pissed on the front gate marking his territory. He used the school as his hunting ground. His control was only temporary. The day would come when Tynan James faced the wrath of vengeance. The day would come when Tynan James begged for forgiveness.

Their trip was silent. Down the street Anthony was forced to take a detour onto the main road that led into Sydney. Extreme weather and mass downpours had lashed the city over recent weeks. Consequently council workers and SES crews were hard at work trying to unblock obstructed pipes. Suddenly the car came to a complete stand still. They hit a traffic jam. The morning traffic was still at its peak. Drivers yelled abuse, waving hands out windows. The overpowering smell of exhaust fumes meant crawling along with the window open for an extended period was not possible. Black smoke, grey and invisible toxic gases pumped into the air. The rotten egg foulness from men and women in their machines on a mission to get to where they needed to go. Buses, trucks, car and motorbikes, everyone was choked by confusion, unlike the accelerated and highly calculated smooth flowing traffic one would observe on an ant highway. Anthony punched his steering wheel. Ben sat silently shaking his head. Blaring horns signified they had just entered a battlefield of angry and impatient drivers. Surely the day could not get any worse. Everything about the day was horrible. Ben closed his eyes; he had just about had enough. Being dead he thought had to be better than what he was going through, life sucked.

"Grab the steering wheel!" a voice demanded.

Ben's eye sprung open and his arms stretched, grabbing the steering wheel he reefed downwards. His actions came from no where. Anthony instinctively pushed him away trying to maintain control of the car.

"What the hell are you doing?" he screamed, "what has gotten into you Ben?"

Ben shrugged his shoulders, his face reddened with embarrassment.

"Sorry, I thought you said grab the wheel."

"I didn't say a bloody thing… oh my god you could have had us both killed."

Shaking his head Anthony maintained a vice like grip on the wheel; he was lost for words.

Sitting in silence a lone tear escaped the corner of Ben's eye. Strange things were happening and he felt as though he was losing control of his mind. Then there was Tynan James, he was a dog. He thought he was the top dog and he behaved as if he were the alpha male in a pack of wolves. Ben felt as if he were a mere lost and lonely puppy, cast aside. Being led to an uncertain future. Trembling with fear. Uncertain as to what would happen next. Apprehensive as to what would unfold. Terrified to face the world without the love and guidance from his mother. Without the direction from his beloved Queenie. Then there was his father who in his mind seesawed between likeable, tolerated and despised.

From the empty silence came a reassuring voice, a whisper. Ben stared. He listened intently to the words. Tuning into the reassurance he inhaled deeply. A faint breeze crossed his face. A faded rainbow decorated the distant skies where dark storm clouds loomed. Rain would soon dance upon the ground, the sweet scent of freshness was in the air. In the distance he could see the gods weeping, bands of rain darkened the northern skies. Ethereal beauty would soon cleanse the earth and his soul. The voices within his mind would guide and comfort him. As he turned towards his father the voices told him their words were private.

Anthony glanced towards the passenger seat. Their eyes met, both smiled.

"It's going to be fine Ben," Anthony said.

Ben nodded.

CHAPTER THIRTEEN

Ben knew it would be fine. He had nothing to worry about. The voices had returned delivering a reassuring message. His father on the other hand needed convincing, he should not go ahead with his plan to uncover and expose the truth.

What happens in the family stays in the family! Ben thought.

His grandmother had repeated these words on numerous occasions. Her instructions were clear. The last time he heard her say them was just before she passed away. He had visited her at the retirement village with his mother. His mum didn't understand the connection he shared with Queenie. No one understood their connection.

"What happens in the family stays in the family!" she snapped as she grabbed the collar of his shirt, pulling his face closer to hers. Her warm breath covering his face, the stench of her garlic infused saliva seeping up his nose. Frozen stiff he dared not blink, afraid the slightest movement may indicate defiance. He was much taller than she was; yet, she still had the ability to scare the pants off him.

"Do you hear me Ben?" Snarling words filled the air.

Nodding his head he motioned his understanding, as her eyes squinted peering deep into his soul. Swallowing hard his eyes were glued on hers.

"I hear you, what happens in the family stays in the family."

"Why? Why does it stay in the family?" Her face contorted in an all-consuming anger, her eyes closed into slits, her nostrils flared and her mouth quivered. Queenie and her words petrified him; the closeness of their encounter made his stomach churn. Her breath was foul. It was as if someone had crapped in her mouth, added a handful of rotten garbage and rancid meat then tossed in ten cloves of garlic and left it all in the sun. Compacted white saliva sat within the intersection of her lips. As she spoke thick and stringy drool bounced around the inside of her mouth, occasionally dancing along her dry and cracking lips.

"Because family comes before anything else…" he whimpered.

"And?" she snapped out her response.

"And…"

"And what?"

"And if I let things out of the family it will destroy us, it will destroy our golden lineage."

"Good boy, that's my boy…good boy and not only that, if you dare let out our secrets you will feel the wrath of the dragon warriors. You must never forget the dragon warriors!" A smile returned to her face as she released her hold on his collar.

Tugging at the bottom of his shirt he straightened himself up and sighed with relief, Queenie would never let him forget what was so crucial to their ongoing existence. It was imperative Ben follow her instructions.

What happens in the family stays in the family! he thought.

His father's words interrupted his reminiscent thoughts.

"Here it is!"

Looking up Ben wanted nothing more than for him to just continue driving. Delving into the past would do no good. Why couldn't his father just sell the house. Surely he didn't need three houses. The house they lived in was as good as any, then there was his grandmother's house and now this one.

"Why don't we just go home?" he asked, "the past isn't going to change anything."

"I know, I know it won't change anything but…" Anthony replied.

"But what? There are no buts, why don't we just leave the past in the past, please dad," Ben pleaded.

"I know you may not understand, but, I have to do this. I need to find out the truth. I need to expose the truth. We are today, a result of what we were yesterday. Our today could have been so different. It could have been so much better, had it not been for your grandmother and her secret and lies. This is where the secrets lie."

Releasing his seat belt there was no stopping him. His mission was to expose the secrets; Ben's responsibility was to stop him. How this would be achieved was anyone's guess. By the time Ben got out of the car his father was fossicking through the boot mumbling about a torch.

"Petrol, crowbar, rope…Ah, there it is, I knew I had a torch in there!" Holding it in his right hand and flicking its switch with his thumb he tapped the torch with his left hand. With a couple of whacks it was working and before Ben had a chance to speak the boot was slammed closed. Anthony crossed the road, he was a man filled with enthusiasm; his brisk pace emphasised by the swinging of his arms.

"Come on, we haven't got all day!" he yelled turning his attention back towards Ben.

"I forgot my jumper, it's in the car."

Reaching into his pocket Anthony retrieved the car keys and threw them across the road.

"Here! I will meet you inside!"

Gulping deeply, Ben wished the world would open up and swallowthem both. Anthony was his father and so he loved him, for without him he would not exist. However Ben also owed his allegiance to Queenie. To go against her would be an act of treason. Only the harshest of punishments were suitable for acts of treason. Dragon warriors would be released; fire and fury would fill the sky. Evil warriors would attack from every angle and he would be cast into the depths of hell to burn for eternity. Queenie knew best, for years she had warned him about the wrath of the Gods. He was the chosen one. This was his test. He had to prove himself. He had to protect his Queen.

Retrieving his jumper he was a bundle of nerves, unsure as to what he should do. His heart was in his mouth. Scanning the scene his mind raced a million miles an hour. His father needed to be stopped. Ben had to stop him.

"Kill him!" came a voice resembling that of Queenie.

Shocked, Ben looked around. He could see no one. There was no one in the street. A few parked cars scattered along the road.

Again the voice spoke, "Do it!"

Ben stood still shaking his head, "I can't." he replied.

An eerie feeling overwhelmed him. A sense prying eyes were watching his every move. Glaring up from behind the car he studied his surroundings. The street was deserted, yet his uneasiness remained.

His father had disappeared from sight. Scanning the street once more he gulped hard. It was then he spotted a dark figure shaded within the trees in the yard of the house next to where his father was. Stepping around the car he raised his right hand to his forehead peering towards the figure. In an instant it was gone. Storm clouds were brewing. An enduring look of trepidation clung to his face as he gazed skywards then towards the house. Fear engulfed his body.

Where the hell had his father gone? A sense of urgency invaded his thinking. A gut level alertness made him believe he was in a struggle against the clock. Time was of the essence. Dashing across the road Ben leaped up the front steps, advancing up them two at a time. Gone were the thoughts of the strange figure. Bursting through the front door he slammed it closed behind him and scanned the room. It was imperative for him to locate his father.

"Dad!" he snapped.

CHAPTER FOURTEEN

Outside nature had unleashed mayhem. It was as if they were being sent a message from the Gods that they should leave. Anthony was standing to the right of the front door in the lounge room. Approaching him Ben wiped webs from his face.

"Maybe we should just go, we could come back another time," he said.

"No! I need to find out the truth of what happened here, I need to find the reason why this place was kept a secret…"

Staring towards Ben he frowned, his face displayed a look of determination and Ben was not sure what his intentions were once he discovered the truth. How far was he prepared to go?

"Your grandmother has made a lot of claims…secrets have been kept for far too long!"

Shaking his head in annoyance, Ben looked out of the front window. He could feel a cool draught on his face that escaped from around the window frame. The wind blew ferociously picking up leaves and small twigs and carrying them high up into the air. It appeared unrelenting and delivered a horrid high pitched whirly whistling noise that sent a shiver down his spine. Bolts of lightning lit up the sky, snapping and cracking like fierce blazing barbed wire whips unleashed by the gods. A warning not to proceed any further.

"It looks like its going to pour down at any moment, we could always come back tomorrow."

Large tree branches whipped about to and fro, hitting the house with a huge thud which made Anthony jump.

"No!" he snapped, "we are here now and we are going to stay here!"

He was like a steamroller, nothing was going to stop him and Ben feared what would happen next. Overwhelmed by the situation he bit down on his lip. He could feel a twitch in his right eye that could have been attributed to nerves or the large volume of dust that had been disturbed by the wind and their moving about. Staring at Anthony he began to feel sick, shifting from one foot to the other he cracked his knuckles and made a suggestion.

"Let's go upstairs…Can we look up there first then come back down here?" he stammered.

"Okay," Anthony nodded, at last he was listening to him and they would be able to leave the lounge room. Being in the lounge brought back so many memories of Queenie. Ben had played in the room. He had sat on the lounge. Cuddled with his grandmother. Listened to her stories.

Proceeding cautiously towards the stairs, Anthony followed in Ben's path. Pausing for a moment at the base. Ben looked up into the darkness as Anthony nudged him to continue on. The creaking sound of their footsteps on the old worn out wooden boards echoed in the silence. Stumbling at about half way up Anthony grabbed Ben by the top of his trousers and asked if he was okay. He was far from okay but understood his insistence to proceed, reaching for the handrail he maintained a vice like grip. With each step the floor boards creaked beneath Anthony's feet. Grabbing the handrail something inside him was telling him to stop, to turn around, to retreat.

The hairs on the back of his neck stood to attention; like fine needles on a pin cushion. A cold sweat drenched his brow, yet he continued to follow Ben. Nervous energy ravaging his body its intensity increasing as the stairs yet to be climbed reduced. The creaking of the stairs sung out like a warning sign, *"Stop! Don't go on!"* but still the inner nagging, that sense of feeling compelled to keep moving forward overrode all sense of concern. What could possibly be so bad it would suggest he abandon his search for the truth?

At the top of the stairs Ben turned his head left and right peering down the hallway. Feeling a poke in his back he moved forward. Anthony grabbed the top of his trousers again.

"Go down there… that door is open," he whispered.

Their journey of discovery continued to the right of the house. Reaching the doorway they were welcomed by a room filled with light. Everything appeared far less dusty upstairs or maybe it was due to the fact the furniture was not draped with clothes, as it had been downstairs. Stopping still in his tracks Anthony pushed passed and walked towards the window which overlooked the front yard. Ben closed the door behind them.

"This is amazing… would you look at this, it's as if we have stepped back in time!" Anthony whispered with excitement.

His jaw dropped as he studied with amazement what appeared to be Claire's grandparent's room. A four-piece bedroom suite sang out pure class. The room carried a strange warmth along with a real romantic and loving feeling. An antique dressing table with bevelled winged mirrors and intricate detail sat to the left of the bed, its dusty mirrors reflecting the light from the window on the opposite side of the room. Two items sat on top of the dresser; the first was an elegant crystal perfume bottle, its contents evaporated years ago. The second item was an empty jewellery box, its contents stripped. The centrepiece of the room was unmistakably the cast iron and brass antique half tester bed. It too had beautiful detailing. At the foot were four porcelain sections that surrounded a circular mirror piece. While at the head a tattered and dusty canopy made of fine lace hug from the half tester. On the base wall, standing opposite the foot of the bed stood a solid double wardrobe with a door either side of a fixed mirror. This sat off the floor on four feet, each door decorated with multi coloured timber inlay flower patterns. Next to this a chest of drawers stood at waist height; three large drawers below two smaller drawers, the iron handles elegantly shaped like teardrops.Opening up the cupboard and drawers Anthony found a few items of clothing. Nothing offered any real answers.

Suddenly a loud thud came from downstairs. Anthony jumped with fright and pulled a face, his forehead crinkled between his eyes. It was an unexpected thud that could indicate they were not alone.

CHAPTER FIFTEEN

Ben was becoming increasingly stressed about them being in the house. His thoughts returned to the strange figure he had seen in the shadows of the house next door. Compounding his anxiety was the fact his voiceshad returned with vengeance. They plagued his every thought. Chattering away like little monkey voices, niggling and chastising, his every move. This was his castle. It had once been Queenie's castle and behind these walls a degree of isolation had been experienced. He liked isolation, for outside life was marked by suspicion. The world was a dark and splintered place. It was his belief, his father was there simply for two reasons. Firstly, he wanted to destroy his family name. Secondly, Ben was convinced his father was out to destroy him. He was jealous. Jealous he was merely a member of the Upper Class, while Ben was the famous and powerful Lord Benami. Ben firmly believed his father despised the acquiesce of this notion.

"Did you hear that?" Anthony whispered, "someone is here!"

Ben stood still with his hands over his ears shaking his head.

"Ben! Ben!…I think someone is in the house."

Creeping towards the bedroom door Anthony's complexion changed to a ghostly white. His breathing became hard, while every little noise resembled an impending threat. Outside an explosive crack of thunder echoed like a gunshot to their ears. This was followed quickly by flashes of lightning that lit up the darkened sky. The storm was upon them. Pouring rain crashed over the house. Howling wind whipped up ripping limbs from the trees. Anthony placed his right hand to his chest and released a loud sigh.

"Oh, bloody hell that scared the bejesus out of me."

Looking towards Ben he gave a half smile as he shook his head.

"Maybe you were right, maybe we should come back another time."

Ben returned his father's smile, at last he was making sense. It was the smartest comment that had left his father's mouth all day.

"Okay we will go. This storm looks like its only going to get worse."

Walking towards the bedroom door Anthony appeared accepting of his decision to return at a later date. Reaching for the door handle he turned the knob in his hand as he looked over his shoulder towards Ben who was relieved by his father's decision.

Whack!

Without warning Anthony was hit hard in the head and knocked off his feet. His body sent hurtling across the room. Ben stood stunned. His feet felt as though they were weighted to the floor. Unable to move. His mouth wide open, eyes looking, staring upon his father who lay motionless on the floor.

"Dad!" Finally, he was able to mutter just one word.

Panic stricken he dropped to his knees. His father's body was contorted, blood seeped from the left side of his forehead. The door creaked. Ben's eyes bulged. His heart raced. His head jolted. His attention turned towards the door. A large figure stood before him.

Monstrously ugly, like an ogre from a fairy tale. Yet this was no fairy tale. His beastly appearance added to the terror. Towering over Ben and Anthony he looked upon them with deadpan eyes. Puffing and panting; not saying a word. His hair was a mess. Teeth crooked and gapped and his upper jaw elongated, maybe the result of extensive thumb sucking. Ben's heart leapt into his throat. The figure stepped forward into the light of the room. The floor creaked beneath his gigantic bare feet. He was filthy from head to toe. His clothes appeared unwashed. His blue and white checker shirt was covered in stains. His oversized jeansripped in both knees. But there was one thing Ben could not ignore. One thing he couldn't take his eyes off. One thing that was of greater threat. Held firmly between his oversized hand was a weapon. A weapon that would instil fear into the most gallant of souls. A sword. A sword with what appeared an extremely sharp blade. Light flickered upon its shiny edge. Ben had seen many swords throughout his life. He and Queenie both possessed a great fondness for these weapons of steel.

Finally, the figure spoke.

"Hello Ben," his voice deep and heavy. A voice that was extremely recognisable.

"Johnnie?" Ben heaved a sigh of relief.

"What are you doing? What have you done? We were leaving."

"I came to protect you."

The sight of Johnnie standing in front of him with his father lying unconscious on the floor infuriated him.

"You need to get out of here. I could have handled this myself. I was handling this myself," he bellowed.

"I thought I was helping," his voice quivered as he

lowered his head avoiding eye contact. His appearance of being somewhat distracted and only half listening further enraged Ben.

"Queenie said you would be back, I promised I would protect you." Tears welled in his eyes, his voice became childlike, "I just wanted to play," he huffed, stomping his feet.

Ben shook his head. How dare Johnnie encroach on what was his. This was his castle. It would serve him well to remember where he stood. He had no right to turn up unannounced. Glaring at him he was disgusted that such a low life would even think he could act as such without his permission. Johnnie was to blame for his predicament. Everything had changed in a blink of an eye due to one idiot's actions and now that idiot stood before him, without even the courage to look at him. The tension in the room was palpable.

Ben stood up and began pacing back and forth. He was becoming increasingly agitated by Johnnie's sniffling. Balling his fingers to a fist he drove them into the wall.

"I am not playing!" he yelled, "I am sick of you!"

Johnnie jumped and stepped back. He was stunned. Ben's voice was thunderous. It was as if he had become another person. Johnnie couldn't concentrate on what he had said only the tone in which he had spoken. Looking at Ben he could see the veins on his forehead popping, his face reddened and eyes glared.

"I'm sorry… I just wanted to help, I wanted to play."

Ben's right hand fisted. Johnnie's words ignited his rage, he glared with blackened eyes and released an inner force pushing Johnnie to the ground. With a single thrust Johnnie landed on his back. Ben stood over him.

"You are an idiot, a stupid useless parasite. You can't get anything right. I saw you the other night. You couldn't even do the blood sacrifice properly. You were supposed to sacrifice the cat, yet, you sat there in the pouring rain cuddling the bloody thing. Don't you want to please the gods? Do you not wish to honour your queen? Do you deny me, your loyalty? What gives you the right to burst in here?

Tears rolled down Johnnie's face, dropping to the floor. He knew he wasn't as smart as many others. His intention was not to disappoint or anger. He wanted to please. Gasping for breath he sobbed uncontrollably, his body shaking. His shoulders rising and falling in time with his wailing pant.

"You hurt me," he whimpered.

"I will do more than hurt you if you don't shut up and let me think."

Johnnie turned his head towards the corner of the room. He couldn't stand it when people raised their voices. Wiping his hands across his face his jagged sniffling continued as he ran the back of his hand and sleeve of his shirt under his running nose.

Suddenly, the pelting rain stopped. Johnnie's sobbing echoed around the room.

Kneeling over his father Ben worried what he should do. Gently he turned his body trying to see how badly he was wounded. Flicking his fingers through his soft hair it looked as if he were searching for fleas on a dog. All he could see was blood, blood and more blood.

His thoughts interrupted by Johnnie's babbling. Without warning Johnnie went berserk. Lunging towards Anthony he launched his foot into his chest and began to kick him repeatedly. Ben swung around trying to push him away. He raised his right hand and formed a fist. He was pissed off that he no longer appeared to be controlling the situation.

"Stop! Stop! Fucken Stop! And shut up! Shut the fuck up!" he yelled as he jumped to his feet. Who the hell did Johnnie think he was to take charge of the situation.

Johnnie froze.

"What the hell are you doing? I told you we were leaving."

"I told you I was trying to help, I was only trying to help."

Hearing a car door slam Ben dashed to the window and peered out. It was Mr. Benson, the gardener. They had met on numerous occasions. His predicament suddenly became so much worse. Mr. Benson could not find them. Mr. Benson had to be stopped.

CHAPTER SIXTEEN

Dropping to the floor Ben lent against the wall deliberating over his next move. The voices in his head plagued his every thought. Niggling away, berating his every action. Johnnie nervously paced back and forth crying like a child. The floorboards creaking with every step. Anthony was still motionless on the floor. The force of Johnnie's hit had rendered him unconscious. Ben needed to act and act fast. The clock was ticking. There was no time to ruminate over the situation or rationalise what was happening. Mr. Benson had disappeared from sight and without action, he could soon be inside the house. He would notice someone had been lurking around. He had walked over to their car, he had studied the number plate and looked inside it. Anthony's car displayed signs for 'White's Plumbing.' Maybe his mother had mentioned Anthony. Mr. Benson may have had no idea Claire had been killed in a car accident. There was no doubt in Ben's mind he would enter the house to investigate. It would be impossible to explain his father's unconscious state. Mr. Benson needed to be stopped.

Smiling broadly towards Johnnie Ben's eyes remained fixed. A plan flashed into his mind. He was a genius. But he needed to act and act fast. The clock was still ticking. The minutes were passing. Mr. Benson had been outside snooping. It was almost certain he would enter. Without action he would soon be in the house. If he made his way inside chances were he would discover Anthony. This could not happen. Stopping Mr. Benson was crucial.

Charles Benson was a modest man in his mid seventies. Extremely active, he loved to tinker in his garage and enjoyed the outdoors. He had been the loyal gardener for over ten years; since he retired from the local council. A proud Australian who served in the Korean War. His next great achievement in life would be celebrating his diamond anniversary with his wife, Agnes. The two had met as childhood sweethearts. For them it was love at first sight. They were soul mates. Time had only strengthened their loving bond. Agnes was a devoted wife, supportive mother and doting grandmother. Three years ago Charles had been faced with a changed playing field. Agnes had been diagnosed with dementia.Recently her condition had deteriorated. Yet Charles insisted he should take care of his wife, it was a man's responsibility to look after his family. Employing the services of external carers allowed him to continue with his gardening duties. The additional cash afforded him the ability to purchase some of the sweeter things in life. Flowers and chocolates for Agnes were at the top of his shopping list.

Johnnie was flicking his fingers. One sure sign of his being nervous was his flicking his fingers. He had been flicking his fingers for at least five minutes. With his frustration building Ben was sure Johnnie wanted to kill all of his problems in the worst way possible. Ben's anger was very different to the anger Johnnie possessed. Ben's was cold and calculating, he did not seek just to destroy. He saw no value in exploding, shouting or throwing things all the time. What he sought was revenge. His anger was persistent. It never faltered, it would not disappear until everything was as the Gods had commanded. In his mind he was the powerful Lord

Benami. Johnnie was a parasite who required direction. It was Ben's duty to instruct. Johnnie's role was to listen and obey his commands.

All of a sudden Johnnie began screaming. Every other word was a profanity. Agitation ravaged his body. He couldn't handle moments of heightened stress. Ben needed to act. He needed to take control.

The sound of the front door opening meant there was no more time for standing still. Inaction was no longer possible. Turning to Johnnie, Ben released his command.

"Kill him!"

Without hesitation Johnnie turned towards the bedroom door, flung it open and charged out of the room.

Ben followed. Peeking from around the corner, he watched. Frozen. Staring. Listening. A loud and deep frenzied howl echoed throughout the house. Reverberating thumping bursts filled Ben's ears. Johnnie leaped down the stairs. The front door was open. Mr. Benson stood at the base of the stairs. A panicked scream screeched from within his tiny body. His eyes popped. Petrified, he was unable to move. Johnnie collided with his body. Mr. Benson hit the floor with a crack. His glasses flung from his face. Flying across the room, they hit the wall and smashed on the dusty floor. Johnnie had not finished. Mr. Benson raised a hand. Covering his face he released a terrifying cry. He was begging.

"No, no…please don't hurt me…please!"

Johnnie towered over him. Releasing his anger he launched a foot into Mr. Benson's chest. Johnnie went berserk. Kick after kick after kick. Knocking the wind out of poor Mr. Benson. He offered no reprieve. A madman on a mission. His mission to kill.

Mr. Benson was curled up on the floor. He struggled to catch his breath. Moaning and groaning. Johnnie's kicking was unrelenting. He towered over his powerless victim. Raising his hands above his head he gripped the sword handle as if it were an axe. He thrust his arms downwards. *Whack!*

Mr. Benson went silent. Agnes would receive no flowers or chocolates. Johnnie stood puffing. Blood spatter covered his clothes and face. He smiled. He was a loyal and committed servant. Lord Benami and the gods would be pleased.

Closing the front door he took a deep breath. He looked down on Mr. Benson's lifeless body. He poked the tip of the blade against Mr. Benson's face. He released a humming sound. He smiled. He had not yet finished. Raising the sword he again thrust it downwards. Again and again. Hack after hack. Slicing, chopping, mutilating, as if he were attempting to kill the same defenceless individual multiple times. Finally he stopped. Huffing and puffing, blood spatter, pieces of skin and flecks of bone soaked his clothes and ran down his face. His attack was vicious and could only be described as barbaric. He smiled. His job was complete.

"I did it! I got you! You evil warrior! I am the gatekeeper, the powerful gatekeeper!" he chanted.

Trudging back up the stairs he held the sword high in the air. Success was his. Puffing out his chest he beamed with happiness. He was a proud parasite. Surely this act would see him elevate within the ranks of their secret society.

CHAPTER SEVENTEEN

Anthony moaned in agony as he began to regain consciousness. Wriggling around on the floor he resembled a slug; his movements slow and uncoordinated. His body bloodied, battered and bruised from the beating Johnnie had subjected him to. Locked in the room. He was now a hostage. Lying on his side the wooden floorboards felt scratchy on his cheek. As he struggled to look around he reached up to hold his pounding head. Everything was dull and he was unsure how much time had passed. Looking at his wrist he could see the sun tanned outline of where he would normally put on his watch. In his haste to find the truth he had left it sitting on the bathroom cabinet. There was no way of knowing the time. The sound of muffled voices entered his ears. The voices unrecognisable. Their words inaudible. Slowly he moved his hand down to his aching jaw feeling a couple of loose teeth. The smell of dust filled his nose, while the metallic taste of blood filled his mouth. Everything appeared blurred and a bit hazy. The room was dark. The window now covered. The door closed. It was as if he was waking up with a bad hangover, although he knew things were much worse. Little glimpses of reality bled through into his haze of speculation and darkness. Snapshots of what had been going on before he had lost consciousness. A thin line separated reality from what was imagined. There was no denying something was seriously wrong.

The last thing he remembered was being at the house. Both he and Ben had heard a noise and he decided they should leave. After that everything went black. The world went silent.

Struggling to his feet he grabbed hold of the wall, staggering and lurching. He attempted to gain and keep his equilibrium as he limped towards the bed.

"Ben," he yelled, "Ben is that you?"

Then silence. The voices stopped. Tears rolled down the side of his face.

The sound of footsteps approaching the door quickly brought him into the now. Letting go of the bed his body teetered to the left and he slammed into the wall. A trail of blood seeped from his left ear.

Again, there was silence.

"Who are you?" he moaned, "what do you want?"

Resting his head against the wall Anthony relaxed his exhausted body, inhaled deeply and released a loud sigh. His right hand braced the left side of his torso as he stared towards the door. In normal circumstances it would have appeared just an ordinary door, but now it appeared large and imposing. If it was locked it would prevent his freedom. In a battered condition he knew it was his only hope but if locked it might as well have been a solid wall, for there was no way he would be able to manage an escape from the window. Extending his hand he felt a lump in his throat. Nervous energy rushed through his body. He slowly grasped the door handle. Pulling downwards. The handle felt cold. He tugged towards his chest. His fear intensified. Wrenching as hard as he could the door remained an impenetrable barrier. Wrenching, yanking and jerking at the handle his fear changed to panic. He was trapped. The straining of his actions heard within his huffing and puffing.

"Fuck!" he screamed at the top of his lungs.

"Ben! Ben! Are you there?" he screeched, his voice more urgent than before. Still there was silence. Defeated by his actions he collapsed to the floor and began to sob. Tears streamed down his face.

Suddenly the hinges of the door squealed like fingernails running down a chalkboard. Anthony looked up expecting to see Ben. But it was not Ben. In front of him stood a stranger. A terrifying intruder. A tall and awkward looking man. Dark crimson spattered across his shirt and over his face. Anthony's eyes fixated on the dark crimson. It resembled scattered freckles and random running lines. But there was nothing random about this crazed eyed intruder. There was nothing confusing about the dark crimson either, Anthony knew it was blood. Fresh dripping blood.

Scampering back across the floor Anthony tried to create distance between them. Frantically, he began to yell.

"Ben, Ben…where are you Ben?"

Fearful his son had been injured or worse.

"Who are you?" he questioned between his sniffles, "what have you done to my son?"

"I am the gatekeeper, my job is to protect my Queen."

"Your Queen, who is your queen? What are you talking about?"

Glancing around the room Anthony tried in earnest to find his son. Fearing the worst he struggled to stand.

"Where is Ben? Where is my son? What have you done with him?"

Johnnie laughed.

"Why are you laughing? Where is he? What have you done?"

"I killed him!"

Anthony erupted into uncontrollable crying. He was hysterical, the thought of Claire flashed through his mind. The image of his son's lifeless body was too hard to imagine.

"No, no…not my son," he blubbered.

Johnnie laughed again.

"You bastard!" Anthony yelled, "I will kill you myself…You bastard!"

Pushing off against the wall Anthony charged towards Johnnie. Johnnie's fist made contact with his face. Anthony flew back hitting the wall in a crumpled mess.

"Shut up or you will be next!"

Anthony grabbed his jaw. Blood appeared on his fingers. His pain intensified. His fear turned to panic. He lost the plot. He yelled at the top of his lungs. He hoped someone would hear. Someone had to hear. Surely someone would come to investigate the commotion.

"Help! Help! Someone help!"

His cries infuriated Johnnie. Johnnie grabbed his ears.

"Shut up! Shut up! Or I will make you shut up!" Johnnie screamed furiously shaking his clenched fists next to his cheeks. His words echoed around the room. His dark eyes stared. "Shut the fuck up!"

Anthony went silent. Frozen. They exchanged twin beams of hate. Glaring. Heavy breathing echoed around the room. Footsteps outside the door. Anthony prayed it was help. He prayed for his son. The footsteps stopped.

He returned his glare towards Johnnie. "You won't get away with this," he murmured.

Johnnie ignored his words and sauntered to the door. Glancing over his shoulder he offered a sinister grin and closed the door behind him.

Anthony was alone. Trapped. Scared. Battered. Bloody and bruised. Closing his eyes he prayed this was all a nightmare. A nightmare he would soon awake from.

Worry flickered in his eyes. He looked at the blood on his arm. He questioned the torn state of his shirt. What the hell had happened in his moments of darkness? He felt the ache in his side, the bruising to his ribs. Struggling to his feet he limped towards the mirror. His reflection was shocking. His face bloodied. His left eye blackened and swollen to a thin slit, offering a puffy slither of sight. Anthony looked away horrified by his own reflection. Glancing back his disbelief remained, his pain failed to diminish. Staring, the look of raw panic entered his eyes. He was petrified. Extending his shaking hands he thought about picking up the jewellery box. It appeared solid; made of either pewter or possibly silver plated. Its floral design softened its appearance yet Anthony could not discount the injury that could be inflicted by its sharp edges if he held it correctly and thrust it into his captor's head. It would be like using a brick. If he stood behind the door he may be able to strike and overpower the deranged intruder. A loud crashing noise broke his silent thought. What the hell had he been thinking? It was a stupid idea. He was trembling and severely injured. In his weakened state any attack would prove fruitless. Scurrying across the room he flopped onto the bed. The bed springs squeaked. He had to come up with another plan. Panic began to seep in and he forced it back down. He studied his wounds. He needed to focus. He looked around the darkened room. Dust filled his nose, his eyes and his mouth. The taste of mildew and mould mixed with blood, twisted his concern and increased his sense of overwhelming dread. Goose bumps covered his skin encasing his body, reflecting his heightened state of fear. How would this nightmare end?

Touching his arm he could feel the pain. He hurt all over, his battered body bruised. Hearing a loud thud from beyond the locked door he jumped. His lips twitched and he bit down tasting blood. Closing his eyes he tried to absorb his pain while attempting to figure out his next move. Wondering why everything had gone so wrong. The smell of petrol entered his nose. Raised voices appeared to argue from the next room. His panic intensified. Did his captors plan on burning the house down with him inside? Placing his ear against the wall he strained to understand the words. They were unrecognisable. A loud thud collided with the wall from the other side. The wall vibrated. Anthony jumped. Inhaling deeply he tried in earnest to sniff out petrol. Being burnt alive he thought would be one of the worst possible ways to die. Moving closer to the door he continued to sniff. Placing his nose next to the crack in the door the only thing he inhaled was dust. A gentle breeze touched his nose. The smell of petrol was no more. Maybe he had only imagined it.

Anthony returned to the bed to rest his battered body.

All was silent.

CHAPTER EIGHTEEN

The sound of footsteps returned. Anthony jolted upright. He could hear voices. Unknown and unrecognisable words. The voices became raised. Anthony began to freak out. His chest was pounding. His breathing became shallow as he struggled for air. Eyes wide and darting. His mind racing. He started to think of all the scenarios. Who was it behind the door? Wiping his sweaty palms down his thighs he felt like his chest was about to burst. What would he do if the door was opened? Should he charge? Attempt an escape? Maybe help was on its way.

Suddenly the voices stopped. The door handle moved. The door creaked open. Anthony leant to his side. Stretching his neck he struggled to see. The door was only slightly ajar. *Bang!* It was reefed shut.

Anthony sighed. He was unsure whether to be relieved or disappointed that he was again alone.

Without time to think the door thrust wide open. Anthony stared. He was in shock. This was not the person he had been expecting. Standing before him was his son. He was alone and unharmed. Overwhelming relief brought tears to his eyes.

"Ben…oh Ben, you are alright."

Ben rushed to his father's side as the door slammed behind him.

"You're okay," Anthony looked his son up and down studying for any injuries but there were none.

"He said he killed you… I thought you were dead," Anthony began to weep.

"You were knocked out. I don't know who he is. I don't know what he wants. He is a madman. He locked me in the other room. I heard him attack someone else. I think he killed them. I heard thudding and thumping, someone's cries then silence. I was terrified, I thought he had attacked you again. Then I heard a repeated hacking noise. It made me sick. I thought he killed you."

Ben's eyes darted around the room, the tremble in his voice made Anthony afraid for their safety.

"Who? Who is it? Why would they do this? This is my house now."

Ben glared at his father, "I have no idea…Why on earth would I know?"

"I don't know but if you have any idea you need to tell me. Did you see anything? How many of them are there? Anything…think Ben…anything?" Anthony pleaded for information.

Ben remained closed lipped shaking his head.

"I don't have the faintest idea."

"Yeah well I didn't think you would…I just thought you may have seen or heard something."

Anthony released a loud sigh as he relaxed his body. He needed to come up with a plan. Surely between the two of them they would be able to over power this madman.

The sound of footsteps outside the door made goose bumps run down Anthony's arms. The bite of fear and danger ran down his spine. The air around them seemed to thicken. Then stillness. An eerie silence hung in the air.

The door flung back open. The madman stood before them.

"You come with me," he commanded pointing towards Ben.

Without hesitation Ben rose to his feet and left the room. Looking over his shoulder towards Anthony his face displayed a look of terror. Eyebrows arched. Eyes wide open. Mouth slightly open and lips turned down. Anthony believed his son complying with the demands would prevent him from being subject to harm. He was pleased he left without resistance. He prayed for his son's safety. The door slammed behind them. Footsteps indicated they were still upstairs. Anthony then heard the sound of another door slamming. This he believed signified his son was being held hostage in another room. Floor boards creaked from outside. The footsteps again approached his door. The door flung open. This time the madman had returned with other items in his hands. Rope and duct tape.

Anthony went berserk.

"Get away from me…this is my house…get away from me!" he screamed, "money, do you want money? I can give you money, I have money, how much, what's your price?…just let us go. We will forget this all happened. I don't know you, please just let us go."

His words were of no consequence. One solid boot to his ribs shut him up quick smart. Leaning over Johnnie grabbed his wrists and wrapped the rope around them. Tugging hard and making a double knot rendered Anthony helpless. But this would not shut Anthony up. He needed answers. He wanted to know why this was happening.

"Who are you?" he stammered. His breathing difficult.

Johnnie turned to him. His eyes appeared vacant. He appeared smug.

"I am the gatekeeper. Lord Benami is my friend. I have watched over him since he was a baby."

His words were sickening. They made Anthony feel as though he would vomit.

"What?" Anthony stared towards Johnnie in shock then glanced towards the door and back towards his captor. Aghast at what he had just heard. How could this be happening? Shirley had bestowed the name of Lord Benami upon Ben. His son had lied. His son was deeply involved. Things immediately catapulted from bad to worse. Deception. Secrets. Lies. Add to the mix violence and possible murder. This was where the secrets lie. How would his nightmare end?

Johnnie had heard too much and said too much. He was sick of talking. Retrieving a stained and crusty handkerchief from his pocket he forced it into Anthony's mouth. Pushing his palm over the top to keep it secure. Grabbing the duct tape he pulled on the end ripping off a long strip. The sound of the cotton mesh tearing signified Anthony's impending silence. Yanking the tape across Anthony's mouth Johnnie showed no regard as the adhesive surface ripped across his face then through his hair. Pulling fiercely, tugging at his skin, ripping out hair roots and all.

Johnnie's duty was complete. He left the room.

Anthony lay petrified and alone. Bound and gagged. Helpless. Terrified as to what would happen next.

Within minutes the door was flung open. In walked Ben. Johnnie stood close behind him. Anthony lay staring. Ben stood staring. Expressionless. His eyes wandered around the room. He turned and looked over his shoulder. Then he looked back towards his father. His calmness made Anthony even more concerned. Why was his son not saying anything? Why did he not come to assist? Why was he participating in such sinister behaviour?

Ben clashed his fist against the wall. His quietness erupted into rage. His eyes widened then changed to staring slits of hate. His jaw tensed and teeth clenched. His nose crinkled like a snarling dog.

"You are an evil warrior and evil warriors must die!" he roared as spit flung from his mouth. The veins in his neck protruding as his fury ignited.

Turning towards Johnnie his yelling continued as he snapped his demand, "Get me the sword!"

Johnnie jumped to attention, turned and limped out of the room. He returned seconds later with the blood smeared sword. Handing it to Ben his eyes shied away as he stared at the floor. Ben approached his father. His eyes appeared vacant. His actions those of an individual possessed by demons. He could see the pain on his father's face, the terror. Rope bound his wrists. His hands strained for freedom. His fingers stretched out like tentacles on a struggling octopus. A dirty handkerchief and duct tape gagged his mouth. Ben was in control. His father, who he believed was Lord Antony was vulnerable, an easy target and his to destroy.

"You stole my mother so now I am going to steal your soul," he screamed.

Ben raised his arms above his shoulders with the sword in hand. His head tilted back as if he were looking towards the ceiling. Gibberish flew from his mouth, his words unrecognisable. He closed his eyes and began to chant indistinguishable mumble. Anthony closed his eyes and prayed for a miracle. He thought of Claire. Trembling with fear. Tears escaped his eyes. He needed a miracle. Any miracle.

A knocking sound interrupted his chanting. Ben's eyes sprung open wide. His intent staring resumed. It was as if he was gazing out to a far horizon, searching for something that did not exist. He lowered the sword next to his waist. He scanned the room. The knocking returned. It was coming from the front door.

"Fuck!" he released a restrained yet forceful word that encapsulated his frustration.

CHAPTER NINETEEN

Hearing a knock at the front door Ben peered out the upstairs window. However the roofline stood between him and the verandah below.

"Bloody hell what else can go wrong," he snarled as he shook his head.

Instructing Johnnie to stand guard at his father's door he handed him the sword and made a dash to another room. He was instantly stunned. What the hell was Rebecca's car doing out the front? How the hell did she know about the house? Leaping down the stairs he knew he could not afford for her to enter. Reaching the door he swung it open, puffing as he greeted her.

"Hey Rebecca what's up? What are you doing here?"

"I need to talk with your father he said you were coming here and the other night…can I talk with him please?"

Ben stood with his hands on his hips blocking her entry and shaking his head.

"Dad is upset…he is upstairs…sorry Rebecca but this is a private family moment…" he paused looking towards her with mournful eyes, "I will get dad to come over when we get home."

Without another word he closed the door. Leaning against the wall he was certain she would leave without an argument and respect his telling her they were having a private family moment. Her fading footsteps indicated he was right. The sound of her car engine starting signalled they were in the clear and so he returned upstairs, annoyed his father would have even dared tell another person about the house.

Upstairs Johnnie became nervous. Standing at the door was not enough. Anthony's face was shadowed in darkness yet he could still feel his eyes. The thought of being watched made him nervous. He stepped inside the room and closed the door. He limped towards Anthony. Expressionless. He waved the sword close to his face. Taunting him. Anthony's eyes darted between the sword blade and his captor. Afraid. He did nothing. He remained perfectly still. Too terrified to move. Frozen at the thought of what would happen next.

Anthony had heard the conversation. He had recognised Rebecca's caring and somewhat singsong voice. It was extremely distinctive in the manner she would make her conversations rise and fall in a musical way. Her words reverberating as if the effervescent effect from eating copious amounts of fruit tingles. She had been the second person who had shown up and thankfully she had been able to leave safely. Maybe there was a chance help would soon arrive. However with his wrists bound and mouth gagged, Anthony knew he was running out of options. Unable to get his son to see reason it ultimatelycame down to attempt an escape or possibly die. His eyes locked onto the window. Maybe an escape was possible. Ben had returned upstairs and pointed for Johnnie to leave the room. Outside in the hallway both were engaged in what sounded like a heated argument. They were squawking like two magpies in a tin can.

Sucking in a deep and pained breath Anthony dragged himself to the wall. With his chest battered and bruised from his repeated beatings, it felt as though he was breathing in mere slithers of oxygen. Struggling to his feet he felt a slight relief as he inhaled. His eyes danced around the room, sweat beaded on his forehead, and his ears filled with white noise. For a moment he found himself standing almost frozen. Unsure if he should continue. His wrists were burning from his continued straining. His restraintsonly slightly loosened from his twisting and turning. The rope had cut in further, mixed together with the salty clamminess that chilled his skin, the pain was nearing intolerable.

He stepped with caution listening for footsteps. The voices outside continued unaware of the creaking floorboards below his feet. Afraid the slightest noise would arouse their return and produce a repeat beating he cautiously edged closer to the window. Arriving there safely he ripped away the blanket they had slung over the curtain rail. Rays of sunlight again shone around the room offering hope. He hoped his angel Claire was watching over him. He prayed she would protect him. He hoped with all his heart that his previous belief about there only being a black hole abyss when one died was not true. If there was any chance angels and spirits of the dead existed now was the time for them to appear. Closing his eyes tightly he thought *I do believe in angels, I do believe in angels.* Surely a person's spirit and soul did not just vanish. Opening up his eyes he glanced around the room. Everything appeared as before. He was alone and it was time to act.

Forcing the window open was achieved quieter than Anthony had anticipated. Holding his breath so not to make any noise he lifted one leg and placed it on the roof that ran along towards the front verandah. In his mind he knew all he had to do would be to make it to the front verandah. Then he would be able to lower himself gently to the ground below. Looking down towards the ground made him dizzy. Anthony was not one for heights, wearing thick socks he said made him nauseous. Yet glancing over his shoulder he feared his attackers would soon return. This may be his last chance at freedom. Holding onto the window above his head he balanced on the sill, supporting his body weight with the foot that he had managed to place upon the roof. The window rattled. Anthony coughed to disguise the noise. The voices outside the door continued oblivious to his break out attempt.

With two feet firmly on the roof Anthony's legs went to jelly. His body a lather of sweat, hands stuck firmly on the window frame above. He began to panic. Unsure if his fear would allow his fingers to release. If he didn't move his legs were going to give out on him. Closing his eyes he huffed and puffed conjuring all the strength required to make that first vital step. Knowing once he started moving every step was another closer to freedom. Releasing his hands he reached high, grabbing hold of the gutter above. However the tight binding around his wrists only allowed one hand to make contact. It was imperative he moved quickly. He had to clear the window so he could not be reefed back inside. Clinging to the gutter he tried to steady himself. His hand was slipping. Once outside the pitch of the roof became a greater challenge. His ankles strained and his feet shuffled as he attempted to calm himself. Lunging upwards he steadied himself. All he had to do would be to get his legs to move. Sliding along the ledge Anthony lost and caught his grip at stop and go intervals. Staring at the wall in front he was not game to look anywhere else.

One foot after the other, one foot after the other, hand, hand, slide. His only thought.

A threatening voice yelled from the window.

"Where do you think you are going?"

Suddenly he changed from escape artist to the hunted. Anthony turned and slipped. Grabbing hold of the gutter he feared it would give way. Thrashing his legs he attempted to steady himself. But his hand was slipping. His body weak. Unable to hold on. His body dropped. His face hit the roof tiles. Smashing his nose and front teeth. In an instant he slid off. His clawing hands unable to stop his momentum.

Hitting the ground hard and with a loud thud he heard the crunchy and cracking of branches and bones. The pain was excruciating, the horrendous sounds were quickly replaced by a high pitch ring that echoed in his ears. Fearing he would pass out he lay staring at the sky with unblinking eyes. He could have been killed. Blood filled his mouth, the force of his face hitting the roof shattered his nose and his teeth had burst through his top lip sending an explosion of blood spatter across his face. His saving grace was a large gardenia he thumped down on. Like him it now appeared a little worse for wear. It was flattened, limbs snapped and flowers sent hurtling with impact. It was not the quiet escape he had hoped for. Staggering to his feet he gasped for breath and shrieked in agony. Desperately he began staggering towards the pathway out. Dazed and confused. Unable to maintain focus. His failing legs stumbled. His body lurched and he collapsed to the ground.

Closing his eyes for a split second he regained his determination. Opening his eyes he was greeted by his worst nightmare. Laying still he was forced to concede defeat. His eyes widened and terrified.

"Well, lookie, lookie...who do we have here?" A sinister smile revealed teeth like a dilapidated picket fence. Anthony knew his nemesis was incapable of making decisions for himself. It was Ben who was controlling all the moves. Ben had a way with words and this awkward moving, odd postured galoot was like a pawn, being played. Trying to reason with him would be useless. Anthony was sure the only thing a brain scan would find in this maniacs head would be white ants. Yet the sight of him made him afraid, well worse than afraid. He was scared witless. There was no reasoning with a madman. He was clearly unbalanced and capable of anything. Charging at him as best he could would prove fruitless. Kicking at him would merely inflict greater pain upon himself. With his stomach in his throat he began to speak, to plead for his release.

Johnnie stood shaking his head, in a calm voice he muttered words Anthony dreaded hearing.

"I have to take you back now."

Anthony had never felt so powerless. A mass of nervous energy invaded his body as he was dragged back towards the front door. The hands of deception tugging on his heart strings stimulating the aching within his chest. His son had betrayed him. The voice of reason spoke, *"You did this!"* Maybe he was the creator of his own destiny. Maybe things would have been very different if he had looked after his wife. If he had listened to his son. Shown the concern every parent should have shown when things started going astray. Maybe this was all his fault. Overcome by guilt Anthony let his body go limp. Succumbing to fear and accepting defeat was inevitable, tears welled within his eyes. No one would save him. He would soon be reunited with Claire.

As his heels hit the steps on the way back into the house, he took one last look at the sky above. Clear blue skies appeared where only hours ago the dark clouds had loomed. Taking one last deep inhalation of the sweet cool air he embraced the beauty and magnificence of Mother Nature. Everything felt so clean and fresh after a downpour. Closing his eyes he could do nothing more than pray and although he was not overly religious, silently pleading for any kind of divine intervention would not go astray.

The front door slammed behind him. Anthony's eyes sprung back open. His limp body slipped along the floor. A strange wetness lashed down his back. Curious as to what could cause this bizarre sensation he turned his head struggling to see from beyond his extended arms that were being tugged at without regard. Instantly he began to gag and heave. His indefensible body was being dragged through the seeping juices of a lifeless body that had oozed, spilled and spattered across the floorboards. A nearly unrecognisable corpse that resembled that of a slaughter carcass you would find in a butcher's shop. Hacked, chopped and partially dismembered remains of an innocent victim. An individual who so happened to be in the wrong place at the wrong time. The repulsive and macabre result, actions of a madman. But who? Was it his son who had committed this heinous and barbaric act or the monstrous creature who yanked at his arms. Anthony could feel a warm foulness rising in his throat. He could feel the blood seeping through his clothing, coating his skin with a layer of tackiness. His body jerked as his heaving continued. Repulsed he closed his eyes. His mind telling him not to look, it couldn't be real. His head telling him it was real. But surely this could not be happening. Looking down towards his dragging feet, he had full view of the gruesome murder his son had spoken of. Again he began to ask himself who really committed this sadistic act? Was his son not only deluded but also capable of murder?

It was all too gruesome to comprehend. He let his body go limp. His heels met each step with a violent and familiar thumping sound. The squeaking of the floorboards below resembled nothing more than his impending doom.

Terrified, beaten down, his body crushed and drained Anthony became emotional. Fear was written over his grief stricken face. Heartbroken by his incommunicative son. Imprisoned by a madman. Judged and kept silent. He had been let down, lied to, mistreated, nagged and subjected to senseless beatings. It was the worst moment in his life. Claire was gone and his son had turned to evil. Squeezing his eyes closed he began to think of Rebecca. She claimed she was able to speak with the dead. He hadn't believed her but maybe just maybe she did hear. If this was the case she may also be capable of hearing his silent cries. Focusing on her, he began to silently plead. He prayed by some miracle she would hear his voice and she would send help. Cynic or not, anything was worth a try. In his mind's eye he could see her. Her blonde wind swept pixie cut hairstyle that complemented her piercing emerald green eyes and caring smile. Her teeth so perfectly straight and white, he was sure she had spent many hours and dollars in visits to the dentist. The word pocket rocket came to mind when he thought of Rebecca. She was always on the go. Always only too willing to assist. Her energy appeared boundless. She was a woman who took pride in her appearance. Beautiful both inside and out. He could smell her, her intense fruity freshness. A mixture of citrus splash and berry fusion. He could feel the warmth from her touch. He began to plead, hoping with all his heart that the impossible was in some weird and wonderful way actually possible.

Rebecca please Rebecca…I need you, look at me, hear me… come on damn it, please I beg of you, please hear me. They are going to kill me, I don't want to die, please Rebecca please! he thought.

But no response came. No caring voice delivered the positive reassurance he prayed for. A lone tear escaped the corner of his eye. Powerless he resigned himself to defeat. Questioning his assailants would only increase the rage. Sadistic individuals required no reason to act. His only hope being if he remained silent his suffering would be minimal.

I am coming to be with you Claire. He thought as he closed his eyes once more and prayed for the end.

CHAPTER TWENTY

Dragging Anthony into the room Johnnie was ordered to throw his debilitated body onto the bed. He followed Ben's rigid commands without resistance or complaint. Johnnie was his loyal servant. Ben retrieved the duct tape from the floor in the corner of the room. Wrapping it around his father's rope bound hands he stretched his father's arms over his head securing them to the bed frame making another escape attempt impossible. Ripping the duct tape from Anthony's mouth and removing his cloth gag, Anthony viewed as a positive action. Maybe his son was open to suggestions as to how they could move forward in a positive way. His fidgeting was a good sign he was nervous and when people were nervous there were generally two options they could take. Firstly they could give in, this would be the best outcome. Alternatively they could attack with great force. Anthony hoped his son had not ventured passed the point of no return. Looking at his father Ben realised everything had gone on for far too long. Glancing towards Johnnie he raised his eyebrows.

"You need to get rid of Mr. Benson's body!" he snapped pointing at Johnnie.

Johnnie nodded.

"Where?" he questioned as his head tilted to the side, confused by the lack of direction.

"Get rid of him under the house! Take him there, you can manage that can't you?" he shouted.

Holding his hands to his ears Johnnie cowered.

"Please don't shout, I don't like it when you shout."

"Then do what I tell you…Do you want to be a parasite forever?"

Johnnie stood still avoiding eye contact.

"No."

"Then do what I say. You must assist me so that you will be rewarded with greatness. I would if I could but I can't…You see Mr. Benson was an evil warrior…"

Ben paused looking at Johnnie, the tone of his voice became gentle almost caring.

"You did good…No, no…You did great, you killed the evil warrior and for that you will be rewarded. But if I touch his poisonous blood even one tiny drop everything will have been for nothing. You don't want to destroy our golden circle lineage? You don't want to go against Queenie do you?"

Straightening up Ben stood at attention, with his right hand over his heart.

"I am Lord Benami, the one and only, the powerful Lord Benami…follow my commands and you will be rewarded."

Johnnie smiled he liked rewards.

Johnnie who was formally known as Jonathon Fox had known Ben virtually all of his life. He along with his young and struggling single mother, Felicity had moved into the house next door to Shirley when he was only four years old. For Shirley, Johnnie filled the void she had been experiencing since her daughter Claire had moved out. Being only four years old Johnnie was extremely impressionable and it didn't take long before Shirley noticed his uniqueness. He was an extremely nervous character, who often found himself flicking his fingers. For Johnnie, routine was crucial, a change in routine would send him into an uncontrollable state of upset and panic. What Johnnie enjoyed most of all was a quiet and habitual existence. Shirley had always loved telling wondrous tales, Johnnie provided her with an audience. As the years passed Shirley's babysitting became increasingly enjoyable. Johnnie would open and close the gate for her as he skipped towards her front door eager to play a hushed game of hide and seek or snuggle on the lounge and listen to her great tales of dragons and evil warriors. It was his enthusiasm in completing the opening and closing of the gate, which led Shirley to name Johnnie the gatekeeper. It was a name that made him proud. Within her tales he was powerful, a dutiful protector. It was the highest honour ever bestowed on the son of a parasite. Shirley tactfully explained how she deduced Johnnie's standing as a parasite. It was his mother's name that gave it away. Felicitys were always nicknamed Flea, and a flea could never amount to anything other than a parasite. However by obeying instruction he would be assured of elevation within the fanciful world she spoke of.Four years later Ben was born and as the years passed Shirley's audience consisted of two extremely captivated individuals. Of course with Ben being her grandson, he belonged to a much higher class. And so Lord Benami was created; he was the chosen one and the gatekeeper was ever compliant in his instruction, to protect and serve at all costs. Shirley or Queenie as they both affectionately called her would secretly bundle both boys into her car and drive to her other house. For this house was what she referred to as her castle with a secret garden. There they would play for hours on end, undisturbed, imagination's running wild. It was a secret that made everything appear so much more special.

They were privileged and those who were privileged in life were always rewarded.

Ben snapped his fingers breaking Johnnie's distant gaze.

"Go on then, do what I say." Snapping his fingers twice more Johnnie nodded his head and left the room.

Alone with his father Ben began to moan and snarl, his muttered words were unidentifiable. Shaking then nodding his head as if he were trapped in an argument. His thoughts changing direction. Darting gibberish flew from his mouth. Anthony lay staring at his son. Aghast at his behaviour and fearful as to what would happen next. He was running out of options.

"You aren't my father! You are a clone from another universe! I know… she told me!" Ben cried.

"Who? Who told you…"

Anthony's words were quickly interrupted by Ben's babble.

"The tracerteps will get you, they will come for us all…You are a traitor…You are Lord Antony, the evil warrior…You want to destroy me!"

Ben paced back and forth waving his hands in the air. His anger seething. His words forceful and full of hate. "I am Lord Benami, the powerful Lord Benami!"

Anthony had to get his son to see reason.

"No!" he yelled.

Ben froze. His babbling stopped. The force in Anthony's voice had broken his thought and so he stood staring at his father with a look of puzzlement. Anthony needed to change his tone, maybe a soft approach would get his son to see reason.

"Can't you see she has corrupted your mind. Poisoned your thinking. She was the evil one, not me.

I am your father, your protector. She was deranged, a habitual liar. A chameleon to her surroundings. She chose an appropriate face for different situations. Her lies have created a ripple effect that has reverberated through the entire world. There is no golden circle. You are Ben. There are no tracerteps. It's all bullshit! She created them in her imaginary world. There is one world. There is no parallel universe. You have to see reason. I am your father. She called me Lord Antony because she didn't like me. She has poisoned you. I can help you…Please Ben…please!"

Standing still Ben's eyes displayed nothing but emptiness, until finally he had heard enough.

"Shut up! Shut up! Shut up!" he roared at the top of his lungs, his fists punching at his thighs. Words spewed from his mouth like lava from an exploding volcano. Its eruption set off by an earthquake deep within its core. Violent outbursts followed by silence, then aftershock after aftershock.

"They are watching us, you know…they watch our every move!"

"Who…who is watching us?"

"The dragon warriors!"

Anthony resisted his urge to argue with his son. He was seriously delusional. It was time he changed tack.

"Let me help you…I can help…I have seen the dragon warriors…I have fought against them and won."

Ben lurched towards his father.

"You have?" he asked and for that moment Anthony believed he may have been able to take control.

"I have and I know they are watching us, I saw them outside. That is why I went out the window. I wasn't trying to escape. I wanted to help you!"

"Oh!" Staring at his father Ben dropped to his knees as he studied his face in awe.

"Tell me about them," he whispered urging his father to speak.

"They told me about you. They said you were powerful. They want me to help you. They wanted to see what was under the house."

Ben jumped back his calm demeanour vanished as his eyes stared and nostrils flared. After a few seconds his face became contorted, his eyes became slits and his mouth quivered.

"You're a liar! You are trying to trick me!" he roared as the veins in the side of his neck popped out and his face became a shade of bright red and purple.

"I am not a liar…It's true!" Anthony begged for his son to believe him, "Queenie told me the stories too."

Shaking his head from side to side Ben again stared into nothingness. Defiant at his father's words.

"Your mother was Princess Clara, you are Lord Benami, I am Lord Antony…You are right…but I am not evil. I have been sent here to protect you…please you have to believe me. The evil warriors are outside. Johnnie has been infected by their virus. You have to believe me. He is not family. What happens in the family needs to stay in the family. You must destroy Johnnie before he destroys us all."

Ben's eyes displayed concern widening more and more as Anthony spoke, darting around the room.

"You need to sit, you need to conserve your energy Lord Benami, I can hear them…they are coming!"

Ben dashed over to the window and peered out. In his mind he was sure an attack was imminent. Anthony's words had begun to make him doubt Johnnie's loyalty. Why was Johnnie taking so long?

"What happens in the family stays in the family… what happens in the family stays in the family…yes,

yes…what happens in the family stays in the family… Johnnie is not family…I must destroy Johnnie…I am the powerful Lord Benami."

Anthony nodded.

Ben walked back from the window and passed his father. Approaching the door he appeared mindful that his footsteps remain quiet. He yanked the door open as if he was expecting to find someone behind it. But there was no one. The hallway was deserted. He scanned into the darkness. He closed the door.

They were alone. Where the hell was Johnnie?

CHAPTER TWENTY ONE

Arriving home the thought of Anthony lingered in Rebecca's mind. Ben had been acting peculiar. The other night her encounter with Anthony had been strained. She had broken contact. She had retreated. Left Anthony standing. Maybe she should have insisted on speaking. Something appeared wrong. An inner sense that something was amiss plagued her mind.

Placing her car keys on the kitchen bench she stared out the window. Looking across at Anthony's house she tried to assure herself she was jumping to conclusions. She did not know how she would react if a loved one had died. But then there were so many things Claire had spoken of. An accusation of murder and cover ups, of secrets and lies. What if…what if there was truth in what she had been told? What if something was wrong? Could Anthony be in danger? But surely Ben would have said something.

Flicking the switch on her kettle she listened as the water began to heat. She watched the tiny bubbles appear until they burst through the water surface. The water churned, steam vapours released. The kettle clicked off. She poured herself a cup of tea and retrieved her latest Sharyn Bradford Lunn novel. She loved the strong characters, the history, the way in which the characters were developed and came to life. Holding the warm mug between her hands, she took a sip. The strong bitter smell with smoky overtones entered her nose as the scorching tea lashed her tongue. Placing her cup of tea on the coffee table she strolled down to her laundry and gathered her dirty clothes. Separating whites from colours she came across her favourite white lace edged handkerchief. It was the handkerchief she had taken to Claire's funeral. Pausing for a moment she thought of her friend. What would Claire have done if she found herself in the same situation? Would returning to the house be viewed as interfering? Unlocking her back door she walked outside and peered over into Anthony's yard. All was quiet. Turning around she walked back inside, threw the colours into the washing machine and commenced a small cycle. Closing the lid she began questioning her feelings and her standing. She certainly did not want to be viewed as interfering. Slipping her hands into her pockets thumbs hooked over the top, she stared into nothingness. Her lips pursed and she released a loud sigh. She assured herself all would be fine. Anthony and Ben would soon be home. She would visit them later that evening. There was no need for worry.

Her thoughts then returned to her cup of tea. A nice cuppa and a relaxing read were sure fire ways in settling her concerns. Strolling up the hallway she floppedonto her lounge, opened her novel to where she had left off and began to read. Engrossed in every word, warm sun streaming onto her body she soon became settled. All concern for Anthony disappeared.

CHAPTER TWENTY TWO

Ben paced back and forth glancing out the window every so often, his nerves intensifying as the minutes passed. His eyes appeared dazed and his hands trembled. He was certainly not acting as the son Anthony had once loved. Gone was his spark for life, the carefree son who once had possessed a squeaky voice. The son who enjoyed a game of soccer and who loved watching comedy movies. But it wasn't the change in his voice as he matured that alarmed Anthony, for this was an expected transition into manhood. It was the alarming conversations he was having with someone Anthony could not see or hear. The irrational thinking and violent temper. The unpredictable antics that stirred from within. His son appeared possessed. His son was no longer his son.

Anthony considered every opportunity. When Ben had his back turned he would twist and turnstruggling to loosen his hands. However each movement was greeted by more agony. The rope scratched, burnt and scraped tearing away the upper layer of hair and skin around his wrists. His efforts to no avail. Fear began to engulf his body. Realising the seriousness of his predicament he needed to foster a new strategy. Panicking would get him nowhere. Maybe he could join in with his son's delusions. Up till now going with the flow of his son's warped thinking had appeared the only thing that had offered him any reprieve. The ache in his chest had only intensified after his attempted escape. A short sharp stabbing pain radiated from beneath the left side of his rib cage making it painful to breath. He was a prisoner bound by ropes, trapped within his son's delusions. If he could convince his son he was on his side then maybe just maybe, there was a way to move forward. Freedom could be possible.

"Lord Benami…we need to protect Queenie and our golden circle lineage," he declared.

Ben's pacing stopped as he stared towards his father. His anger disappeared. He spoke in a soft voice saying only one word.

"Yes!"

"I can help you…I want to help you…how can I help you?"

As he spoke Anthony watched his son's every move.

Ben stood still. Anthony could have been lying to him. But he wanted to believe him. Looking deeply into his father's eyes the suffering contortions within his stomach dissolved. His fidgeting hands relaxed. His burning rage was extinguished. A visible calmness washed over him.

And so Anthony continued.

"To truly understand your quest you must tell me more…I am your loyal servant. I am here to assist you. Together we will fight this battle. Great evil is stirring. I can feel it."

Anthony's words set his son off like a firecracker. Dashing towards the window his head jerked erratically from left to right and back again.

"They are out there. They want to destroy my Queenie's name. They want to ruin us all. The devils of darkness have returned. The fate of our golden circle lineage is in my hands," he snapped.

"Then we have little time. We must act now! Tell me your plan. I will assist! We must defeat the devils of darkness!"

Ben turned his attention from outside looking towards Anthony he smiled. His father's words were pleasing. Calm quickly returned to his body. He nodded, sauntered towards the bed and grinned faintly. Perching up next to his father he appeared relaxed. His eyes rolled back into his head as if he was slipping into a hypnotic state.

"To move forward my Lord Benami, we must first go back. Take me back, tell me Queenie's tales and arm me with the knowledge so we can defeat the devils of darkness. You are Lord Benami, the chosen one. I am your loyal servant, your protector." Maintaining a soft a reassuring voice Anthony urged Ben to impart to him details he hoped would not only buy him valuable time, but possibly aid in his release.

"I have been here many times," Ben sighed as he relaxed his body leaning against the bed head next to his fathers restrained hands. "Darius is a dragon warrior, she introduced me to him when I was a boy. She never treated me like a boy. I was always Lord Benami. Queenie was always Queenie. You know she had to kill her parents. They were devil warriors. They wanted to control her every move. She thought she would be able to remove their evil, but that was not possible. They are under the house. But this is not any ordinary house. This is a castle and it has a secret garden."

Anthony was stunned by his son's words. Exceedingly concerned about his disturbed thinking. And tremendously shocked by his allegations. But he had to learn more. He needed to find out the truth. Ben could be the key to revealing all. But then again he could have been lying. His irrational thinking had resulted in totally unpredictable actions. His son was far from being of sound mind.

"What do you mean? Tell me more."

"Queenie was hand picked by the gods. You know they spoke to her from the moment she was born. She was the ruler of all. She had proven powers and could read people's minds. She knew what they were thinking. I am a member of the inner circle of strength. She picked me to take up where she left off. It's all pretty simple. Our secret society has existed since the beginning of time. If you dig deep down into the earth surface far below the layers of sand, rock and clay you will find the ancient remains of a lost city. A city where Queenie's predecessors ruled. You will find fossils that belong to prehistoric creatures. It was a grand city..." Ben paused and made a grunting noise as he cleared his throat. It was clear he had emotionally immersed himself within the stories he had been told. His eyes glared as his jaw tensed.

"That was before the evil warriors attacked and they were forced to a parallel universe," he snarled.

Anthony shivered. Suddenly he became worried. His eyes widened. He wondered if his suggestion to get Ben to talk was wrong.

"But that is not going to happen again, I am here to protect and serve," he said attempting to keep Ben calm.

Ben closed his eyes and smiled. Anthony urged him to continue with his story.

"Tell me about it, please Lord Benami...tell me more."

Ben opened his eyes and looked towards the window. He chuckled then turned towards his father. A stolid look blanketed his face. Silence. Staring intently with vacant eyes Anthony was reminded of his son's unpredictable behaviour. Frozen by fear he dared not to break eye contact with his son. His soft panting appeared synchronised with Ben's gentle snuffling. Minutes passed with complete stillness. Anthony's arms were beginning to ache from his restraints. He wanted to go home. He thought of Claire, wishing he could go back in time. Back to before it all went wrong. Tears welled in his eyes. He could not give up.

"Roar!" Ben released a deep thunderous and terrifying animal cry as his eyes sprung wide open.

Anthony jumped then jerked his head back trying to create distance. With his hands still bound he was going nowhere.

Ben burst out laughing.

"Oh my god, you should have seen your face," slapping his hand against his side his laughter continued. "That was so funny, I scared the crap out of you." Rocking back and forth Ben's eyes sparkled and his teeth flashed. The last time Anthony had witnessed his son's joking manner had been when Claire had been alive. Months earlier, when they had taken a family holiday on the Hawkesbury River. Maybe his son was coming to his senses. But as fast as his hope for a returned son came, it quickly disappeared. Ben snappedback into all seriousness, his formidable storytelling continued. Anthony lay shaking his head wondering what the hell had just happened.

"Just like in feudal Japan we have great warriors called tracerteps. Our society runs parallel to here on earth. I sit at the top now. I have the inner circle strength, my class is the golden circle. You are in the Upper class, that is below me. Then there are the inhabitants and last of all the parasites. Johnnie is a parasite. His mum is flea. And you can't forget the dragons. You people here on earth see them as simple dragonflies, but they are really dragons in disguise and if invoked by anger they can transform into their true giant form, lashing out and destroying all who dare to go against the greater good of all."

Speaking with great enthusiasm Ben was no longer guarded in his actions. His hands waved around as he described the flight patterns of the dragonflies, how they would hover and swoop. It appeared Shirley had created a large array of warriors. It was inevitable one day an evil wrath would descend. Fire spitting dragons would appear in the sky, replacing the dragonflies. Harmless butterflies had the ability to transform into large flapping mystical creatures; with broad long wings allowing them to soar high above the earth. Like the dragons they were capable of putting on spectacular aerial displays, including death-defying swoops. When they were called into duty the taste receptors on their feet instantly transformed into sharp talons capable of killing and carrying prey. Unlike the dragons these loyal servants had wings with razor edges. Magnificent wings that gave them the ability to fly at great speeds, to swoop down on their prey and slice their enemy in two. Bull ants would emerge from beneath the earth, and transform into giant thunderous and fierce beasts, capable of trampling their opponents to death. Notorious for their stinging fury, an army of bull ants was willing to defend to the death. These monsters were powerfully armed soldiers. A formidable force to be reckoned with.

Ben's words excited him, his eyes lit up like a child on Christmas morning. But he was no child, he was nearing manhood. Leaping from the bed hecolourfully described the transformation of the bull ant into a large thunderous beast with its impenetrable body. Without Lord Benami the world would be engulfed into great darkness, evil would rein supreme.

Suddenly Ben stopped speaking, glancing around the room a look of suspicion returned to his face.

"Shhh!" he whispered, "you can not forget the evil warriors, they are hidden and take on various forms inconspicuously blending into everyday life. The are intent on destroying Queenie's name and all who served beneath her. That includes you!"

Staring towards Anthony he was completely immersed within his story telling. He no longer viewed his father as an evil warrior.

Slowly, slowly. Little by little. Piece by piece. Anthony began to put the fragments together. His son clearly believed himself to be the powerful Lord Benami. There were four distinctive levels within his secret society and a parallel universe did exist, along with evil warriors and devils of darkness. The tales his grandmother had spoken of had come to life. She had brain washed him. His mind had been poisoned. He heard voices in his head. It was clear his son was trapped within his delusions and prepared to take whatever steps necessary in order to maintain his existence within these delusions.

It was time for Anthony to throw a spanner in the works.

CHAPTER TWENTY THREE

Johnnie is going to kill you."

Six powerful words escaped Anthony's lips. Six words he hoped would create doubt. Words he prayed would be capable of defeating their delusional teamwork. He had to destroy their combined allegiance.

Ben turned towards his father with a look of horror. His face paled, as his eyes became filled with tears. Anthony nodded reinforcing what he had just stated to be the truth. Doubt entered Ben's eyes, they began darting around filled with suspicion. Nodding his head it appeared he was having a conversation, yet no words escaped his lips. Then stillness. Ben froze glaring towards Anthony. His intent stare accompanied by his heavy breathing.

"He told me. He told me when you left the room to speak with Rebecca."

"What did he tell you?" Ben exploded angrily, "what did he say?"

"He said he was the powerful gatekeeper. His actions please the Gods. Queenie speaks to him. Queenie has told him he is the ruler of all."

Ben's face instantly turned red. His eyebrows lowered and his lips became a thin line. Grabbing Anthony by the shirt he clenched his teeth together so tightly that his jaw ached. Raising one hand he slammed his fist into the bed. He was livid. Words leapt from his mouth like furious uncontrollable flames.

"He is NOT!" he screamed, "I am the powerful Lord

Benami! He is a parasite! I will teach him right from wrong!"

A cruel smirk came across his face.

Anthony nodded in agreement.

And then silence. Anthony lay still on the bed watching his son's intent staring into nothingness.

Finally Ben spoke calmly.

"I want to tell you a story...I want to show you something. Let me tell you a secret. Let me tell you something I have never told anyone before."

Anthony lay watching his every move. His son had the ability to leap from one subject to the next faster than Anthony could blink. His hair-trigger temperament and volatile behaviour had Anthony terrified.

He was fearful of this erratic behaviour yet relieved his son was for that moment composed and had been obliging to share the basis of his belief. Maybe an escape was still possible. He had planted a seed of doubt within Ben's mind and his son appeared to trust him.

Ben reached his right hand around into the back pocket of his jeans and retrieved a tattered envelope. Immediately Anthony recognised it as the one he had been left from his grandmother when she had passed away.

"See this!" he smiled as he flapped the envelope in Anthony's face, "this is the answer to all our problems."

"Why? How? What is it?" Anthony questioned.

"It's a confession to the murders...it explains what happened to the devil warriors under the house and who killed them," Ben laughed, "she was a genius. My Queenie thought of everything."

"It's her confession?"

"No stupid, it's Billy Bunbagel's confession," he

laughed again, "this is what will maintain Queenie's dignity in death. And as for all of this here, don't worry about this mess… I too have a plan."

Anthony stared intensely. Who the hell was Billy Bunbagel? How did his son intend on covering up Mr. Benson's murder? Was he to be his son's sacrificial lamb?

"Johnnie boy!" Ben burst out suddenly before laughing hysterically, acting totally disconnected.

"He will do anything for his Queen. He has the blood on his hands, not me."

"Untie me then…can you untie me so I can help you?" Anthony pleaded believing his son was convinced he was no longer a threat.

"No!" snarled Ben, "you are the evil Lord Antony. The gatekeeper is going to deal with you. Then I am going to deal with him."

Pacing back and forth Ben's rage returned. In his mind he believed Lord Antony had evolved and now it was him against the world. Distant and disconnected his frustration deepened. Clenching his fists he punched them against the wall then flew to the window. Looking out his agitation intensified.

"Where is he? Where the fuck is that moron? I want this over with," he barked impatiently.

Delivering the grim reality of the situation his voice became loud, as his words escaped from behindclenched teeth. Eyes bent into a dark and threatening black. Nostrils flared. Face reddened. Veins protruded. There was no denying the inner burning rage. His ability to maintain a rational and logical conversation had dissolved like a soluble aspirin dropped into a glass of water, all that remained was murkiness.

"I am Lord Benami. I am the chosen one. You are the

evil Lord Antony. You are to die. Johnnie is the gatekeeper. Johnnie is a traitor. He knows he must sacrifice himself. Sacrifices bring rewards. Johnnie loves rewards. He is a servant of the Queen. He accepts he must do anything in order to protect Queenie's name. He accepts this as a privilege and great honour. Offering his life to the Gods guarantees he will be destined to return with far greater status in the next life. Johnnie is willing to do anything to obtain power. He knows sacrifices are essential."

"Ben please!" Anthony pleaded, his words delivered in heaving gasps, "please Ben!"

Tugging on the rope that bound his hands Anthony wriggled and jerked his body attempting to break his restraints. It was no use. The rope only ate further into his skin. Freedom would only come at the hands of another. The only other person present was mad. Rebecca had left. Anthony was tied up like an animal.

Returning a deathly stare of blackened fury eyes Ben's rage erupted.

"Shut up! Shut the fuck up! I have had enough of you."

Pacing back and forth he appeared to be on a march of madness. Gibberish flew from his frothing mouth. His eyes darted and his ranting exploded.

"All you humans are going to die! The tracerteps are going to destroy you all. Earth is ruined. You have destroyed everything. All of your hatred. The Gods have spoken. I the powerful Lord Benami. I will reign supreme. The tracerteps are powerful, the tracerteps are going to crush you all."

Ben threw his head back and released a blood curdling cry, "Darius!"

Anthony watched on in horror. He had seen too

much. He had heard too much. Witnessed too much. He knew far too much. He had to be silenced.

"Traitors will die and so will YOU!"

CHAPTER TWENTY FOUR

Broken and desperate. Everything appeared warped and twisted. Shadows danced around the room laughing at his suffering. The voices tortured Ben's mind. Interrupting even the most basic of thoughts. Yet he could not admit he had a problem that existed within his mind. Battling the voices in his head was becoming more and more difficult. Ben now teetered on the precipice of destruction. His every thought disturbed. Like the screeching of nails down a schoolroom chalkboard. They were sickening. All consuming. Cringe-inducing. All he wanted was for the voices to stop. But the voices would not stop. Nothing could make them stop. They had invaded like a swarm of ravenous locusts within a wheat field infesting his mind, munching, crunching, grinding, destroying and devouring what was once.

Suddenly he burst into tears. Placing his hands over his ears he rocked back and forth. He appeared inconsolable. His behaviour a total contradiction of the antics he displayed moments ago. Anthony was shocked. He wanted to help his son. He wanted to ease his pain. Helplessly watching his son was devastating. But he was his hostage and had no way of knowing when Ben would catapult back into his paranoid delusions.

"Tell me about Billy," he said quietly.

Ben raised his head. His rocking stopped. His voices fell silent.

"Billy…Oh Billy Bunbagel," Ben chuckled shaking his head. His voice appeared to take on that of another.

Anthony nodded.

He hoped having Ben focus on a story would maintain his calm. It could buy him valuable time. He was unsure whether Billy Bunbagel was real, a fictitious character created by Shirley or simply a figment of his own imagination.

"Bad Boy Billy Bunbagel was a real sadistic bastard. A sneaky little scumbag. He grew up near Queenie, you know. Raised in the school of hard knocks Billy Bunbagel suffered the bitter sting of rejection and let no one stand in his way. He was infatuated with Queenie. He was a cruel, perverted prick." Ben paused chuckling, "his reputation preceded him. Queenie admired his strength and courage. Other children feared him while adults were unnerved by him. He was wicked even from a young age. His actions left even some adults fearful. He enjoyed thrill kills. Wounding birds with slingshots then kicking and beating them to death with sticks. He pelted houses with rocks and enjoyed smashing windows. At the pool he would take great delight in tying hair around the necks of struggling flies. Jumping into the deepest water he would release them from within his clasped hands and watch as their bodies exploded from the water pressure. On warm summer days he would trap ants and carefully turn his magnifying glass above them until they would meet a hot and smoky death. Nothing was safe. As his age increased so did the boldness of his antics. Seagulls, rabbits, cats and dogs were his victims. Seagulls were hunted with a fishing rod, on the end of the hook danced bread. As soon as the seagull swooped he would tug on the line and the seagull commenced its battle in the air. Only when Billy became bored would he cut the bird free. Cats met their death struggling within the confines of plastic bags tossed into the raging surf. He took delight in slitting the throats of rabbits and beat dogs to death with rocks and branches. Oh yes, Billy Bunbagel was a real sadistic bastard. He feared no one and no amount of punishment would deter his actions. He was a real piece of work." Ben paused and then erupted into laughter. "I remember Queenie telling me a story, one Easter they were on an Easter egg hunt. Billy decided to add a little action." Ben paused again slapping his hands on his thighs, he began to laugh hysterically. Anthony watched and listened wondering what his son would say next. His sense of humour mirrored his deranged thinking.

"Well…the kids were all sneaking around, it was an exciting time. Billy disappeared and got a rabbit he had stashed away in a wooden crate. The best was yet to come. Petra one of Queenie's friends unsuspectingly turned the corner, Billy leaped out. He had slit that rabbit's throat and thrust its lifeless body in Petra's face. Blood spattered everywhere. Oh my god Queenie said she squealed like a stuffed pig, turned as white as a ghost and ran off screaming."

Anthony couldn't believe his ears. His son spoke with such excitement. The story was sickening.

"And he killed your great grandparents?" he questioned.

"No, no silly…don't be stupid. I told you Queenie had to kill them as they wanted to destroy her," Ben giggled, "but this confession signed by Billy will see him proudly take the credit. Oh my Queenie thought of everything."

Leaning against the wall Ben retrieved the hand written note from his pocket and flapped it about.

"But what about Billy?"

"Billy is dead. He died years ago. Queenie said he ended up in and out of goal. I told you he was a real sadistic prick. He did murder. Actually he murdered a couple of people. Anyway no harm, no foul. No one will care. Queenie said no one even turned up at his funeral. She did though. She went to make sure the miserable bastard was dead. She wanted to make sure her secrets would be safe. I told you he was infatuated by her didn't I? She said he was like a love sick puppy. He had no qualms in doing anything she asked. She was sure he would have had no problem in helping her dispose of her parents too, so it only seems fitting he takes the fall. Oh my Queenie she thought of everything."

Anthony lay still. Shocked at what he was hearing. His son spoke with great enthusiasm. He was proud of his grandmother's evil deeds. He appeared proud of her manipulative ways.

"Oh but you haven't heard the best of it. That book that you have, the one that claims to be about her secret life, oh how that made us laugh. She would read me selected paragraphs and we would laugh together. Sometimes we would laugh so hard I thought I would wet myself. Don't get me wrong there are many facts in it. But Dunberry, now that was a classic. Originally she said she was going to call it Dumberry but she thought that would be too obvious." Ben laughed hysterically. "I bet the location of that town will have a few people stumped. Then there was Bugsy. Oh poor Bugsy. From what she told me he did exist and he did in fact propose to her. Well poor Bugsy, he too was infatuated by Queenie's charm and he did help her get rid of her parents' bodies. But the silly bastard couldn't contain his guilt. He started whingeing and whining saying what they did was wrong and how they should just go to the police. Now she couldn't have that, could she? So she had to put plan B into motion. As history goes Bugsy was no more."

Anthony was astounded, his son spoke with great excitement.

"What was plan B?" he questioned.

"Billy…Bad Boy Billy…Billy Bunbagel, of course."

"Oh my god! He killed Bugsy?"

"Of course he did. Queenie went to Billy and told him what had happened. Billy was stoked to think she had killed her parents. The news excited him. Well of course she had to show him proof. And she did. Then she explained how Bugsy was going to expose what she did. Billy couldn't have her go to goal. His infatuation peaked. Her wish was his command. And so Bugsy had a terrible car accident. Bugsy was no more. Poor little Bugsy. He couldn't keep his mouth shut. He couldn't keep a secret."

Anthony couldn't believe his ears. Ben was operating in a different world. A mental world full of illusions, a world he had created himself with the assistance of his grandmother. His son acknowledged his grandmother's evil acts, he boasted about her ability to manipulate, yet he still insisted he belonged to a golden circle lineage. How could he dispel one notion and be so accepting of another? Lord Benami, a parallel universe, evil warriors, simple bugs transforming into giant lashing beasts. All of his warped thinking had stemmed from one evil bitch – Shirley Rumming.

Tethered by the wrists with rope Anthony struggled and strained. His body shook with rage. He was exhausted. His thrashing about proved fruitless. His son had lost the plot. Yet still he wanted to see the best in him.

He wanted to believe not all was lost. What would his loving wife Claire have done if faced by this madness? He had to get through to him. He had to make his son see sense.

"Please Ben please…you must listen to me. I am your father. She has contaminated your mind. I see the hatred in your eyes. I hear insanity seeping into your words. The madness in your voice. Your grandmother was evil, cold and calculating, a master of manipulation."

Turning towards Anthony Ben seemed to listen. His face held no anger. His eyes held no rage or confusion and his lips appeared relaxed.

"Please Ben please…do not succumb to the darkness. Please don't let the delusional thoughts of your grandmother destroy you. Your grandmother loved to bend her elbow just as much as she loved to bend the truth. Surely you must see this. I can help you. You need help."

Snap! Ben's agitation metastasised. The voices returned with vengeance. Loud, forceful and demanding instructions snapped from within. Grabbing his head he pulled at his hair begging for silence. He was vulnerable, powerless, useless. He was at the mercy of the voices. An inner compulsion was driving him.

"What the fuck are you looking at? You wouldn't have a fucken clue," he screamed glaring towards Anthony. Stepping closer to the bed he bent over. His face within centimetres of his father's face. Anthony could feel his warm breath. He could hear his son's huffing. He was terrified. His son appeared possessed. Ben was studying his face as if he was searching for something. The closeness of their encounter made Anthony feel as though he was suffocating. Swallowing hard he was afraid even the slightest of sounds would send Ben into an uncontrollable rage. Pursing his lips together Ben pushed his tongue forward and released the pressure within his mouth producing a popping sound. Tiny spit particles hit Anthony's face.

Anthony closed his eyes. For the first time since his ordeal began he had a strange thought. The thought of food appeared in his mind. He was not hungry. Yet the only thing he could think about was food. How nice it would be to be enjoying a deliciously tender pepper steak with a garlic smashed potato and nice crisp side salad. The steak so tender it could be cut with a bread and butter knife. Or maybe a slow cooked lamb roast decorated with garlic and rosemary. Crunchy baked potatoes, sweet carrots, roasted pumpkin slightly blackened on the edges and fresh minted peas, all covered in lashings of rich succulent gravy made with the juices from the meat. And at the end to finish the meal with a hot baked potato sandwich on fresh white bread covered with lashings of butter, not margarine and a sprinkler of pepper and salt. When you ate it the butter would run down your arm signifying your delight. Besides the apricot chicken made by Rebecca, Anthony hadn't enjoyed any meal he had consumed over recent times. The consuming of food had only been completed in order to maintain routine and of course his life. A life that appeared to be crumbling before his very eyes. Maybe his thoughts of food represented him and his life being devoured. One did not have to be old to die, a life could end at any moment, for any reason. Woven into his thoughts of food was the image of Claire. Claire had died long before her time. Among many things, Claire was a wonderful cook. She had the ability to conjure up the most amazing meals within minutes.

Her garlic roast pumpkin, fetta and roast capsicum salad was to die for. Piled high on the plate, decorated with kalamata olives, blanched snow peas and crunchy roasted cashews. Anthony described it as the salad of all salads. Little had he known last New Years Eve would be the final time he would enjoy such a wonderful creation. Had he thanked Claire for her magnificent cooking? Did he show her how much he loved her? Did she know how much he appreciated her in his life? If only he could turn back time. This morning he had been so eager to discover the truth behind Shirley's words he had left the house without breakfast. Were his thoughts merely a sign? For it wasn't the food he longed for, but the opportunities he missed. To sit and to have enjoyed breakfast. To observe his son. He hadn't enjoyed a meal with his son for some time. Maybe the thinking of his meals simply highlighted what he had been missing all along. Family time. He had cast Ben aside. If only he had insisted on sharing time together then surely he would have noticed an issue. Ben could have sought medical assistance. It was he who was responsible for this current situation. His son was ill but as his father it had been his responsibility to seek out help. He had failed as a father. His regret appeared as tears in the corner of his eyes running down his cheeks. Only time would tell where they would finally rest. Only time would tell what price Anthony would have to pay for his failure to act as a loving, caring and observant father.

Opening his reddened eyes his vision was blurred. Ben continued to study his father carefully although he had created a small distance between them. His eyes wandered to his father's restrained hands. His gaze constant as his peering continued down beyond his father's face. Pausing at his torn and battered shirt he poked hard into his chest. He showed no regard for the misery he inflicted, as if Anthony were a piece of discarded meat.

Anthony winced in pain. There was no doubt in his mind if his son got his way, he would soon be killed.

CHAPTER TWENTY FIVE

The thudding noise of Johnnie's distinctive footsteps coming up the stairs signified their alone time would soon end. Anthony knew his fate would soon be determined by his son. He had run out of options.

Bursting through the door Johnnie was covered in blood. In his hand he held a sword, its blade dripping with blood. Anthony could not imagine what suffering Mr. Benson experienced. He had witnessed the brutal murder scene. He had been dragged through Mr. Benson's drained life force. Johnnie was sick. Ben was deranged. Both were totally unpredictable.

Overwhelmed by his feeling of impending doom Anthony lost control of his excretory habits and began to pee where he lay.

"What happens in the family, stays in the family!" Ben yelled.

Anthony had heard enough he was sick of his son's threats. He knew being let go was not an option. What was the use in trying to reason, there was no reasoning.

The tension in the room was palpable. Johnnie stood shaking uncontrollably. The floor boards creaking beneath his feet as he rocked from one foot to the next. Pacing back and forth Ben was becoming increasingly agitated at his father's defiance. Anthony lay strapped to the bed not willing to conform to what he believed were his son's unreasonable demands. Thrashing his head from side to side he struggled with stuttered and muffled words.

"This is not about emotion Ben, your grandmother was deranged, a habitual liar. She was a person just like you and me. She was no Queen. This is about the truth. You have to listen to me."

"I am not Ben, I am Lord Benami! She warned me about you. She told me how you could not be trusted, how the evil forces had their claw securely embedded in you. You think I am stupid. But I am not. I know about you too, Lord Antony… I know you are an evil warrior."

"I am not Lord Antony, I am Anthony your father. Can't you see she has corrupted your mind, poisoned your thinking. She was the evil one, not me, I am you father, your protector."

Closing his eyes Ben tried with all his might to hear Queenie's voice. She had assured him she would never leave his side in his time of need even if the time came when her physical presence was no longer.

"Shut up, shut up with you!" he yelled, "I need silence so I can hear my Queen!"

With his eyes closed he clenched his fists tight and inhaled deeply shutting out the muffling of his father's voice. Finally he could hear her, he knew she would never abandon him.

"Its time to stand up for who you are Lord Benami, the princess and I watch over you. You must protect your people, don't be fooled. Remember evil Lord Antony awaits commands from the dark side. He is trying to trick you. He waits to destroy what he can not rule. The future of our family is in your hands."

Anthony began sobbing then the floodgates opened deep guttural wailing, uncontrollable shaking and hysteria engulfed his body. Drool that could not be contained in his mouth ran down the sides of his cheeks.

"Shut up or I will make you shut up!" Ben snapped.

"Just let me go everything will be alright, I will make sure you get help."

This was not the response Ben had been seeking. He did not need his help. He needed his father tolisten. He was in command. His father was in no position to bargain. Tightening the rope around his wrists he violently added more duct tape. Wrapping it around his head he tried to gag his mouth but missed it all together instead his father's chin was now plastered by the restrictive tape. Ben believed he was in control. His father was vulnerable, an easy target and in Ben's mind he was clearly the enemy.

Looking upon his father as the restrained and weak individual only increased the strength Ben felt from within. Engulfed by a feeling of disdain and total repugnance his pacing resumed. Johnnie appeared overwhelmed. He didn't like confrontation and despised loud noises. Everything was becoming too much. Johnnie was close to breaking point.

"Please I beg of you… please just let me go… I promise I won't tell, " murmured Anthony.

"Ah so at last you're starting to grasp the concept," Ben sniggered, "you are a joke… you think I am the fool but I know better   for it's you that can't be trusted."

Looking down upon his restrained body Ben laughed. His grandmother was right. He was Lord Benami ruler of the world, enforcer of the laws and punisher of those who failed to obey. Johnnie was the gatekeeper. He was his loyal and trusted servant, his unscrupulous supporter, his henchman.

Johnnie walked towards Ben and stood by his side. For a moment Ben stood still, very calm, very composed, very measured. Gazing up at the ceiling his eyes locked as he stared into thin air. To Anthony he appeared deep in thought. His son had clearly stated his intentions. His son was hearing, seeing and feeling things others could not. Hallucinating wild beasts, monster-like creatures. Voices appeared to catch him by surprise, sending him on a roller coaster between insanity and lucidity. Polluting his mind, clawing away all sense of normality. Things changed rapidly when the demons appeared. Talking demons, instructing him to hurt, hit, cut and kill.

Ben was marching into madness, hunted by illusions and stalked by voices. Resistance was futile.

"Stay there and watch him. Make sure he doesn't move," he snapped at Johnnie.

Johnnie limped over next to the doorway. Inside he was seething but he knew he should never argue with the powerful Lord Benami for arguing could result in grim consequences.

"Yes my lord," he replied submissively not daring to question his instruction.

CHAPTER TWENTY SIX

Retreating down stairs Ben sought solace. The constant chattering in his mind continued to plague his every move yet he longed to hear Queenie's voice. He understood the concept that what happened in the family should stay in the family, however he was unsure as to what he should do next. He wanted nothing more than to please his Queen. He was in desperate need of peace. Space in which he could think and listen for instruction. Removing the dust covered sheets from the lounge he sat down. Relaxing his tired body he tucked his feet under his buttocks and lent to the side. Resting against the softness, his body sank into the sagging cushions. A smooth sponge of sweat and grime stained leather embraced him with coolness that soon turned to warmth. It was a well loved lounge, natural wear and tear had created fine spider web cracks all over but it was not torn. A couple of cigarette burns were evident on the right arm and the wooden legs could do with a polish but considering its age and neglect it was holding up reasonably well. As his eyes gently scanned the room he began to smile and then chuckle. The dark tan colour of the lounge made it look like a hundred year old dead cow, and it smelled like faint woody tobacco. But the lounge was more than just a simple piece of furniture, it held a treasure trove of memories to his senses.

Closing his eyes he thought of Queenie; the scones she loved to bake and serve with soft butter, homemade strawberry jam and lashings of whipped cream. Her fresh blackberry pies with their sugar sparkled pie crust. The light and fluffy sponge cakes covered in tangy passionfruit icing and how could he forget her famous slow cooked roast lamb covered in homemade gravy, using the juices from the meat in the roasting tray. With his eyes closed he could almost smell her presence. The floral like Chanel No. 5 Queenie doused herself in, the mixture of lanoline and talcum powder; gentle fragrances that lingered for hours. When she cuddled him the scent would transfer onto his clothing; sniffing it reminded him of her enduring love. With his eyes still closed and his mind full of so many happy memories Ben could almost see her standing before him. She always maintained immaculately styled hair; firmly held in place by her ever reliable Cedel hairspray. Opening his eyes once more he scanned the room listening to his persistent nattering murmurs. Closing his eyes he inhaled deeply. He calmed his mind. He let his thoughts drift to a happier time. Immersing himself within one of Queenie's many tales was always pleasurable. He smiled. He cherished the time they shared. All the wonderful memories were so vividly etched within his mind. Queenie had so many amazing tales. Ben felt privileged to have shared in such precious moments.

CHAPTER TWENTY SEVEN

Closing his eyes Anthony became fatalistic about his future. His situation heartbreaking. His son, his enemy. All he could do was wait. He cherished all the good moments, the wonderful memories. The love and warmth he felt holding hands with his adorable wife, Claire. The quiet times they shared. He missed her more than words could explain. The ache he felt within his heart was unfathomable. It was as if part of him had died along with her. Emptiness, his heart was like a barren desert, a dark starless night. He also missed the laughter he shared as he joked with his son Ben. There were so many special memories. With his eyes closed an escape was possible, if only for a brief period.

Sparkling tears trickled down his face yet their warmth offered no comfort. All was silent. His pain evident, as was his fear. Stretched out on the bed his body began to shake. His creased forehead and tense shoulders highlighted his haunted look as invading thoughts entered his mind. Would he be rescued from this nightmare? Would anyone save him from this crumbling mess? He was not sure how long had passed since they had arrived at the dreaded house, but the coolness in the air made him believe it was getting late in the afternoon.

Desperate for the truth and realising this may be the only chance he had to escape the madness Anthony seized the moment to talk with Johnnie. Ben had left them alone. Unaccompanied and with no clear direction Johnnie appeared fragile and uncertain.Unsure of what made this lunatic tick Anthony knew he had to choose his words wisely. He needed to find out what role this villainous nutcase played? What drove him to partake in such a horrific affair? Why would someone commit murder? He knew his son's actions were being controlled by delusions. His son was so deranged, so wrong, yet so adamant he was right. Did Johnnie share his son's views? Was Johnnie being played? Maybe he could convince Johnnie the only way forward was with his release. Sitting in silence would get him no where. He had to try.

"Who are you?" he questioned in a soft voice, "why are you doing this?"

Johnnie looked towards Anthony and studied his face. His eyes squinting and head cocked to the side as if he was unsure and baffled by the words.

"Who are you?" he questioned again, "what's your name?"

"Johnnie…Jonathon Fox."

"And where does Jonathon Fox fit into this picture?"

"Picture? What picture?"

Johnnie looked around the room trying to find a picture but there was none. Wiping his eyes with his hands he appeared confused.

"I mean, why are you here? How do you know my son?" Anthony asked anxiously.

"Oh," Johnnie grinned as he walked to the bed and sat on the edge. Wriggling around he straightened his back and cleared his throat, "we have known each other forever. Lord Benami was only a baby. I am older than Lord Benami. I promised to protect him. I am protecting him. I am the gatekeeper."

It appeared Jonathon Fox was also out of his mind, yet Anthony needed to know more. Urging him to continue he relaxed on the bed listening to his words, while also listening out for his son's return. He knew Ben would hit the roof if the two were engaged in conversation. On the other hand Johnnie appeared to enjoy the quiet moment. He loved the attention. He hadn't experienced many instances where individuals were interested in him. When he began to talk his words flew from his mouth like verbal diarrhoea.

"My mum is Felicity, we live next to Queenie. Well we did. Queenie is dead now. Queenie looked after me. My mum had to work. Queenie said I am the gatekeeper. I liked Queenie. Queenie was my friend. Lord Benami is my friend. He likes me even though I am just a parasite. He said if I help him I will be rewarded. I like rewards. He said I will make my family proud. My mum knows Queenie. My pop knew Queenie too. My pop was a powerful man. The evil warriors took him away. They banished him to a far away place and locked him up. I never saw my pop again. The evil warriors wanted my pop to tell them what he knew but he didn't. He didn't give in. My pop is dead now. Queenie is dead too."

Anthony lay on the bed listening to the galoot's babble. So far the information he had imparted meant nothing. It was useless drivel. Surely he must have missed something.

"Where is your mum?" he questioned.

"Oh she is at home. She said I could go out and play. I like playing here. I play here all the time. Sometimes I have to hide. Queenie said I would be in big trouble if I got caught here, so I hide. I have lots of hidey holes."

The enthusiasm with which he spoke gave Anthony an idea.

"Do you want to play a game?"

Johnnie nodded, his face lit up with excitement.
"Can we?"

"Of course we can but you need to untie me first."

Johnnie nodded again and stood up. Walking over to the window he retrieved the sword that had been placed onto the floor next to the wardrobe. Turning towards Anthony he could no longer contain his excitement as he swung the sword through the air. Waving it around he made swooshing sounds. The reflection of the blade flickered as it caught the light from the window. Bright flashes danced over the walls and ceiling. The breeze of Johnnie's movement stirred dust within the room. All of a sudden he stopped and stood still.

"I tried to play with Princess Claira the other week but she didn't want to play. She never liked playing. She was boring. Princess Claira is dead now."

Anthony saw red. Johnnie's words were void of sorrow. He spoke in a nonchalant manner as if Claire held no significance. Alive one minute and dead the next. What the hell had this bastard done to his wife? How did he know she was dead? Had he played a role in her death?

Burning pain radiated through his chest like a million angry fire ants attacking from within. Attempting to move only accentuated the stabbing pain in his shoulder blade. It felt as though his chest muscles had been ripped from his ribs. Turning his head to the side he struggled to look beyond his bound arms that were extended high above his head. The smell of fear entered his nostrils. It was a rancid stench comparable to fermented blue cheese and two week old beef rendang curry that had been left in the sun. Under his arms his shirt was stained by sweat, dirt and who knows what else. Leaning forward he strained his head closer to his armpit. He stunk to high heaven but more concerning was the fact Johnnie had moved from view. Anthony's breath became rapid, small beads of sweat decorated his forehead and his chest felt as though it would explode. Silence. Besides his breath there was no noise just a deathly silence. Johnnie had the sword and now he had vanished from his field of vision. He could attack at any moment. Looking around the room its contents took on a different significance. A railing from the bed, if removed successfully could be used as a weapon. The old timber panelled cupboard could be used as a hiding place. All he had to do was convince his captor to release his ties. If left alone he could prise open the window. Make out he had successfully jumped free. They would leave the house to give chase. And he would walk out a free man.

Anthony could not give up on hope. Hope was one thing he still had. One thing that could not be taken from him.

"What did you do to my wife?" he screamed.

Johnnie leaped back into view.

"Nothing, well…"

"What did you do? You bastard, you just wait."

"Nothing!" Johnnie exclaimed shaking his head, "I just pushed her…but she got up I was playing and she came and found my hidey hole under the house. I didn't hurt her, I just knocked her off her feet and I ran off. I think I frightened her though," he burst out laughing.

Closing his eyes Anthony relaxed his neck. This madman was as deluded as his son. One minute he would be speaking in a somewhat deep monotone voice. The next minute he would be propelled into baby talk and useless babble. How could anyone reason with a lunatic?

With his head cushioned by the soft dustcovered pillow the familiar smell of mildew entered his nose. The floor boards creaked next to the bed and he opened his eyes to see Johnnie standing next to him. The sword was no where in sight. Instead Johnnie was innocently playing with a piece of string. Wrapping it around his finger. Curling and twirling. Pulling and tugging. Releasing his spring formed creation before he recommenced his twisting process.

"Look…look, it looks like a curly pig tail," he giggled proudly before switching to all seriousness.

"I used to have a pig," he mumbled tearfully, "Pop made me slit its throat and we ate it for Christmas dinner."

Anthony was stunned. What sort of deranged grandfather would make a child partake in such an atrocious act?

"No way," he exclaimed.

"I did, his name was Mr. E. Pop said his name stood for Mr. Eaten and that's what we did. I was only a boy and Mr. E was huge. I could barely lift him. He squealed and kicked. The blood spurted everywhere. There was so much blood. It was warm and tasted foul. I had blood all over me. Pop said that was all part of the fun. It didn't take long for Mr. E to stop moving. I missed him but Pop said things and people dying was a part of life and sometimes it was kill or be killed."

Anthony couldn't believe what he was hearing. Johnnie's childhood recollection belonged in a horror story.

"You said the evil warriors took your pop away?"

Johnnie nodded.

"Queenie didn't help him. She let them take him

away," he sobbed, "she said he would never talk and he didn't. He needed to sacrifice himself for the good of all. He was loyal and they couldn't make him talk. He kept his promise."

"Queenie knew your pop?"

Johnnie nodded again.

"They were friends."

Anthony began to wonder who the hell this grandfather was. How did he fit into the scheme of things?

"What was your grandfather's name?" he questioned unsure as to whether he wanted to hear his answer. Everything was becoming so strange. Stories were warped and twisted, details became intertwined. Startling revelations only became stranger and more bizarre.

"William."

"William, who?" he asked anxiously.

"Bunbagel."

Anthony's mouth dropped wide open, his eyes staring as he gasped for breath.

"No way, you're kidding."

Shaking his head he could not believe what he had just heard. How the hell could this be happening? William Bunbagel...Bad Boy Billy...Billy Bunbagel was a vile human being. Jonathon Fox was his bloody grandson. Was Jonathon Fox really as thick as he portrayed? Did Jonathon Fox have his own agenda? Maybe he wanted revenge as he held Queenie responsible for losing his pop? Maybe his submissive behaviour was a part of an act? Everything changed in an instant.

"Holy shit... this is where secrets lie!" Anthony exclaimed shaking his head.

And then the penny dropped. Surely he was being played.

"Hang on a minute, your last name is Fox."

Johnnie raised his eyebrows and glared towards Anthony.

"Mum changed it she said to run with the best of them we had to be as cunning as a Fox."

Johnnie began giggling then erupted into a full bellied laughter. With his hands on his hips he tilted his head back and released a blood curdling howl. Anthony was floored, this lunatic had lost the plot. A normal man did not howl like a dog. Anthony had been terrorised and brutalised. The not knowing what would happen next was torture. Overwhelmed by an avalanche of exposed and collapsing secrets, he lay on the bed shaking his head. Evil actions and perverted views intertwined with deluded thoughts. Was his son aware of the relationship shared by Billy and Johnnie? Was Johnnie really his grandson? Ben appeared cocksure and proud proclaiming Billy to be the fall guy for past murders. Maybe Johnnie had discovered his plan and had a different plan altogether. Either way Anthony knew neither could be trusted. Thrashing around on the bed he screamed in agony, praying someone would come to his rescue. Johnnie lunged forward and planted his closed fist into the side of Anthony's head. The force of the pounding sent dust into the air. A high pitched ringing entered Anthony's ears. Short, sharp flashes appeared behind his closed eyes. Clasping his hands together he tried to absorb the pain, praying his suffering would soon end.

Johnnie hated threats he also hated loud noises and never ending questions. When someone questioned him he felt as though he was on the receiving end of an interrogation. He was also prone to headaches. He had had a headache all day and it was beginning to get worse. It was like someone was banging a hammer into his head. Not any normal hammer, more like an ice pick. The intense pain erasing his ability to think clearly. Lashing out was the only way he knew he could gain stillness. When Johnnie lashed out everyone paid attention. Glaring down upon Anthony he released the sword from his grasp. The clang of it hitting the floor echoed around the room. Anthony lay sobbing on the bed. Johnnie's outburst had achieved his desired result. The questions stopped. Johnnie collapsed back against the wall and slid down to the floor. Both were exhausted.

Anthony was terrified. Nothing logical could explain his captors' erratic behaviour. Their seemingly unprovoked outbursts of violence. The delusional ranting. It was all but certain someone would die.

All of a sudden Johnnie leaped from the floor and lunged onto Anthony; like a cat he pounced onto his prey. Dark and evil forces reflected from within his blackened eyes. His intense stare void of emotion. His actions forceful. Driven. His face tense. Jaw clenched. Forehead wrinkled. Nostrils flared. His breath warm and wheezing. His large hands applied pressure. Squeezing tightly they covered Anthony's nose and mouth. Cutting off oxygen. Anthony's eyes stared. Bulging. Pleading for help. Struggling for breath. He was being smothered. His panic escalated as his body was forced into the soft mattress. His legs thrashed. His eyes darted. He could feel the fear in this throat. His breath restricted. The pressure against his face was increasing. A high pitched buzzing sound entered his ears. Black spots invaded his vision.

The room became fuzzy. The room became blurred. Heat surrounded his face. Coolness encased his body. His pain disappeared. Floating weightlessness. Blackness. He plunged into a vacuum of nothingness.

The world was still and silent. Black.

Johnnie released his hands and collapsed to the floor. Leaning against the bed he felt great relief.

Silence at last.

CHAPTER TWENTY EIGHT

Anthony's body lay motionless on the bed. Johnnie sat slumped over on the floor. Glancing over his shoulder he could not bear to look at Anthony's stillness. His face limp. Expressionless. His instruction had been to watch him, "Stay there and watch him. Make sure he doesn't move." Was what Ben had instructed. Anthony wasn't moving. But what would Ben think when he returned? Had he overstepped the mark?

Alone with the dead anything could happen. But to be alone with a dead evil warrior, the possibilities were endless. Had Anthony released a silent scream that would result in an attack from above?

Johnnie's eyes darted around the room. His ears pricked as he listened, his head tilted to the side. He suddenly became extremely scared. Panicked. The slightest breeze from outside could be the result of evil forces gathering. Evil forces ready to unleash fire and fury. Pushing himself to his knees he crawled closer to Anthony's face. He stared with horror studying Anthony's eyes. Thin slits. Thin slits between his eyelids exposed the whites of his eyeballs. No colour, just thin white slithers of nothingness. Cautiously he raised his right hand. Extending his finger he poked Anthony's cheek. No reaction. Anxiously kneeling next to the bed he watched and listened for anything. Only silent stillness followed. Extending his finger he poked again, this time a little harder. The eerie silence continued. Johnnie became terror-stricken. Anthony's mouth was slightly ajar. Was he calling for help? Was it possible for an evil warrior to talk beyond the darkness?

No longer able to maintain closeness Johnnie jumped to his feet. Shaking his head in disbelief he kicked the bed. Surely his foot colliding with the mattress would jolt him back to life.

Diddly.

Shocked by the consequences of his actions and fearful of the repercussions, Johnnie needed to escape. Eager to create distance he lunged towards the door. Under pressure he could not think. Being so close to the dead made thinking impossible. How would he explain his death to the one and only Lord Benami? Confusion clouded his mind as he exited the room. Marching into the bathroom he believed he would be able to lock himself away. If Ben returned he would claim he knew nothing. He would insist all had been fine when he left Anthony to relieve himself. He would deny any involvement. Anthony's death would be the result of evil. Standing in front of the toilet Johnnie struggled to pee straight. Nerves ravaged his body; his hands trembled. Nothing could possibly prepare him for the wrath of the almighty Lord Benami.

Looking into the mirror he searched out an excuse, a plausible story. It had to involve something Ben would not link to himself. But what?

Zipping up his pants Johnnie studied his reflection in front of the bathroom mirror. Wiping is face he began to chuckle. He looked like an Indian with war paint smeared across his cheeks. Placing his hand to his mouth he released a soft war cry. He reassured himself he was a brave soldier and he would win. Glancing at his watch he became alarmed at the time. He had promised his mother he would be home for lunch. Lunch time had well and truly been and gone. Johnnie hated seeing his mother upset. He knew she worried about him. He knew he had to go home. If he didn't return home soon she would begin searching for him. She always looked for him when he went walkabout. Leaving the bathroom he tiptoed up the hallway peeking in where Anthony lay. He had not moved.

"Shit!" Johnnie swallowed hard and nervously crept down the stairs.

In the lounge room Ben was fast asleep on the lounge. His snoring gave Johnnie hope he would be able to return home, check in and return. His absence would go unnoticed.

CHAPTER TWENTY NINE

The gentle ring of the bell hanging above the door indicated someone had just entered the shop. Mr. Vassallo looked up from behind the pages of the local paper. It had been a quiet afternoon and so he had been catching up on the news as he rested against the glass counter of the lolly display.

"Wow! Johnnie my man what have you been up to today?" he questioned stunned by his dishevelled appearance.

Seeing a customer enter his shop with rope tied around their head, a feather in their hair and what resembled stripes of blood red war paint smeared across their cheeks was not a usual occurrence, but with Jonathon Fox anything was possible. Last year he had nearly scared Mr. Vassallo half to death as he staggered in with a sword jutting out from his chest. On that occasion he claimed he was a pirate who was in desperate need of eyeballs to feed the angry sea serpents. Mr. Vassallo had made Johnnie promise never to enter with shocking wounds ever again; he could handle his strange clothes and the fake blood but when it came to protruding weapons and acts of near death antics Mr. Vassallo said enough was enough.

"I've been fighting evil warriors...and Cowboys and Indians," Johnnie puffed as he staggered towards the counter. His eyes scanning to see if anyone else was behind the magazine rack to his left. Mr. Vassallo could do nothing but shake his head and wonder if and when he would ever start acting his age.

"That's great, so what's your name? Are you Chief Big Cloud or Indian Warrior Brave Horse?"

"No, I am the gatekeeper, the powerful gatekeeper."

Proudly boasting his title Johnnie stood tall, his shoulders back and pointing to his chest.

"And this is blood…real blood from the evil warriors I killed," he said nodding his head.

Mr. Vassallo laughed, "Well I can tell you now, your mum isn't going to be too happy with you. Paint is so hard to get out of clothes. She may have to throw those ones out."

"I didn't say paint…I said it was blood," Johnnie's voiced became raised, "and my mum loves me. I protect her from bad people. She will be proud I killed the evil warriors."

Mr. Vassallo stepped back from the counter he knew his words had upset Johnnie. He had seen his temper as a child when people had not agreed with his stories. Many years had passed since they first met. Johnnie was close to twenty years old now and he towered over him. Close to six foot tall, solid build and with hands like spades. Mr. Vassallo certainly didn't want him to throw a temper tantrum. It was much easier to go along with his story.

"So what can I get for you…Maybe some bullets so you get reload your weapons?"

"Oh yes please Mr. Vassallo I need some chocolate bullets and do you have any of those bags of gold."

"The gold gum?"

Johnnie nodded with excitement.

Reaching down Mr. Vassallo retrieved a bag of gum and placed it on the counter.

"How many bullets do you need?"

"Twenty…and can I have some strawberries and cream too, mum loves strawberries and cream lollies."

"Sure I'll put them in a separate bag."

Kneeling down behind the counter he began to count out the lollies and Johnnie became relaxed. He would soon be home and the gift he was purchasing for his mum would help get him out of strife for missing lunch.

"You know the other night I wrestled with a huge wild cat."

Looking up from behind the counter Mr. Vassallo could only wonder what Johnnie would say next.

"Really? Well you are lucky it didn't rip you to pieces." He smiled.

Pulling up his sleeves Johnnie showed off his scratch free arms.

"Not me, I was too quick. I snapped its neck with my bare hands and then I bashed him to smithereens."

Twisting and turning his hands, Johnnie demonstrated how he had used brute force to annihilate his opponent. Punching into the air he released a snarl closer to a growl and his face changed.

"Oh my goodness you sound like a wild cat yourself. I hope you didn't swallow him," Mr. Vassallolaughed.

"Ha ha! You are so funny, of course I didn't swallow him."

"Well all I can say is you are definitely one tough guy. I'll tell you what, I will throw in some extra bullets to keep on your good side."

Johnnie nodded and smiled he liked rewards; Mr Vassallo always managed to throw in a surprise.

Handing over the money in exchange for his lollies he headed for the door.

"Thanks I had better hurry and get back to the castle before the dead come back to life. They are evil warriors you know."

Mr. Vassallo stood shaking his head nothing Johnnie said could surprise him. His childhood imagination had continued into adulthood. His vivid fantasies, along with the enthusiasm with which he spoke about his creative and bizarre experiences would have many folk believing they contained a degree of truth.

Sitting back in his chair Mr. Vassallo picked up the newspaper and returned to his reading not giving Johnnie a second thought.

CHAPTER THIRTY

Sneaking around to the back of the house Johnnie scanned the sky. He knew he was in trouble. The slightest sound could be that of evil warriors seeking revenge. Lord Benami could wake at any moment and discover he was gone. His absence could be interpreted as an act of desertion. And if Lord Benami discovered Lord Antony's lifeless body, he could be accused of treason. He knew he had to get back to the castle without delay. Grabbing the door handle he gave it a gentle twist. It released a loud squeak. Johnnie swallowed hard. He moved forward up the back step. He pushed the door open. He came face to face with the last person he wanted to see; his mother. She was far from happy. Her forehead wrinkled, eyebrows lowered, her despondent eyes stared and her lips pursed together. Opening her mouth was not necessary, Johnnie had seen this look before. It was a mix of upset, disappointment and worry. He knew his dishevelled state would only exacerbate the situation but there was no turning back.

"Oh my God where have you been? You should have been home ages ago. I told you I wanted you home for lunch," she snapped holding her left hand on her hip. She began waving her hands around like a crazed conductor. Her finger pointing close to his face. Stepping forward he could feel her warm breath on his face.

Johnnie lowered his head and stepped back a little. Her outburst upset him. Staring at the floor he maintained a stolid and gloomy expression. He was not game to make contact with his mother. His breathing ragged. He felt a flush of apprehension and fear warm his face. Startled by the intensity of her anger and agitated, by her words he was unsure how he should interpret her words and actions. Should he speak up or remain silent? Sweat ran down the side of his face. Rocking back and forth his hands remained in his pockets. Hidden, his fingers twitched as his anxiety increased. He owed his mother an apology but what would he offer as an explanation?

Looking him up and down Felicity's annoyance mutated, replaced by concern. Her son was filthy. Johnnie was a grown man yet he acted as a large child. His wild imagination, obsessive behaviour and difficulty in foreseeing the consequences of his actions left him extremely vulnerable when it came to finding trouble. The rope around his head and feather in his hair did nothing more than increase her concern. In her mind, ripped clothes covered in mud and spattered red all proclaimed trouble. Something was definitely wrong and she needed answers. Johnnie's face became ashen, eyes staring and vacant.

"Where have you been? What have you done?" she questioned in great haste, "you look like you have just come from a battle field. Are you hurt?" Grabbing him by the shoulders she forced her son to look at her.

Johnnie knew his mother's questions could not go unanswered. He could no longer hold his tongue. He had to be honest.

"I went to the castle…I did a bad thing…" he blurted shaking his head, still refusing to look at her.

His mother was always so caring and loving, so supportive and understanding. How would she ever understand his actions? Actions that would bring great shame to their family. The last thing he wanted was to upset his mother.

Removing his right hand from his pocket he offered her the bag full of strawberries and cream lollies.

Accepting the bag from her son Felicity looked inside the bag, shook her head and huffed. Throwing it onto the kitchen table, she again shook her head. Looking up to her son Felicity's concern intensified. Her heart began to race. A gift of lollies would not keep her silent. Strawberries and cream would not erase her concern. Physically Johnnie held a startling resemblance to her father and now the words he had just spoken were also shockingly familiar. She didn't want to think about it, but couldn't help it.

Felicity's mind turned to her father; William Bunbagel. A big, heavy-set and extremely volatile man. She had not thought of him in years. He was a man whose reputation preceded him. He was aggressive, manipulative, argumentative, domineering, controlling, spiteful and deceitful. A man many locals once described as evil. Billy Bunbagel was well known by the police. He had been implicated in several disappearances, charged with four counts of armed robbery and two assaults. If Billy Bunbagel did not like you, you could be guaranteed he would make your life a living hell. Felicity had grown up watching her father's scheming and conniving ways. She had witnessed his rage, listened to his threats, been on the receiving end of his violent outbursts and painful punishments. She knew some of his most guarded secrets. He had claimed there were numerous bodies yet to be discovered; bodies he had buried. Her past with all its mysteries was littered with violence, betrayal, secrets and lies. The actions of those before her had the ability to taint her future and destroy all hope, if she allowed them. As a child she was tarnished by her father's reputation. Taunted and teased. As she approached her teenage years she realised detachment from negative elements was essential for positive growth and advancement in life. Bad boy Billy Bunbagel was the reason she left home so young. He was the reason why she ultimately changed her name. A new identity granted her freedom and the ability to breathe easy without shame.

Johnnie had inherited so many of her father's features; gapped teeth, the large hands, large build, piercing eyes that gazed off into the distance or stared straight through you. She could only pray these were the only things he had inherited from the Bunbagels. Great fear swept through her; her face turned a ghostly white. Johnnie's response triggered internal alarm bells. Her father had spoken of a castle. It was a scary castle. She never knew its location. However the context in which he spoke was extremely clear. They were words she never forgot. It was a castle she associated with death. Bodies were hidden under the castle. She recalled the threatening words; words he had clearly stated on numerous occasions.

"Continue with your insolence and you will no longer walk this earth my girl. I will bury you under the castle and no one will ever find you. I have done it before so you mark my words. Mind your tongue or you will soon draw your last breath and I will bury you under the castle with the others," he would threaten.

Felicity was haunted by his remarks. Her father terrified her. As soon as she was old enough she moved out of home, got a job and forged ahead with her own life. Creating distance between herself and Billy Bunbagel was crucial. Years passed with no contact. Living in Bondi with her boyfriend, Felicity fell pregnant. Three months later her boyfriend was gone and Felicity resigned herself to the fact she would raise her child as a single parent.

Then she received news her father was gravely ill with limited time. As a daughter she felt compelled to assist and so she returned to his side. Felicity was stunned. William Bunbagel was near unrecognisable, a shadow of the man he once was, frail. Bent over from the shoulders down, his body lacked muscular strength and appeared feeble. He needed assistance in showering, getting dressed and with meals. He insisted he was, 'stuffed,' 'buggered' and 'not long for the world.' With no motivation to leave his bed William Bunbagel was close to death's door. Felicity did what she thought was right. She knew she would never change him but that would not stop her doing what she believed in her heart was a daughter's duty. Time, effort, sleepless nights and endless arguments finally paid off. William began to gain weight. He reduced his time in bed. He regained his ability to wash and dress. His assisted shuffling became powerful strides. His back straightened. Gone were the arguments associated with his refusal to eat. These were replaced by demands on what he wanted to eat and complaints about the quantity and quality of the meals. Six months passed. Felicity gave birth to her beautiful baby boy Jonathon; her father returned to his bullying and drinking ways.

For the next four years Felicity reluctantly stayed living with her father. Stashing any extra cash in the bank; her intention was to leave without warning as soon as she had enough for a deposit on her own house.

Her mother had left them years ago. Initially Felicity felt betrayed by her mother abandoning them. However in time she understood this action. Her mother was a victim; subject to repeated threats, psychological and physical abuse. Her mother had been a sufferer of domestic violence for as long as Felicity could remember. Felicity's father had bashed, bruised, cut, threatened and strangled and enough was enough. She was eight years old when her mother left. She remembered the evening as if it were yesterday. Her mother was crying, begging for forgiveness. Her eyes were blackened and swollen. Her hair a mess; great clumps of hair lay on the kitchen floor from where her father had yanked her. Her clothes covered in the remains of the gravy, squashed peas and chunks of mashed potato she had been dragged through. Felicity's father was drunk. He was generally drunk when he launched his assault. On that night his explosion occurred due to the fact his dinner was not what he wanted. In seconds of it being placed before him it flew across the kitchen and splattered on the wall. The plate smashed. His fist first collided with the table and then with her mother's body. His threats collided with her pleas and apologies. Felicity sat terrified at the table; she cried and screamed and begged. As usual, he ignored and continued. He continued until he was exhausted and his wife was a bleeding, blackened mess. All because his dinner was not what he wanted. After he was finished he simply retrieved another drink from the refrigerator, walked into the lounge room, quenched his thirst and passed out. An upset Felicity ate her dinner and went to bed as instructed. Ten minutes passed. Her bedroom door opened. Her mother entered holding a small brown suitcase. Resting over her arm was her favourite pink knitted cardigan. Distraught, her mother begged Felicity for understanding. He threatened he would kill them both if they ever left. He said he would track them down. Felicity was *his* child. He had never raised his hand to *his* child but, he would have no hesitation in tracking them down and killing her then her mother, if her mother ever defied his instruction. Her mother believed his threats. She said if she didn't leave he would eventually kill her. Her mother promised when she had herself established she would return and take Felicity to a new safe life. Her mother hugged her, told her she loved her and left her bedroom weeping, suitcase and cardigan in hand. That was the last time Felicity would ever see her mum. Some would view her decision as selfish, Felicity knew her mother's words were true. It was easier that she accepted her mother as gone but alive, as opposed to gone and gone for good. One day, she hoped, she prayed, they would be reunited. A woman, no matter what woman, should never be subject to psychological or physical abuse.

Billy was enraged when he realised his wife had disappeared. He threatened if he ever saw her he would kill her. He said her actions had made him look a fool. He accused her of having affairs behind his back. He labelled her a lazy bitch and good for nothing slut. Nothing was ever his fault. He justified his assaults by saying he simply reacted to her insolence and stupidity. It was a man's duty to keep his wife in line. It was a wife's duty to honour and obey her husband. When her mother left Felicity took on the washing chores, she quickly learnt how to cook and did the best she could to stay out of her father's way especially when he had been drinking. Felicity never suffered the degree of abuse her mother did and that was something she was grateful for.

When she fell pregnant she vowed she would always

protect her child. Her child would never know violence. By all means she would set boundaries and guidelines, but she would never raise her hand with the excuse of discipline. When she gave birth she promised no matter what happened she would never abandon her beautiful bundle of joy; Jonathon. When she returned home with her newborn all her efforts were to limit the interaction between grandfather and grandson. The warped sense of humour her son possessed was extremely similar to her father, frighteningly similar.

Back on his feet trouble followed Billy around like a shadow. As soon as Jonathon was old enough to walk he followed his grandfather around like a lost puppy. Years passed. Finally Felicity's prayers were answered. In the middle of the night there was a knock at the front door. The law caught up with him. Billy was dragged out of the house kicking and screaming.

"You evil bastards, I'll kill you, you evil bastards."

He was drunk and never went down without a fight. Billy was sentenced to gaol for two counts of armed robbery and one count of assault with a deadly weapon. Felicity cheered when he went to gaol. Jonathon cried. He had heard his grandfather's bellowing rage. He had witnessed him being dragged off into the dark of the night. Felicity hoped her father would be involved in additional offences behind bars. She needed a clear break from the Bunbagel name. A new name. A new look. A new life. This time there would be no going back. Felicity Bunbagel became Felicity Fox; *to run with the best of them I have to be as cunning as a fox*, she thought. She prayed he would not bother to look for them when released.

Seven months later she danced and sang. It was the day she found out he was dead. It was an inevitable ending; his big mouth, his demise. Even behind bars restraint was impossible. In gaol a person could be killed for various reasons; outside issues which come to gaol, drug debts, one prisoner may not like the look of another, racial issues, anything really. Some prisoners were simply mad. Weapons could be made of anything sharpened; a toothbrush, toilet brush or a bit of metal. They could be bashed, stabbed with a spike made from sharpened wire, or simply jumped on until their head popped. Attacks were opportunistic; shower areas and the oval were known hot spots. Billy found death in the shower block, a shiv made from a sharpened tooth brush embedded in the side of his neck. His head stomped on till it popped. No one witnessed the attack. No one was charged with his murder. William Bunbagel picked a fight with the wrong person at the wrong time. Ultimately he lived in violence and finally he got his just desserts and died by violence. We all have choices, he made his.

When Felicity heard the news the only thing she could think of was, "*Do unto others as you would have them do unto you, finally the bastard has met his match.* It was bitter sweet. She would miss her father, but she would not miss the man she despised. She hoped he would burn for eternity in the pits of hell.

Placing her thoughts aside Felicity's priority now was to focus on her son who remained closed mouth, nervously rocking back and forth. She knew something was wrong he hadn't lifted his head.More startling than Johnnie's words was the partially crusted crimson spatter that covered his shirt. Spatter similar to that she had seen on her father years before; the night their neighbours cat howled for the last time. To her father it was one big joke. As he entered the kitchen Felicity could not believe her eyes. At first she thought he was holding some kind of fur. That was until she noticed the trail of blood. Her father was laughing. Repeatedly howling and laughing. It was not a fur but the remains of Whiskey; the cat next door. In his left hand he held its limp body, blood dripping from the neck. And if that wasn't bad enough; holding up his right hand his fingers cupped tightly around its head. Fleeing the room in tears Felicity dashed to the bathroom. His actions were sickening. His killing a poor defenceless cat reinforced her fear. Anything was possible. Her father was an unpredictable monster. The bathroom was her safety zone. It was the only room in the house with a lock on the door. Locked inside she would not have to face the horror. Five minutes passed. Ten minutes. Her father was drunk, his yelling echoed up the hallway. He was tossing up the idea of placing the head on a garden stake and sticking it smack bang in the middle of the neighbours' front lawn. Felicity wanted no part of it, she remained silent.

"At least we will sleep well tonight with no howling," he laughed.

Crouched down in front of the toilet Felicity closed her eyes and vomited, cringing at what would happen next. Her father was deranged. Five more minutes passed. The back door slammed, then silence. Locked inside she would spend the night laying on a pile of bath towels.

The next morning her father was no where to be seen. Felicity cleaned up the bloodied floor and transferred Whiskey's remains from the kitchen tidy bin to the outside garbage where she hid them under old rubbish. That night she heard her neighbours continued cries, "Whiskey, Whiskey…here puss, Whiskey, Whiskey…

come on puss, puss, puss." The calling and cries continued for hours, out the back, in the front, up and down the street. Felicity sat in her room in tears. Whiskey hadn't deserved to die. Her father was a monster. When asked about Whiskey she told her neighbours she had no clue. How could she possibly tell them the grizzly truth. Her father was deranged. When he returned home he acted as if nothing had happened. Whiskey was never mentioned again.

Johnnie's continued silence and lack of eye contact increased her frustration, she wanted answers and was becoming annoyed at his ignorance.

"I asked you a question and I expect an honest answer!" she demanded.

"I told you, I went to the castle."

Jonathon nervously flicked his fingers. The increased pitch in his mother's tone was making it so he could not concentrate. He was becoming annoyed, super annoyed; so annoyed he felt he would lash out in anger. He couldn't deal with her screeching voice. He needed her to stop but Felicity was determined to get answers.

"You said you were going to the doctors. You needed a doctors certificate for work. You said you would be home for lunch. Don't you care that I worry? I want to know where you have been. What castle?"

Looking towards his mother Jonathon replied sheepishly, "The secret castle."

Felicity exploded, she seas sick of his stupid make believe, "Stop…stop playing with me. I am not playing Jonathon Fox. I want you to tell me the truth."

Tears welled in his eyes. He knew she was upset. He knew he was not allowed to reveal the location of the castle. He knew he had yet again disappointed his mother. If she didn't shut up, he also knew he would not be able to control himself. He needed to shut her up.

"I am telling you the truth…I went to the castle," he yelled, stomping his foot. Jonathon clenched his fists and glared towards his mother. "Stop telling me I am lying and stop butting your nose into my business. I told you where I was. I said sorry I was late and now I am going to my room."

Storming off down the hallway Jonathon felt defeated. Felicity was left dumbfounded. Shaking her head she feared she could do nothing more. If he continued on this path of behaviour she knew he would soon self destruct. It was just a matter of time. He would be out of yet another job. Jonathon had been in the workforce for over two years and had changed his jobs more frequently than most people went on holidays. Motivating him to go to work was like trying to train a cat to swim; it was fought with great resistance. Today his excuse for not going was a headache. Yesterday it had been an upset stomach. Felicity acknowledged he was easily distracted, lacked motivation and appeared oblivious to the consequences of his actions. She worried about what he would do if she was not around to offer encouragement. His current employer, Mr. Tyler had employed Jonathon only five weeks ago. Mr. Tyler was a friend of a friend, he owned a home wares business. He was a lovely man, caring, open minded and willing to give anyone a go. Jonathon was employed as a warehouse clerk. His herculean appearancegave him the physical advantage required in moving around large pieces of furniture. Felicity had given her word; her son would be reliable and punctual. Five weeks into the job Jonathon had been late, argued with his supervisor, gone missing in action and now it appeared he just couldn't be bothered going any more. For Jonathon it was always one excuse after another.

Sitting down at the kitchen table Felicity burst into tears. Was her son beyond help? Sobbing into her handkerchief she felt alone. How muchmore would she be able to take? How long would she be able to support her son who appeared so resistant to the basic elements of adulthood? Every living adult had a responsibility to get off their backsides and go and get a job. Work was not something you chose one day and ignored the next. If you didn't work you would never get ahead in life. Felicity didn't want people to regard her son as a bludger. The harder a person worked the luckier a person became. Ten minutes passed. Felicity's anger and frustration had eased. It was time for a quiet chat. Anger and frustration would never result in abandonment.

Knocking on his door Felicity waited for a response. Nothing. All was quiet.

"Jonathon can I come in?" She knocked again. Silence.

Opening the door she was shocked. His room was empty. He was gone. No note. No explanation. Just gone. Staring at his open window her mind turned back to the words he had spoken. Jonathon had a great imagination, but why would he say he went to a castle? Was mentioning a castle, a coincidence? Were his words echoes from the grave? There were no castles nearby so why would he say he went to a castle? The manner in which her son was acting was more than a little concerning. Was he genetically infected? His appearance, what he said, the way in which he was acting and now his unusual disappearance left her questioning if she should contact the police. But would such contact be an act of betrayal?

A mother's duty was to protect, not betray. Closing his bedroom door Felicity dropped to the floor and burst into tears. She prayed for his safety and hoped with all her heart her son was not beyond help.

She remained silent.

CHAPTER THIRTY ONE

With his eyes gently closed it wasn't too long before Ben fell into a deep trance. He could hear Queenie's voice and in his mind he could see her words. He inhaled deeply and released a gentle sigh. The planets had rotated. The stars were aligned. He felt the warmth of her hand as it brushed against his cheek. Her voice and his mind took him back to a time of a great battle. Gazing upwards he saw beautiful skies; like nothing he had ever seen before. The red and pinkish glow of windswept clouds appeared as fires burning in the vault of heaven. It was obvious the gods were looking over them. The skies sent a message; a message only his Queen had the powers to read.

They were together. Ben was once again transformed into the powerful Lord Benami. He sat proudly to the right of his loving Queen. They were in her castle. He watched on as she snapped at her forces, barking orders. She snarled when things did not run as she commanded. Yet when she turned towards Benami calm and a caring gentleness welcomed his ever-watchful eyes. Queenie wrapped her arm around his waist, assuring him all would be fine. Her words delivered like the comforting touch of a soft warm blanket on a cool winter's night. Benami's concern eased. Queenie was a woman of her word. She had survived many attacks and assured him this time would be no different. Victory would be theirs. Her confidence overflowed. Loyal servants accepted sacrifices were essential. Death was not feared. Those who died protecting the cause were guaranteed to return with a far greater status in the next life. The warmth and love Queenie conveyed towards Benami reinforced the safety he felt within the confines of her impenetrable castle. It was a castle as formidable as Queenie herself and a true symbol of her power.

Surrounded by a deep moat and with the added defence of a drawbridge, opponents soon deemed battering rams worthless weapons. Detection on approach was guaranteed; armed guards manned watchtowers, constantly peering through arrow slits. A long winding passage wrapped around the castle dominated the landscape, and served as a plain that provided ample time to spot approaching intruders who emerged from the darkened forest. Incoming visitors had no way of concealing their advance.

Concentric in design; it was a stone castle with two rings of outer walls, one inside the other. In essence, it was a castle inside a castle. Magnificent in construction, to seize the castle attackers first had to successfully make their way over the outer curtain wall. Then they would enter a barren strip of grass called, 'the death area.' Archers firing incessantly from the walls above, death was almost certain, there was nowhere to run or hide. If this assault were survived, opponents would then have to breach the second inner wall. Needless to say Queenie's castle had never been invaded.

Perched high upon the royal throne made of gold and decorated in jewels, Benami inhaled his power as he cast his eye over what would one day be his. Grand marble stairs flowed down to a huge cobblestone quadrangle. Eagerly he watched on. He clasped her hand as he scrutinised her staunch defence. A messenger had arrived sending word an attack from evil forces was imminent. The barbaric sixth battalion of the evil King Henry was intent on destroying what was rightfully hers. Evil warriors had advanced over the northern mountains. They had infiltrated her outlying regiments and viciously slaughtered those villagers who lived in dwellings on the banks of the river to the west. Queenie's forces waited for instruction. Armed loyal subjects and giant earthly bug transformations made up a five thousand strong force.Queenie definitely had the upper hand; no other earthly leader possessed powers giving them the ability to control fighter insects. The thunderous sound of fierce bull ant troops marched into formation within the quadrangle awaiting her command. The ground shook below the thudding noise. Above the sky darkened as it filled with giant fire spitting dragons and butterfly warriors; like hundreds of fighter jets.

Unlike her earthly servants who took years to mature and mold, these giant creatures in some instances took only a matter of weeks. This element added to her continued strength. The creation of a butterfly warrior took place in four weeks and consisted of four stages; egg to caterpillar to chrysalis and finally the emergence of the butterfly. Butterfly warriors possessed giant lethal wingspans capable of slicing opponents. Normal butterflies were cold blooded; these giant transformations were cold-blooded killers. The giant butterfly warriors appeared like colossal raptors, resembling prehistoric pterodactyls. Their shrilling screech cut through the air and served as a warning. The bull ant warrior also developed in four stages with a timeframe of only eight to twelves weeks between egg and adult fighter. These powerful ants had the capability of lifting twenty times their body weight. Queen ants produced millions of babies and the adults had an innate determination that would see them fighting to the death. Bull ant warriors were a tenacious force to be reckoned with when transformed into warrior mode their size equalled that of a car. Although the finest and most revered warrior by far was the dragonfly. Dragonflies took considerably longer with development from their larval stage to adulthood taking up to two years. However their extreme capabilities far outweighed this short fall in reproduction. Dragonflies could attack alone or in swarms. They were efficient hunters who would swoop down on prey and catch it in their feet. When transformed into their giant dragon form these fire-spitting creatures attacked turning enemies to ash. Leading the bug transformations was Darius; this was the name bestowed on all dragonfly leaders. A title reserved for the most gallant of souls; a fierce supreme commander who was both admired and revered. Darius would fight to the death, defend until the last breath left his body, surrendering was not an option.

With his body relaxed Benami listened intently. In his mind's eye he saw butterfly scouts in the distant skies. Butterfly warriors were at the ready. Dragonflies hovered. Guarding. Protecting. Dying in the name of Queenie was an honour. Cowardice in the face of the enemy was punishable by death. No one dared go against his or her Queen.

Enemy soldiers advanced rapidly through the surrounding forest. Shouting could be heard from within the canopy of darkness. A crashing noise followed the shouting. The top of trees moved as the sound of cracking branches from the dense under wood echoed. Something of considerable size was working its way through the forest towards the castle.

Queenie's forces stood silent. Watching and waiting. Benami sat with his eyes wide open, sometimes holding his breath, his knees shaking. No one dared move.

Suddenly an explosion echoed from the east. A messenger returned. Enemy forces were surrounding the castle. Within minutes of the announcement monstrous weapons of war emerged from the forest. Enemy forces in the thousands' advanced rapidly along the grassy plains. A barrage of gunfire accompanied the charging warriors. There was no time to wait; the castle was being attacked from all sides. Queenie's forces stormed into action, to remain inside the confines of the walls would not demonstrate her power. Queenie wanted to annihilate her enemy.With anger filled eyes she turned towards Benami and reminded him of the consequences, "I will pulverise those against me."

Snapping instructions to lower the drawbridge she ordered her troops to annihilate the enemy.

Benami was mesmerised.

Bull ant warriors charged thunderously towards the battlefield. The earth shook below. A hail of gunfire hit the approaching enemy's first line of attack. Blood spattered and screams released as many fell. Others staggered and lurched forward trying to keep pace with the attacking line, until finally they collapsed. Within minutes the forces collided. The bull ant warriors relentlessly continued forward. Bulldozing, stampeding and crushing their opponents. The attacking was ruthless, for every fallen opponent five more appeared from the forest. Defence forces streamed from the castle gates. Butterfly and dragon warriors invaded the sky, swooping down they sliced the enemy. Others were set alight. Black puffs of smoke followed leaping flames, the smell of burning flesh carried upwards by the heat. On the ground only ash remained. Evil warriors were decapitated, limbs and flesh flew into the air as the body count mounted. Possessed by evil, they fought on until they fell senseless from the loss of blood. Splinters of wood were sent flying. The ear splitting and almost deafening roar of exploding bombs echoed. Crashing steel against toughened armour clanged. Bullets whizzed. The cries of injured soldiers accompanied death wails of the dying. Bodies piled up in heaps. The fighting continued for hours. Agonising moans and groans filled Ben's ears, offering him a sense of power. Gruesome cries and screams, sorrowful echoes of final escaping breath heaving upwards, reinforced his egotistical and narcissistic belief. He was the chosen one. Listening to Queenie and accepting her every word would deliver greatness. Closing his eyes he inhaled deeply. A gentle breeze danced across his face. Breathing in through his nose the smell of excrement, blood, gore and charred remains tantalised his senses. These odours were not offensive, but captivating, rich and enticing. His future had been foretold by Queenie, all enemies required destroying to make way forthe supreme leader; Lord Benami. The future was in his hands. Opening his eyes he watched on relishing the thought of what would one day be his. He loved being in control. Power delivered ultimate control.

Night time approached. The enemy unable to gain any ground.

All of a sudden a distant trumpet sounded and the enemy ceased fire. The evil forces retreated in great haste, fleeing like madmen. Hundreds of corpses strewn in every direction lay scattered across the scarred battlefield.

Complete silence.

Queenie's forces suffered considerable losses. Thousands of dead souls littered the bloody battlefield. A chaotic mixture of black, grey, green and red covered the landscape. Then without warning a ghostly glow brightened the nearing night skies. This time it was the beam of spirits searching out those souls from the departed. Strong winds whipped over the plains. The heavens darkened, only soulless bodies remained as the gateway to beyond closed. All was still. The stars sparkled. The peaceful moon shone. Victory was theirs.

Ben's eyes sprung open. The message was clear. This house was his castle. He was the chosen one, the powerful Lord Benami. He knew what he had to do. He had to annihilate his enemy. He was more resolute than ever to keep his word. He had promised Queenie he would honour and protect her. It was imperative he maintained her dignity in death. What happens in the family, stays in the family. Determination drove him off the lounge. Balling his fists he punched himself in the chest several times then began slapping himself in the face. His eyes stared. He began huffing and puffing, moaning and groaning. Squinting his eyes he clenched his teeth, his nostrils flared. *I am Lord Benami. I am the ruler of all. No one messes with the powerful Lord Benami,* he thought. It was his responsibility to put an end to the threats. Queenie had spoken. He had heard her words. He would follow her instruction.

CHAPTER THIRTY TWO

His eyes flickered and then went still. Blackness. Time passed. Nothing. All was silent. Panicked he gasped for breath. His eyes flickered once more. Hearing a rustle, he believed it emanated from the wind as it travelled through the trees. He lay still in his world of darkness. His mind fuzzy. His body heavy. His breathing painful. Feeling the rise and fall within his chest he focused on that alone. Inhaling deeply he could smell the freshly cut lucerne hay. He could feel the dryness of the small pieces as they touched his cheeks. A warmth touched his face. *It must be the sun,* he thought. Several minutes later he drew in deeper breaths. The air appeared thick. His eyes flickered. His eyes opened slightly. Fine particles scratched his eyeballs. Shaking his head vigorously reality began to bleed into his understanding. There was no field of lucerne. Fine needles danced within his eyes. Burning pain from which there was no escape. Opening his eyes wider he struggled to restore his vision to normal. Everything was so dark. His head throbbed. His body ached. The world appeared spinning. Sucking in air he whipped his head from side to side. A loud scrunching noise entered his ears; like writing paper being crumpled into a small ball. Fine particles fell across his face. The rich sweet earthy smell he inhaled was much closer than any field and far more restricting. His consciousness began to return as did his shocking realisation that his head was encased in a bag. His darting eyes battled to gain sight. Nervously he bit on his bottom lip. He listened but heard nothing. When he remained still there was silence. He could hear nothing but his breath. It sounded echoed like when you place you ear next to a sea shell. The air around his face felt damp, humid. He must have been restrained for some time for the moisture to have been trapped and thick.

The silence broke. A loud clanging noise entered his ears. A sudden jolt hit his legs. Chains rattled. Scratching metal. Footsteps boomed. The commotion appeared to be coming from all directions. Was he under attack from multiple persons? He burst into tears. Uncontrollable torrents of wetness escaped his eyes. Poking and prodding collided with his restrained body. Laughter echoed and taunted his agony. Then silence. Stillness. The door slammed. Muffled voices from outside were followed by yelling. Indecipherable words. The door creaked. He listened. He swallowed hard.

Whack!

Black nothingness.

His eyes flickered and then went still. An unknown time passed. Tugging at his head. Pulling around his neck. His eyes sprung open. Hazy. Painful scratching returned to his eyes. Loud voices entered his ears. The bag was ripped from his head. He struggled to see. A blurred vision of his son looked over him. Blinking he stared upward trying to focus. The moist lucerne air was gone. The scratchiness in his eyes continued. How long would he have to endure his suffering? Coagulated blood lingered in the outer corner of his left eye. Remnants of his earlier beating. His hands still tied above his head; the rope anchored to the metal bed head. His body was bruised and battered. He felt a stabbing pain in the left side of his abdomen every time he inhaled. A few broken ribs, he suspected. His breaths short and ragged.

"What the fuck have you done?" Ben screamed turning his attention to Johnnie who was standing to his left. "How dare you, who do you think you are?'

"I thought I was helping," Johnnie quivered, "he was dead. The evil warriors killed him. I put a bag on his head so they would not see his eyes. If he could not see them then they would not see him and we would be safe. I did it for you. I thought I was helping."

Ben's rage churned like a giant ocean undertow. The wild voices whipped up. Lashed over. Swirled from beneath. Taunting his every move. They disputed his logic. Sucking him down into the depths of delusion. An inescapable place in which he was drowning. His henchman was trying to steal his power. His father continued to argue. Ben's anger was mounting. His frustration was growing. Lord Antony was far more powerful and resilient than he had ever anticipated.

"Your grandmother was a young spoilt brat who grew into a conniving and manipulative woman. She kept secrets and told lies. The problem with secrets and lies is they fester, and they consume. Greed drove her until finally she withered into a mean, disturbed, bitter and twisted old woman. She hated those who ignored her rule. She played with those who believed her. She despised what she could not control. Greed, power, selfishness, envy, jealousy, all of these things drove her to destroy. She was a narcissistic bitch who played us all. You were her pawn. We were all pawns in her warped little world. Please Ben…please…I beg of you, please. It's your innocence that doesn't allow you to accept her deceit and subterfuge. It's your illness that drives your madness. You are sick. I can get you help. I will get you help. I promise you, please son." Anthony's pleading echoed through the house. Surely his son had to see reason. Surely there was still time to stop with the madness.

"You leave Queenie out of this. This is nothing to do with her. This is between you and me. My nightmare started the day you killed my mother. Today your nightmare is just beginning."

"Listen to me, please it's not too late. I didn't kill your mother. I loved her. I am your father. I love you. I want to help you. I can help you."

Anthony could not control his grief. Ben's emotions began to stir. He paced back and forth. Johnnie stood silent in the corner of the room, his hands covered his ears.

"You loved to hate her; you hated Queenie."

"I didn't hate her. I could see through her. Your grandmother was so rude and forever angry at the world. On many visits she offered us nothing more than a hot tongue and cold shoulder. Surely you remember this, surely you remember your mother's tears."

"My grandmother was a great woman. Her actions were merely reactions to the evil that surrounded her."

"Come on Ben…surely you don't believe that. She was evil. We are all bound by the decisions we make, irrespective as to whether they are made in haste or under pressure. She just gave her excuses names. It was easier for her to blame something or someone else. She pulled you into her twisted world. The power of persuasion on a young and innocent mind can have devastating consequences. She played you from the very start. She groomed you over many years. You are living in a world of your own creation."

Ben endured his father's diatribe for as long as he could stand.Releasing adeep throated explosion he became verbally abusive and threatening. Johnnie sunk to the floor, crippled by nerves. He couldn't stand yelling. Holding his hands over his ears he silently prayed for silence.

"You need help Ben. It's all in your mind, your imagination. It's not real."

"You're lying. I know what I know. If it were in my mind I would be able to see and hear them when I wanted. They are real and they come to me when they want. Queenie will never desert me. She will never betray me. You are the one who wants to destroy me…they told me. The voices have spoken."

"Who? Who are they?" Anthony pleaded.

Ben raised an eyebrow and looked closely at his father. Internal bickering prevented him from answering his questions. A brutal battle was being waged within his mind. He was absorbed and influenced by his grandmother's stories. Plagued by voices and hallucinations. He knew his thinking was wrong. He understood his behaviour was warped. Yet he felt compelled to believe. Driven to act. He was drawn in by the voices. Trapped by his delusions. Resistance was futile. Portals to another world opened amazing doors to adventures. The evil warriors would seek vengeance if he did not comply. Great forces of darkness were at work. The intrusive thoughts consumed his time. Battling against his beliefs drained his energy. The loss of his mother had left him empty. Abandoned. With his grandmother gone he felt alone. Anthony's words were obsessive, suffocating.

"Shut up…they are talking now. You are trying to confuse me."

Anthony looked around the room; Johnnie was the only one with them and he remained closed lipped, huddled over in the corner of the room. The room was silent yet Ben insisted he could hear voices. Caught up in the fantasies her stories became so entrenched in his mind. They appeared real. Anthony was fighting an up hill battle. A battle it appeared he was losing. Ben's dark side over shadowed all brightness. His once spark for life, smothered. Choked by his ever consuming and increasingly paranoid delusions. His rage was volcanic. Ben was deranged, disturbed to the very core of his soul. Full of conflicting emotions. He heard silent voices twist in the wind. His imagination carried in the breeze. Silent voices appeared as real as the earth he stood on and the air he breathed.

"I know. I remember. I saw Darius. You weren't there. He is real. The evil warriors are real. I am Lord Benami. You are the evil Lord Antony. Shut up…I demand that you shut up," he yelled.

Anthony closed his mouth. Enough was enough. There was no way of getting his son to see reason. Recollections of the conversation he had had with Johnnie bled into Anthony's mind. The thought of what would happen next was paralysing. His eyes locked onto his son. He was more cunning than Anthony had ever anticipated. But now Anthony recalled his son's plan. He was convinced his son was willing to do anything. These latest revelations only exacerbated his concern. His son appeared lost and totally immersed within his delusions. Johnnie was the perfect fall guy, his connection to Billy Bunbagel linked him to the scene. His stupidity would allow him to follow instruction. Johnnie's stupidity was enabling him to be manipulated. But there was no time to think about that. Johnnie would have to fend for himself.

Closing his eyes Anthony recommenced his silent pleading. Rebecca had to hear. She just had to hear him. Maybe she already had. Maybe she was on her way. He felt like screaming out at the top of his lungs. He felt like bursting into tears. He felt like smashing his captors to smithereens.

"Fuck, fuck, fuck!" he screeched, "let me go."

His body thrashed. His face reddened. His legs kicked wildly. His head shook. His mouth frothed. Eyes wide and darting.

Ben pounced. His hand covered Anthony's mouth. Both locked in an intense stare.

"Shut up…or I will shut you up!" Ben snarled.

Anthony closed his eyes. His son made him feel sick. He was repulsive. Warped.

Rebecca please Rebecca…I need you, look at me, hear me… come on damn it, please I beg of you, please hear me. They are going to kill me, I don't want to die, please Rebecca please! he thought.

CHAPTER THIRTY THREE

Time passed. Waking in fright Rebecca wiped her eyes. Her body a lather of sweat. She had heard Anthony. For the most part she thought she had heard his voice calling to her. It was as if he had paid her a visit while she was sleeping. An eerie feeling engulfed her body. In her mind she saw him. He was surrounded by darkness. He had called to her from a frightening place. He was begging, pleading to be heard. Looking at the clock she noticed several hours had passed. Walking over to the window she glanced over to his house. It was getting late. She rubbed her temples. Why did he appear so lost and scared? Her conscious thoughts focused on Anthony. Surely both he and Ben should have been home by now, yet there was no sign of activity next door. The niggling feeling of unease persisted. Why was he calling to her?

Rebecca began to think of Claire. Tears entered her eyes. She missed her friend. She loved her friend. Warm tears flowed down her face. They had shared a beautiful connection. A warm and cherished friendship. Now all that lingered within was a heaviness in her heart. A longing to be close once more. To be able to smile and joke. To sit and enjoy. To share in quiet moments. Claire exemplified friendship. She was loyal and trustworthy. She was protective, respectful and understanding. She heard and never judged, offered advice but never dictated. She was a person who was thoughtful and took other people's feelings into consideration. Supportive, encouraging, Claire joined in with happiness. She consoled and stuck by you when others did not. Most of all Claire knew all Rebecca's faults and frailties and accepted no one was perfect. She cared. She loved. She laughed. She listened. She was the perfect friend. And now she was gone. Rebecca burst into tears. Everything seemed to be falling apart. Everything was silent. Up till only days ago Rebecca had possessed something special. An ability some would argue wasn't possible, while others would regard it as either a blessing or a curse. Rebecca had received a visit. A life changing visit. A visit that in her mind proved the existence of earthbound ghosts. At first she had been shocked. She stood stupefied not believing her eyes and ears. How could a friend who had just passed away be standing in front of her? Surely it was not possible. People would think she was mad. When a person died many believed they entered into heaven. Others believed they disappeared into black nothingness. How could someone possibly die, yet remain visible to earthly beings?

After death her friend had reappeared and more than that, she had spoken to Rebecca. They had engaged in lengthy discussions in which Claire had imparted to Rebecca information pertaining to unspeakable acts of violence, murder, cover ups and deeply guarded secrets. Claire's death was indirectly linked to her efforts in trying to uncover and reveal the truth. Rebecca had spoken to Anthony about her experience. Anthony had dismissed her words. Anthony was now at the house from which so many of the details emanated.

"Oh shit!" she cried, "Anthony."

All her concerns returned to Anthony. The feeling something was drastically wrong intensified from within. She could no longer stay put. She needed to act. Grabbing her car keys she raced out the front door slamming it behind her. Troubling thoughts kept playing through her mind making her shiver. A sense of urgency overwhelmed her as she jumped into her car.

Turning the key she heard a click. The engine failed to fire. Disengaging the key she tried again. Again, it clicked.

"Come on!" she yelled, "come on!"

Turning the key once more she heard the familiar clicking noise. This time it was followed by a faint whirl. Frantically she turned the key again and again. Click, whirl, click, whirl. Her frustration growing as the intensity in her flicking of the key increased. It wouldn't start. Reaching down she found the release button for the bonnet then leaped out of the car. She hadn't experienced any car troubles of late. Finding the bonnet catch she pushed it with her fingers and with both arms thrust the bonnet upwards.

"What the fuck." One of the leads connecting to the battery terminal had dislodged. Pushing it back into position she raced around flung open the driver's door and turned the key. The engine roared into life. Within seconds the bonnet was slammed shut and Rebecca was on her way back to the other house.

CHAPTER THIRTY FOUR

Ben bellowed across the room. He was fuming. "Get up on your feet. You whiney little parasite. I am sick of your defiance. I am sick of your sniffling." Johnnie jumped to his feet and moved slowly towards him. He appeared scared. Ben put his arm around his neck and whispered into his ear. "You had better do what I tell you or Mr. Benson won't be the only one in the hole."

Johnnie cringed shaking his head as Ben tightened his grip. Animosity and stress was building. Signs of friction were favourable to Anthony. Something or someone was about to snap. This realisation lifted his hopes. Resentment and tension between his captors increased his ability to destroy them. Divided they were weak. But Anthony wondered if he would have the energy to flee or fight if given the opportunity. He had been deprived of all food and water and bashed within an inch of his life.

Releasing his hold Ben turned glaring towards Anthony. Things weren't going to plan. Frustration was growing. Anthony lay still. Staring. Unwilling to show his pain and fear he needed to remain calm. Waiting. Watching. Surely his son would realise he was fighting a losing battle. Surely he would come to his senses before it was too late. Johnnie's continued sniffling triggered Ben's rage. Flipping around he released a roar as he launched his assault. Grabbing Johnnie around the throat he slammed him into the wall. Pushing his thumb into his adam's apple Johnnie began to cough and splutter.

Heaving he gasped for breath. Ben laughed. He released his hold. Johnnie burst into tears. To Ben it appeared as one big joke.

"You hurt me…why did you hurt me?" he sobbed.

"Oh come on…I was playing with you," he chuckled.

Johnnie stood shaking. In his mind Ben's actions did not reflect those of someone who was playing.

"What's wrong with you, you need to toughen up… don't you want to prove your allegiance?"

"Yes."

"Well can't you take a joke?"

"Yes."

"Then what's your problem?"

Johnnie shook his head. He was not game to speak. Ben smiled. He turned his head, looked at the door and gave Johnnie a small nod. Both locked eyes, Johnnie's mouth twitched as his fingers flicked. His eyebrows came together confirming his confusion.

"Well what are you waiting for?" Ben shouted in a voice that made Johnnie jump.

"Huh."

"Grab his legs… we don't have all day."

Johnnie nodded but remained still. Confronted by his hesitation Ben's anger began to stir. Delivering a savage blow with his closed fist to the back of Johnnie's head he attempted to knock some sense into his accomplice. He was furious. They had come too far now to think about turning back. Johnnie released a loud cry, squinted his eyes but said nothing. Anthony could see tears release in the corner of his eyes. The friction between his captors was definitely mounting. Without saying another word Johnnie moved towards the end of the bed. Standing still he glanced at Ben. A frown came over his face. His head tilted towards the floor. He released a loud sigh. He hesitated. He gingerly raised a finger.

"What's wrong with you?" Ben shouted.

"I need to pee," Johnnie quivered, not daring to look in his direction.

"Well go and bloody pee…for fuck sake, you are really starting to piss me off."

Turning around Johnnie walked away. His face remained looking towards the floor. His hands rubbed the back of his head. His slamming the door on the way out triggered Ben's fury. Alone with Anthony he began to rant and rave. His conversation held no direction. His words darted off in tangents. Any attempt to cut him off only escalated his irritation. Totally out of control his words flew thick and fast. His rage intensifying, eyes blackened and darting wildly. Adamant Anthony was plotting against him and convinced Johnnie was nothing more than a weakening scrap of pond scum he became crazy with destruction. Pacing around the room he picked up the perfume bottle from the dressing table and hurled it into the wall. Anthony watched on in horror as it smashed into tiny pieces. His son was a walking time bomb.

Trying to remain inconspicuous in his movements Anthony twisted his hands trying with all his might to grab the knot that held him trapped in what was a near inconceivable predicament. Johnnie would soon return. His son was out of control. Anthony's struggling was to no avail. He could only pray for a miracle. Maybe someone would hear them. Maybe someone would see them. He would soon be dragged outside. He would soon be faced with the hole under the house.

Minutes passed. Johnnie returned and Ben ordered

him to grab the rope from the corner of the room. Johnnie appeared upset his eyes were red and puffy. Anthony believed he may have been crying, yet he submissively followed Ben's demands like a robot. Complying with his instruction reduced the tension.

Handing over the rope Johnnie stood back and waited for his next command. Ben pulled Anthony's legs together and wrapped the rope around, tugging hard as he tied a knot. Looking up Anthony gave Johnnie a half smile. Johnnie looked at him with no expression, just blinking eyes. Anthony said nothing. Johnnie looked away.

Ben tugged at his father. The bed springs squeaked. A feeling of dread and doom filled Anthony's body. He was exhausted. The situation appeared surreal.

"Grab his legs," Ben snapped.

Johnnie reached over. His fingers wrapped around the knotted rope. His breath became puffed. Sweat decorated his forehead. His chest ached. His head pounded. He felt sick. Nervous.

"Lift him… for fuck sake do I have to do everything."

Tears filled Johnnie's eyes as he lifted Anthony's bound legs.

Making their way out of the house Ben pulled at Anthony's arms as he took off down the stairs with a determined stride. His voices had returned. This time they were louder and more forceful than ever before. Berating his every action. Johnnie followed visibly exhausted and appearing somewhat withdrawn and defeated.

Pausing at the front door Ben dropped his father's body without warning and went to the window. The street was clear. It was now or never. It was time to put an end to everything. His frustration increasing. His thoughts disturbed. Every thought interrupted by yet another annoying comment.

"Shut up, shut up, shut up!" he screamed, "shut up or I will make you shut up!"

Johnnie jumped. Anthony flinched. They had heard nothing. For Ben the voices became intense. The nagging demons ravaged his mind. Snatching at his father's arms he dragged him out the front door. Panicked and increasingly nervous Johnnie followed. His eyes scanned the street. His heart raced.

At last they were behind the front fence. Anthony's body hit the ground with a thud. Moaning in agony he closed his eyes and prayed his pain would soon end.

Buckling over Johnnie collapsed to his knees. He was a mess.

Ben paced back and forth. Gibberish flew from his mouth. Everything he felt said yes, but still he was forced to question the legitimacy of his voices. Conflicting forces continued to argue. All he needed was for a sign, any sign. Looking at his restrained father his mind was a mass of confusion.

Johnnie looked towards Ben for instruction. Anthony looked towards Ben for release. And that was when Ben received it. That was when the wind picked up and leaves began to blow creating a clapping sound as if the Gods were cheering, demanding he go further.

The end was near.

CHAPTER THIRTY FIVE

Y ou must finish your job!" Ben roared as a sense of panic engulfed his body.

Anthony's eyes were wide like saucers; fear painted his face. A muffling sound escaped his partially gagged mouth. Nodding his head up and down, he was frantic. Working his jaw he struggled to open his mouth, pushing his tongue against the tape. He could feel the skin on his lips ripping. Floundering around on the ground he was like a fish out of water; his legs bound at the ankles thrusting back and forth. A cloud of finely powdered earth whisked up into the air with each erratic thrust. There was no way he was going to die without one last attempt. He needed his son to hear his words. In Ben's mind his father needed nothing more than to be silenced.

"You are the gatekeeper, it must be you who inflicts the fatal blow!" Ben screamed.

Staring at Johnnie he feared he would not do as he instructed.

"This is your test, you must prove your allegiance!"

Peering towards Ben then down towards Anthony who lay stretched out next to the hole, a wheezing noise escaped Johnnie's mouth. His right hand grasped the brass hilt of his sword. A look of confusion came over his face. Fearing he doubted his commands, Ben snapped.

"Do it!" he bellowed as his heart raced faster and faster. Anger rushed through his body; a fire of fury erupted, his breath temporarily stolen. Opening his mouth wide he gasped for oxygen as dirt particles reminiscent of the taste of gritty potatoes danced on his tongue. Clenching his jaw in frustration the dirt particles crunched between his teeth. The tension was nearing an unbearable level. Sweat covered his brow and ran down the side of his cheek. Someone needed to act. He could see the pain on Lord Antony's face. The terror in his eyes. He feared the evil forces might attack if he was not silenced.

"You stole my mother…so now I am going to steal your soul…Goodbye Antony!" he yelled staring at his father. Turning his glare towards Johnnie he screamed at the top of his lungs, "Do it, kill him!"

Johnnie raised his arms above his shoulders. The sword firmly in his hands. With all the force he could muster he thrust his arms downward. Anthony kicked his feet. His body pushed to the side. The blade made contact. Anthony was struck. His attempt to save himself from a fatal blow resulted in a slice to the side of his head. The momentum of his kick saw his body propelled into the pit. He hit the bottom with a thud. He was alive. He was lying on the dismembered remains of an aged stranger. Terrified. Still. Staring. His face within millimetres of the hacked up corpse. *Maybe they will think I am dead*, he thought.

Ben glared at Johnnie, "Finish him!"

Anthony lay face down. Unable to see what was happening. Too terrified to move. Frozen by fear. The venom and determination behind his son's words led him to believe these would be his final moments alive. In a hole. Under a house. His remains would be covered over for eternity.

Johnnie turned his head slowly towards Ben; blood splatter glistened on his cheeks. His expression sent goosebumps down Ben's spine and a smile to his face.

"Finish him!"

Anthony could no longer remain silent. Tormenting sobs echoed from below. Staring into the hole Ben studied his father's battered body. His arms and legs tightly bound. The rope cutting into his skin.

"You low life pond scum parasite," he snarled glaring at Johnnie, "finish him off or I will release the dragon warriors onto you and you will burn in hell for eternity!"

Anthony inhaled deeply. Clenching his eyes tightly he waited to be struck. He prayed there was more after death than just a black hole of abyss. *Claire I am coming to join you*, he thought.

Tightening his grip around the sword handle a look of determination came onto Johnnie's face. There was no second guessing as to what he had to do. It was kill or be killed; demonstrate allegiance to his Queen and the unblemished chosen one or prove disloyalty and suffer the consequences. He jumped into the hole. Anthony felt the earth move around him. Johnnie held no regard for where he stood. Anthony moaned.

The job was nearly complete. Peering down Ben was struck by the harsh reality of his actions. There was no way he was going down for murder. It was time to create a new legend. His idea brought a smile to his face. The legend of the gatekeeper would be born. A demonic individual of epic proportion. His eyes went cold as he stared expressionless. Johnnie would do anything to please the gods.

CHAPTER THIRTY SIX

Hearing a car door slam Ben dashed out from under the house. He peered out the gate. He couldn't believe his eyes. This couldn't be happening. How the hell could this be happening? She was back! Rebecca had returned. Queenie had claimed she would always watch over him. Her words were true. The gods were assisting. He couldn't have planned things any better. With Johnnie preoccupied he ran across the lawn. He yelled at Rebecca to get back in the car. She did as instructed.

Anthony had also heard the car door. But more importantly he had heard his son dash away. Johnnie and he were alone. He needed to seize the moment. Johnnie was a fool. Anthony shook his head. He had to act but also maintain calm. He needed to appear in control. His eyes widened. His determination returned. Claire would have to wait. The black hole of abyss would have to remain a mystery. Frantically he began nodding his head. He stopped. Then he began shaking his body. Thrashing his legs around. Johnnie jumped. Unsure as to what would happen next. Anthony shook violently at stop and start intervals. Finally he rolled over. Frozen still. He glared. Johnnie stood over him. His hands trembled. Johnnie looked frightened. Anthony began nodding his head. Johnnie's face became shrouded in confusion and he too began nodding. Mimicking the strange actions. Confused. Anthony began shaking his head from left to right. The sudden change in his behaviour left Johnnie baffled. Stepping back he created space between the two of them. With his back up against the dirt wall Johnnie feared what would happen next. And that was when things changed. Anthony began to mutter strained words.

"In the name of our Queen and almighty gods I order you to stop."

Johnnie's mouth dropped wide open. He couldn't believe what he was hearing.

"You are my loyal gatekeeper and as King of the tracerteps and ruler of all, I order you to stop!"

Anthony's voice was firm yet convincingly calm.

Johnnie stared, confused at what he had just heard.

"What?" A lone word escaped his lips. His eyebrows raised, displaying a look of puzzlement.

"I am your King. I am King Antony of the tracerteps."

Johnnie tilted his head to the side like a confused dog that had just heard a strange noise.

"Huh?" he gulped, bewildered at what he was hearing. How did he know about the tracerteps?

"I am King Antony. Queenie has spoken. She has demanded I reveal my true self…Darius is guarding from outside. Lord Benami has been infected by the evil warriors. You must let me free or I will not be able to save him."

Johnnie couldn't believe what he was hearing. Not only did he know about the tracerteps he also knew of Darius. Anthony's words went down like a poop in a pool. Johnnie didn't know where to look or if he should flee and hide. Hearing that Lord Benami had been infected terrified him. The powerful Lord Benami was his protector. He could not let harm come to his Lord Benami. He could not harm King Antony of the tracerteps. A King was more powerful than a Lord. It would be up to the King to protect them all. Looking out of the hole he scanned for his friend. Nothing. He was no where to be seen. Where was Lord Benami? Anthony could be lying. But if he wasn't then not helping him could risk the safety of his friend.

"I don't know what to do," he sobbed.

"Help me…you must free me or I will not be able to save us."

Reaching down he grabbed Anthony's bound hands. Johnnie had hands like shovels; large, solid and powerful. His quick response gave Anthony hope. But Johnnie froze. Staring. His breathing ragged. It was necessary for Anthony to maintain eye contact. He gave Johnnie a reassuring smile. He nodded. Johnnie said nothing. He copied Anthony's nodding motion. His unblinking eyes fixed on Anthony's face. His mouth twitched. He licked his lips. He released his hold on Anthony's hands. He glanced out of the hole. Nothing. The clock was ticking. Anthony became concerned by his hesitation. He felt like screaming. Clenching his jaw he knew it was imperative to remain calm. He inhaled. He stared. He nodded again.

"I am King Antony of the tracerteps. I order you to release me."

Johnnie blinked. He gulped in air. Shook his head. He stretched his arms. The blade of the sword danced within millimetres of Anthony's face. Johnnie dropped his arms. The blade hovered above Anthony's chest. Johnnie peered out of the hole. Still nothing. Anthony maintained eye contact with the blade. One thrust and it could all be over. Johnnie nodded. Shrugged his shoulder and cut the rope. He released Anthony's hands. Pausing for a moment he giggled and grinned. He moved quickly towards Anthony's feet. He repeated the slicing action.

Anthony was dumbfounded. The big galoot had believed him. His reaction was almost too ridiculous for words. Not only had he released his restraints he was helping him out of the hole.

Dusting himself down Anthony instructed Johnnie to stand silently near the house.

"If you face the wall eyes closed and ears covered the evil may not detect you."

Johnnie meekly did as he was directed. Anthony peeked from behind the gate. He could hear Rebecca; she was sitting in her car. Her voice appeared panicked. Ben was leaning into the car window talking to her. Blocking her view of the gate. Ben was waving his hands around. Shaking as he expected a person would who feared for their life. Instructing Rebecca to leave quickly and race to the police. Anthony grappled with one question. What would he do to protect his family? If he attempted an escape now the consequences could be horrendous. Rebecca sat in striking distance of Ben. Ben could snap. He could kill her. Johnnie stood near the house confused and unpredictable. He could snap.

Anthony's heart pounded. He couldn't risk endangering Rebecca. A split second decision was required.He was terrified. There was no time for procrastination. Ideas flew through his mind. He couldn't take his eyes off Rebecca's car. He held his breath. Run for it and risk her life or stay and risk his. He was stuck. Undecided. Nausea was choking him. A split second decision was necessary. A split second decision would change everything. He had to act. Hesitation could mean the difference between life and death. His entire body began to tremble. Looking over his shoulder he saw Johnnie. He had his back to him. His hands were placed against his ears. His body shaking. Anthony spotted the shovel. It stood resting against the wall of the house. He could hear Ben and Rebecca.

"It's going to be okay," Anthony whispered, "I will protect you."

Johnnie nodded not daring to turn. The thought of an attack from the evil warriors terrified him. He began to sob. His head tilted forward. His hands remained next to his ears as if he were trying to block out all noise. Anthony edged close to the house. Gently he wrapped his hand around the handle of the shovel. Picking it up he prayed Johnnie would not hear his movements. He prayed his son would not return. Dealing with two of them at once in his battered state would be impossible. With the shovel in hand and within striking distance of Johnnie he paused. Standing still, he listened. Ben was still immersed in conversation with Rebecca. The time to strike was now. If the talking stopped it was almost guaranteed Ben would hear. Raising the shovel above his head Anthony thrust the nose down as hard as he could. It made contact with the back of Johnnie's head. A dull thud echoed. Anthony held his breath. Johnnie's hands dropped to his side. His knees buckled. His body collapsed. He hit the ground with a thump. Anthony cautiously approached his body. Nudging him with his foot he got no response. Silently he cheered. He had just dealt with Johnnie. He couldn't believe how gullible one individual could be. Like Ben, Johnnie had immersed himself within Shirley's wild stories. He whole heartedly believed an attack was imminent. He had been brain washed. All it took was for Anthony to announce himself as the King, deliver an instruction for Johnnie to turn away then *whack!* Johnnie was knocked out cold.

But how would the internal nightmare of suffering end? Tears welled in his eyes. Nerves invaded his every pore. He would soon face a mind in chaos. His son was hell bent on seeing him dead. His delusions and hallucinations implicated Anthony in a sinister conspiracy from which there appeared no escaping. The gentle soul he had known as his son had been devoured by demons. He had succumbed to an inner world. More than any other time in his life Anthony stood at a very dangerous crossroad. A pivotal decision was paramount. An instantaneous and crucial determination that would weigh on his conscience forever. Some things were worth protecting. Some things were worth being kept a secret.

Resting against the fence he listened. He waited for his son's return. It was imperative he kept Rebecca safe.

CHAPTER THIRTY SEVEN

Go, go! You have to get the police. I need to get back in there. I need to help dad. He is attacking dad!"

Rebecca was stunned, she couldn't believe what she was hearing. Since leaving hours earlier she hadn't been able to get Anthony out of her mind. She gripped her steering wheel. Panic engulfed her body. Surely this couldn't be happening. How could this be true? Glancing towards Ben concern for his safety escalated. He looked terrified.

"What about you? Come with me," she urged, "you will be safe, together we will get help."

"I can't…I need to help dad. He is going to kill him."

"Ben no…"

Shaking his head Ben pleaded with her to leave.

"Go! I can look after myself. I need to help dad. Go! Get the police," he screamed.

Turning the key into the ignition her car roared into life. Foot down on the accelerator she took off from the gutter. Her heart pounding. Her palms sweaty. Glancing in her rear vision mirror she could no longer see Ben.

Why the hell hadn't she listened to her little voice? Why had she ignored her gut instincts? A persistent niggle had screamed out alerting her to the fact something was not right. Poor Ben, he must have been frantic for his father. Poor Anthony, oh my god Anthony could be dead. She prayed for their safety. Her hands tightened around the steering wheel. She was determined to get help. Determined to save them both.

Images of her earlier visit flashed through her mind. Ben stood at the front door. The door had only been ajar. He said Anthony hadn't wanted to see her. He said Anthony was upset. She should have realised something was wrong. Anthony had cried within her arms before. He was not the type of guy who was embarrassed to show his emotions. Maybe the madman stood on the other side of the door threatening his silence. Had she missed a secret signal from Ben? Confused by the events Rebecca became angry with herself. She cared for them both. She had promised Claire she would look after them. And now they were in extreme danger. She had ignored her gut instinct. She had had a bloody nap.

Overwhelmed by panic tears welled in her eyes. Her vision blurred. A stream of tears cascaded down her cheeks. She began to feel sick. A rotten taste entered her mouth. Her body trembled. If something happened it would be her fault. She had failed to keep her promised to Claire. Blame would be on her head. How would she ever be able to forgive herself?

Rebecca rocketed through the intersection. She ignored the give way sign. She scanned the road ahead. She checked her mirrors. She wasn't familiar with the backstreets. She had never been to the police station. She knew where it was. But she was uncertain of her current surrounds. Was she heading the right way? Should she turn? *I need to head to the right more,* she thought. She glanced at the fuel gauge. The needle was on empty. The warning light was on. *Damn!* Blood drained from her face. There was no time to stop. She prayed her car would keep going. She turned at the next street she saw. Tyres skidding. The back end of her car fish tailed. Her chest pounded. Her hands battled to maintain control. Foot to the floor. Her speed increased. Parked cars and houses became blurred. Her panicked eyes scanned. Ahead someone was reversing out their driveway. Oblivious to her approaching speed. Her foot hard against the accelerator. *Stop! Get out of my way!* They continued onto the road. She jumped on the brake. Tyres skidding. Horn blaring. Closer and closer. She gripped the steering wheel. She held her breath. She braced for impact. Tyres screeched. Burning rubber. Her car came to a halt. She narrowly avoided a collision with the white sedan.

"Get out of my way!" she screamed. Her hand repeatedly striking the horn. The other car jolted forward. Her path was clear. Her foot returned to the accelerator. She took off. At last she was on Cascade Street. Familiarity. A sharp right into Paddington Street. No obstructions. Deep breaths. Body trembling. Hands gripped the steering wheel. Left into William Street. The road narrowed. William Street was one way. Her speeding continued. 40km speed signs ignored. Foot to the floor. Flying past parked cars on the left. Indistinct pedestrians. Blurred houses and shop fronts. *Damn!* Up ahead there was traffic. A T-intersection. Hand on horn she screamed. "Get out of my way!" Forcing her way onto Oxford Street. She hit a complete stand still. Her panic skyrocketed. Two lanes filled with cars and trucks. Bottleneck traffic.

Shaking her head thoughts of Anthony flashed through her mind. The closeness they had experienced. The warmth of his body. His strong embrace. Wandering hands. Could there be more? Claire had described Anthony as an amazing lover. She had said his love making ability made her toes curl. They were best friends who had shared their most private thoughts.

Rebecca now wanted what Claire had had. She recalled New Years Eve on Sydney Harbour, three years ago. The encounter Anthony and she had shared. It was an awkward moment below the decks. Bodies bumped together. Hands clumsily placed. Eyes locked. Lips met. Hands wandered. Hearts fluttered. Euphoria and satisfaction struggled against guilt and conscience. It was a moment that could destroy. Claire meant so much to them both. Knowledge of a passionate exchange could devastate. Claire had not witnessed. Nor would she ever know. Both agreed it was a line crossed that would never be crossed again. A passionate exchange, kept secret. Tears streamed down her face. Rebecca wanted more. A sense of urgency exploded from within. She had to get help. Her car edged forward. Tail gating the car in front. She checked her mirror. She glanced around wildly. There was a break in the right lane. She swerved. She gained speed. Jumping from accelerator to brake. She weaved in and out of traffic. Palms sweaty. Heart racing. Head pounding. Churning knots in her stomach. Thoughts of Anthony's naked body next to hers. She ignored the traffic light turning yellow. Past Paddington Public School. Congestion cleared. A distant green light. A break in the left lane. She skidded narrowly avoiding a cyclist. Sweaty palms gripped the steering wheel. Determination. She swerved again this time into the bus lane. Undercutting cars. She tore up Oxford Street. Jetting past shops. There was no slowing down. A sharp left into Jersey Street. The blue and white checkered sign ahead. Police. Bountiful happiness and relief.

Yanking down on the steering wheel her car clipped a police car parked out front. But there was no time to think about that. Her tyres screeched. Foot hard on the brake. She came to a sudden halt under the blue and white checkered sign. She didn't care that the tail of her car protruded into the lane of traffic. Ignoring the blaring car horns she flung open her door and ran as fast as she could towards the main entrance.

CHAPTER THIRTY EIGHT

Strolling across the lawn Ben felt nothing other than complete and utter cockiness. Unbeknown to him this conceited self assurance could be wiped right out from under him. The voices, that had badgered his mind could soon be knocked silent. Approaching the gate he turned looking over his shoulder to make sure no one was watching. The coast was clear. His plan was coming together. This was his house. This was his castle. *What happens in the family stays in the family*, he thought. He stepped through the gate.

Whack!

Anthony thrust the shovel into the side of Ben's head. Ben hit the ground like a sack of potatoes. The gate slammed behind his crumpled body. Impact had removed his smirk and ignited his fiery rage. Stunned he glared upwards, as pain exploded deep within his skull. It had been an unexpected attack. A frantic confusion crossed his face. His frenzied eyes darted. Blood seeped down the side of his pounding head. Leaping to his feet he staggered then charged. Hurtling towards Anthony his shoulders collided into Anthony's ribs. Releasing a loud heaving noise Anthony hit the dirt with Ben on top. He weighed far more than Anthony had remembered. Thrashing around Anthony roared with pain. Dirt filled his mouth. Grit covered his teeth. He was sure more ribs were broken. The image of Claire flashed through his mind. He didn't want to die.

"Get off me!" he screamed, "get off me!" Reefing his hands upwards he tried to push Ben away.

Exchanging blows their battle for survival had

just begun. Both were intent on destroying the other. Punching and kicking. Swinging arms and legs. Savagely pulling at each others ears. Thumbs poked andstabbed in eye sockets. Fingers ripped at mouths. Nails scratched and clawed faces. Like two wild creatures their contest was fierce.

Launching his fist into Ben's side Anthony was able to free himself. Ben flung over to his back screaming in pain. But the struggle was far from over. Scurrying on hands and knees Anthony dashed towards the gate. Freedom was in his reach. He needed to get away. He was desperate to escape. He couldn't handle the thought of violence. He didn't want to hurt his son. He loved Ben even after all the madness.

Powerful hands grabbed his right ankle. Tugging and pulling. Panic stricken he glanced over his shoulder. A bloodied Ben frantically attempted to drag him back.

Crack!

The sound of Ben's teeth smashing together made Anthony sick. His foot had made contact with his son's face. Ben's nose shattered. He screamed in pain. Blood spattered to the ground. He toppled backwards. He hit the side of the house and collapsed to the ground. Blinded by sweat, puffing and panting. His eyes crazed, burned with rage. It was a fight in which there would be only one winner.

Anthony grabbed the back of the gate and pulled himself to his feet using one arm, struggling in pain. His pain was intense. His other hand clenched his chest. He was sure bones were broken. The metallic taste of blood filled his mouth. Both were exhausted. Faces and bodies, bruised, battered and bloodied, clothes ripped and covered in dirt.

Looking towards the house his son appeared defeated. Ben looked up. His eyes changed to sad and sorrowful. Limping towards him, Anthony extended his hand. His son needed help. A father could not abandon his child. Their eyes locked. Ben moved his right hand down next to his thigh while extending his left hand. Anthony gave a half smile. Hope. Ben's extended hand represented hope. Ben's eyes beamed as he returned a grin. Leaning forward Anthony groaned as a stabbing pain invaded his chest.

"Are you okay dad?"

Hobbling closer Anthony nodded. A noise out the front caught his attention. He turned removing his eyes from his son. Standing there for a moment he realised it was the postman zooming past on his motor scooter. He knew help would soon arrive.

Turning back he wanted to reassure his son all would be fine.

CHAPTER THIRTY NINE

Rebecca burst through the front door of the police station. Heart racing. Head pounding. Tears streaming down her face. Her legs felt like jelly. Her chest felt as though it would explode. Her eyes were wide and darting. Would her legs hold out? Would she make it in time? Would they believe her claims?

Senior Constable Murphy stood leaning against the front counter. It was the beginning of his shift. His meticulously neat appearance and unblemished uniform with its faultless creases exemplified the pride he took in his career. He was proud police officer who had served the force for nearly thirteen years. Well respected for his professionalism, dedication and passion for truth and justice. In his years of employment he had developed a strong belief that police worked in partnership with the communities they served. Maintaining law and order, preventing crime, protecting all persons and property was paramount in a civilised society. The world was a changing place, offences against the law, violence, extremists, terrorists, radicalisation and drugs impacted on the lives of so many innocent people. During his time as an officer, Senior Constable Murphy had seen countless nut jobs. He had heard many crazy claims. He had been subject to receiving various hoax calls used to attract the attention of the police. Some people were simply crazy. Some thought it funny to waste police resources, while others made bogus claims as a ploy to draw police away from an area where they were about to commit a crime. This time was different. With one look at Rebecca he instantly knew this stumbling woman was in trouble. Something was grave. A ghostly panicked female waving her hands around and stumbling towards the counter was not a daily occurrence. This woman needed his urgent attention.

Rebecca's chest was heaving. Her mind racing. She was on the verge of hysteria. Convinced she would be too late. Frantic she tripped over a step that was not there. Staring forward her eyes met with Senior Constable Murphy. Her arms waved. Her hands grabbed forward into thin air as she tried to save herself from falling flat on her face. Her efforts to no avail. Her body hit the floor with a thud. Impact knocked the wind out from her chest as she released a painful cry. Clawing at the floor she continued on her knees until finally she made it back to her feet and dashed limpingly towards the counter.

"Help, I need help!" she screamed hysterically.

Lunging towards the counter her body shook uncontrollably.

"Help, I need help!" her bellowing echoed around the room.She had his complete attention.

"How can I help you?" he replied in a calm voice.

"He's going to kill him, he's going to kill them…you need to save them."

"Please Miss, please you must calm down, what's your name."

"Rebecca, Rebecca Baxter, but my name is irrelevant they need you…they need you now."

Hearing the commotion two more officers entered from the back office. It was obvious the woman standing before them was extremely panicked but until they ascertained all the information they would be unable to assist. They needed to get her into an interview room, gather all information and determine any required action.

Time appeared to pass with infinite slowness. Rebecca's head throbbed. Her knees ached. Her knowledge was limited. The threat to lives of those she loved was very real. Extreme. Immediately she was ushered into an interview room to the left of the front counter. Shaking uncontrollably she viewed the actions of the police a waste of time. Why didn't they just send a police car? Why were they wasting crucial time?

"Where are you taking me?" she stammered.

"You need to get there," she pleaded.

"He is going to kill him…he is going to kill them." She burst into tears. Petrified any delay could meanthe difference between life and death. She battled with their pleas to calm down and follow them to the room.

"Please Rebecca…you must calm down."

Turning his head towards the other officer Senior Constable Murphy indicated they should get some squad cars ready and requested a cup of water. Closing the door behind them he insisted Rebecca take a seat. Throwing herself into the chair her fingers fanned out on the desk. Her palms sweaty, faced down. Nails scratching. Tears streamed down her face as she answered all the questions.

Reaching across the desk Senior Constable Murphy rested his hand upon Rebecca's.

"Now we are going to help you Rebecca, but you need to take a deep breath and calm down," he said in a reassuring manner while nodding his head.

"Okay." Rebecca returned a nod.

"I need to ask you some questions, we will help."

"Okay."

Sitting upright she struggled to inhale. Shaking and

blubbering. Fidgeting she couldn't keep still. Her hands ran back and forth through her hair. Her legs jiggled. Her knees bounced up and down. Tears continued to stream down her face. She was distraught.

"We need to know all the who, what, when, where, why and how's…Who are you talking about? Where are they? How do you know?"

"My neighbour Anthony and his son Ben… I went to their house…" she blurted, spit flying from her mouth.

"Where do they live? What's their address?"

"No, no…not their address, they just inherited a house. They're there."

Providing the officer with all the information she knew Rebecca began to feel help would soon arrive.

Senior Constable Murphy called for assistance and requested a female officer come into the room. Constable Carrie Burns entered carrying a box of tissues and sat opposite her superior and to the right ofRebecca. Handing her some tissues she sat quietly watching as the interview proceeded.

"Do you know if anyone is injured?"

"No, Ben told me his father was being bashed, that they were going to kill him."

"Who is they?"

"I don't know, I don't know… please you need to help them," she cried.

"We are going to help them, just a few more questions… do you know if there are any firearms or weapons at the scene?"

"No, I don't know, I don't know anything, he said to get help."

"Why didn't you phone? Why didn't he phone?"

"I left my mobile at home… he didn't have one, I

didn't want to waste time… I just drove here as quickly as I could, oh shit maybe I should have just phoned. I could have gone to someone's house. It will be my fault if they die." Rebecca began to howl. Why hadn't she just gone to a house and phoned for help?

"It's okay, you did the right thing. You are doing great… Now was he injured? Was Ben injured? Is there any history of family domestic violence? Do you know if drugs or alcohol are involved?"

"No, you don't understand, it's not Ben or Anthony. They are at their house, someone else is there trying to kill them. You are wasting time. You need to help them. Stop wasting time," she screeched.

Typing the details into the computer Senior Constable Murphy remained calm and assured Rebecca they were not wasting time. Their action taken was based on an assessment of the incident. All information provided assisted in the safety of all concerned. Safety was paramount.

"You don't understand they just lost Claire… she was my friend… Anthony's wife… Ben's mother, they can't lose each other."

And with those few words the situation became personal. Senior Constable Murphy had lost his best mate just over a year ago. His mate was 44, married, and had a teenaged son. He had promised he would look after his family. Senior Constable Murphy was a man of his word. Putting himself in her position he clarified everything they were doing. It was imperative Rebecca knew what they were doing and why. Reiterating that the primary responsibility in responding to such reports was to put safety first which included the safety of police and all persons present at the scene, he continued to speak in a reassuring manner. At last the questions were over. Advising Rebecca he would attend the scene, Senior Constable Murphy instructed Constable Burns to remain where she was and to ensure Rebecca was taken care of.

A priority two call was broadcast. Police needed to respond, there was an imminent threat to life. Senior Constable Murphy would lead the charge teamed up with Probationary Constable Walden. Their car would enter the street from the northern end. A second car, also despatched from the station contained Constable Smith and Probationary Constable Bunting. They would enter the street from the southern end. A request for further back up was communicated.

Glancing out the door Rebecca saw the officers run through the foyer.

Screeching tyres and blaring sirens signalled help would soon arrive.Rebecca collapsed forward. Exhausted. Arms folded. Head buried within her arms. She broke down. Her hair a mess; as if she had just climbed out of bed. Uncontrollable sobbing echoed around the room. Her body trembled. She was aghast. Terrified. How could this be happening?

Constable Burns placed her reassuring hand around Rebecca's shoulders.

"Its going to be fine…they will be okay."

Rebecca nodded. Her head remained buried within her arms. Suddenly she sat bolt upright.

"I need to get there."

"You need to stay here, where you are safe."

"I need to be there."

"You are safe here."

" I don't care about me. I know I am safe. I need to be there for them. You can't make me stay."

" No… no I can't."

"Then I am going…I am going there and you can't stop me."

Jumping up she pushed her chair back. It flipped over banging against the floor. Blood rushed to her head then drained just as quick. The room began to spin. Her head pounded. Her face went white. Tiny stars flashed within her eyes. A wave of nausea overwhelmed her. Her legs lost strength. The room spun. Rebecca collapsed.

"I need help in here!" screamed Constable Burns.

Dropping to her knees she knelt at Rebecca's side. Tapping her cheek she urged her to wake up.

"Rebecca…come on Rebecca, wake up…come on."

Rebecca grabbed her chest.

"No!" she screamed. Clenching her eyes tight. She shook her head.

"No, no, no!" she howled. Her eyes sprung open.

"It's okay, it's going to be okay, you are safe."

The hands of reassurance resting against her shoulder offered no relief. Sitting up Rebecca continued to shake her head.

"It's not going to be okay. Something bad is happening. I can feel it. I know. Something bad is happening."

Tears streamed down her face. Her body shook. The female officer with the help of another assisted her to the chair. Rebecca collapsed head forward onto the table. Her face buried within her folded arms.

"Stop, make him stop. He is going to kill him. I know he is going to kill him."

Her muffled words and sobbing echoed around the room.

Would they make it there in time? Would they

save Anthony and Ben?Or would her falling asleep and ignoring her little voice cost them their lives?

CHAPTER FORTY

Snapping forward Ben's evil eyes glared. The demons had returned. The voices screamed *kill him!* He slung a handful of dirt at Anthony's eyes. Anthony howled. It felt like one million needles. Blinding, cutting, excruciating. Screaming in agony Anthony thought he was going to die. How many times did a person think they would die before they actually would?

Ben charged. Shovel in hand. Blurred and muddy vision alone could not hinder Anthony's reaction. The image of Claire flashed through his mind. He didn't want to die. It was her love and strength that had carried him through tough times before. He could not let this strength die now. Anthony leapedfor protection. He grabbed the sword. Ben tripped and stumbled. With the heavy shovel he overcompensated his balance. Anthony thrust the sword forward. The metal blade sliced into Ben's chest and out his back like a hot poker through a block of butter. A heaving noise echoed upwards. Ben dropped to one knee, attempted to stand and dropped again. Coughing and spluttering, blood seeped from the side of his mouth. On his knees he appeared in a painful prayer. His wounds zapped all his strength. Unable to maintain balance on his knees his body crumpled. His buttocks precariously balanced on his heels. Blood flowed from his chest. Gurgling. He struggled to breathe. Terror entered his eyes. He was barking up blood. Trying to speak. His lips quivered. Reaching out towards his father his eyes begged for forgiveness. His hands trembled with fear. A lone tear escaped the corner of his eye. Anthony stood frozen. Fear prevented him from reaching out. Ben's body convulsed. He collapsed forward. The chattering noises in his head fell silent. Ben was dead.

It was a fight in which there would be only one winner. But really could surviving be referred to as winning. Anthony was alive however, the whole ordeal had been brutal and his saga was far from over. Johnnie lay unconscious. He was oblivious to the bedlam. Watching his son suffer as life drained from him had brought back all of the horrible visions he held within of Claire and her dying moments. Had Claire suffered a similar pain?

Exhausted, Anthony staggered backwards hitting the gate hard. His face and body battered and bloody. It was all too much to handle. He collapsed to the ground. On his hands and knees he was crying out.

"I'm sorry, I'm sorry."

But it was too late for sorry. Desperation and self preservation had forced him to act. This was now paired with denial and heartache. Everything was so messed up, inside out and upside down all at the same time. A lump the size of a rubik's cube instantly appeared in his throat. A pain a millions times more excruciating than the most severe case of indigestion he had ever experienced. Like a solid square of timber lodged in his throat. Its sharp corners gouging into his oesophagus. The flat porous sides absorbing all saliva, making it near impossible to swallow. An ache radiated to his jaw. Pain shot into his forehead. Branching out, all consuming it quickly spread across his chest. Reefing at his shirt he could see no forcible restriction only blood, sweat and dirt. Swallowing hard or coughing would not extinguish his torment. He needed to act. To think fast. He was gutted. Shattered. Devastated.

He went nuts. Staggering to his feet he began kicking his son, "Why? Why? Why?" he screamed.

Tears streamed down his face. The burning sensation in his side was excruciating. Blood seeped from his wounds. Yet this searing pain would not stop his unrelenting kicking. Unleashed from within were all of his frustration and aggression, all the hatred and the despair he had endured. His son had been evil. His son had been his enemy. Surely his actions were justified. It was the only way he could be stopped. But even with all his madness his son had made some extremely valid points. Surely there was no use in telling all. Some secrets should remain just that, a secret.

He needed to act. It was vital he cleaned up the mess. A father's job was to protect his family. The bible said, the father should not suffer for the iniquity of the son. Dragging Ben's body to the hole it was time to put an end to the madness. One last boot to the torso sent his lifeless body down into the hole and onto the dismembered remains of Mr. Benson. Anthony knew he had to protect the family name. *What happens in the family, stays in the family!* he thought as he turned his attention towards Johnnie.

Time was of the essence.

CHAPTER FORTY ONE

The realisation he had come within a whisker of death had Anthony fuming. Plunged into a vacuum of nothingness he peered down upon Johnnie. He looked dead. *Surely, he can't be dead.* The thought of him being bereft of life terrified Anthony. If his assumption was correct who the hell could be blamed? The dead could not be punished for their wrongdoings. This man needed to be held accountable for the pain he had caused. This was the man responsible for his agony and suffering. A monstrous, giant ape-like Neanderthal. He needed to pay for the misery he had caused. Vicious feelings and the desire for revenge pounced into his mind. Anthony stared towards him. Still, he wasn't moving. Was he dead? Surely he couldn't be. Edging closer he became concerned. Johnnie's face was frozen with a neutral expression. His bushy eyebrows framed his larger than life eye sockets. Eyebrows that resembled static steel wool. All was still. The only noise that of Anthony trying to regain his breath.

His world had been torn apart the moment Johnnie appeared. He needed Johnnie to be alive. Dead people could not be punished.

Glancing around the yard and then back to under the house there was no way of hiding the daylight recognition of his actions and the current situation. The seriousness of his predicament. Taunting confusion attached and strangled all sense of reason. Everything had gone to shit from the moment he stepped foot into the house.

However there was no time to lament over what was or what could have been. Time was of the essence. He needed to take control. This menacing individual needed to be held accountable for his actions. He needed to be alive. It was vital Anthony protect his family. If Johnnie was in fact dead the plan Anthony played out in his mind would be ruined.

What happens in the family stays in the family. He thought.

Edging closer his face came within centimetres of Johnnie's. Relief soon followed. He could feel the breeze of his warm breath. He could smell the caustic odour of bacteria build up being released between his slack jawed mouth. A faint wheezing noise escaped his lips. From behind his closed eyes an ever soslight twitching was visible.

Kneeling down next to him Anthony urged him to wake. Clutching his shoulders he gave him a gentle shake. The clock was ticking. He feared Rebecca would soon return with the police. He needed to act quickly. He shook him a little harder. No response. Overcome by panic he grabbed his shoulders firmly between his hands andshook Johnnie violently. Johnnie moaned. Anthony sighed with relief.

"Wake up Johnnie…wake up."

Johnnie opened his puzzled eyes and looked towards him.

Anthony sighed again and smiled. He was alive. All he had to do now would be to convince him to go along with his story. It was imperative Johnnie believed his words and followed his direction.

"Johnnie…the evil warriors attacked! They took control of your body and made you kill Lord Benami! They knocked you to the ground!"

Johnnie's pained eyes became wide and full of concern. Anthony continued.

"They tried to kill me too…you must help me or we will fail!"

Johnnie sprung upright holding the right side of his face. He grimaced in pain. Blood covered his palm as it trickled from his wound. Squinting he wiped his hand across the corner of his eye. The sight of blood on his hand signified the seriousness of the situation.

"What can I do my King?" he questioned in his familiar monotone voice.

"I have been injured. My energies are depleted. I have been contaminated by the blood of evil. You must get me inside. An attack is imminent! The dragon warriors will soon be upon us!"

Johnnie jumped to his feet. Wrapped his oversized hands around Anthony. Anthony squealed in agony. It was crucial Johnnie get him inside without being seen. He threw his arm around Johnnie's shoulder and with Johnnie's hand firmly around his waist pressure was taken from his throbbing ankles.

"Hold on, I will protect you my King."

Anthony nodded and released a painful moan. Glancing over his shoulder he looked under the house. His son was gone. He burst into tears. He couldn't believe what had transpired. How was it things could get so far out of hand? His body began to shake. Shock took hold. His pain increasing with every heaving breath. Disbelief. Looking towards Johnnie his anger began to build. He clenched his teeth. He closed his eyes. Looking at him made him feel sick. It should have been Johnnie who was dead. Fisting his hands the only thoughts that raced within his mind were that of revenge.

I am going to make you pay, he thought.

Panicked by the prospect of an impending attack from evil warriors Johnnie scanned the sky. Supporting Anthony's weight they edged closer to the front gate. They paused. They peered out. The street was quiet. Anthony nodded. It was now or never. They had to get inside. Johnnie tightened his grip. His breath became rapid. Huffing and puffing. He began to count down. "Three, two, one"… they were off. Launching into long strides Johnnie dragged Anthony along as if he were a rag doll. His manoeuvres resembling the kind you would use in a battlefield. His staring eyes, highlighted his conviction. It was imperative they make it inside without being seen. Leaping up the stairs he released a grunting determination. Bursting into the house he swivelled around and slammed the front door. They had made it. Both heaved a long sigh of relief.

Dropping Anthony onto the lounge Johnnie dashed towards the front window. He tugged at the curtains. He scanned the street. Stillness. Dust filled the air. Tiny powder particles floated about in search of a new resting place. The taste of dirt and mould filled their mouths. All was quiet. Johnnie released a roaring sneeze. Anthony jumped. He grit his teeth through the pain. His body ached beyond explanation. Staring at Johnnie he was seething. Anger and hatred filled his heart as he renewed his vow to make him pay. He worried and wondered about all the 'what if' scenarios. All he wanted was for it to be over. Johnnie had to be punished. If he had the strength he would kill him with his bare hands. But that would get him nowhere. He had to stay cool. Releasing a loud groan Anthony tried to straighten himself up. He needed to focus. The clock is ticking. The pain emanating from his wounds was nowhere near as terrifying as grappling with the consequences should the police arrive before his plan was put into motion.

Overwhelmed by fear Johnnie began to tremble. Tears welled in his eyes. He could see no evil warriors. It was up to Anthony to keep him calm. To reassure him all would be fine. Sacrifices were essential.

Anthony smiled and signalled for Johnnie to come closer. Johnnie nodded.

"You did great and you will be rewarded," he said as his raised his eyebrows, nodding his head.

Johnnie's face lit up, he loved rewards. He stepped towards the lounge releasing a loud sigh.

Anthony's plan was working. His enemy was now his ally. Soon he would be his sacrifice. Like a lamb to the slaughter.

The image of Ben's lifeless body slumped across Mr. Benson's remains flashed through his mind. Blood... there was so much blood. It announced itself in crimson red fury. Spurting, cascading, oozing and seeping from within. Death was in the air. Looking upwards all Anthony could see was hair. It was as wild as the jungle. An untameable mass of knots and tangle. Johnnie's hair conveyed the confusion he displayed. This half wit had committed the most heinous of crimes yet he lacked the ability to maintain the most basic of hygiene elements.

"Sit with me," Anthony pointed towards the table that ran in front of the lounge, "sit there my loyal friend we must work out a plan."

Johnnie's smile lit up his face. His King referred to him as his friend. He lowered himself onto the coffee table. Sitting still he stared towards Anthony and waited for instruction.

Closing his eyes Anthony was instantly reminded of blood. Luminous clouds of crimson red seeped into the stillness. It was an inescapable haunting vision. Seeping. Oozing. Spilling from Ben's chest. *Oh my fucking god.* He had killed his son. The young man he was supposed to protect. How could this be? A father's duty was to protect, not kill. Overcome by grief he began to sob. Johnnie sat silent. Confused by his King's outburst. Afraid to speak. Anthony's body shook. He was unable to stop his overwhelming grief. Consumed by guilt he feared living. For living would be a fate worse than death. Had his actions resulted in the death of those he loved? Had his words driven Claire to her demise? It was by his own hand that his son had drawn his last breath. Howling echoed around the still room. Internal yearning twisted from within. Anthony silently begged for his nightmare to end. He prayed he would open his eyes to a time when there was happiness. He longed to be reunited within his loving family. If he wished hard enough would he too draw his last breath. Surely death would be far better than the hell he found himself in. He remembered the dirt and grit that filled his mouth. His arm outstretched holding the sword. His son's painful look. Those final gasps. The lifeless staring eyes. The frozen expression of horror as it transitioned to one of peace. He would never forget the knock on his front door. The officer telling him his wife, his loving Claire was no longer alive. How could he continue on with a life void of those he loved? A barren life was no life at all. Questioning his own existence Anthony believed it was he who was the monster. Maybe he was the gatekeeper for he had opened up the can of worms. It was he who wanted to know all. He believed it necessary to reveal the truth, to expose the secrets. He had driven Claire away and Ben to the house. If only he had been able to draw a line in the sand and leave the past in the past. For he had committed the worse sin of all; murder. Opening his eyes he stared into nothingness. He began to whisper. Johnnie watched on afraid as to what would happen next. Unable to decipher Anthony's words.

Anticipating the arrival of the police Anthony toiled with the idea of handing himself in. His mind a mass of confusion, going through a million thoughts and emotions all at once. If you live by the sword then surely you should die by the sword. For fuck sake he had killed with a sword. Would spending the rest of his life in goal be a suitable punishment? Maybe he deserved to die. His whispering continued. And at that moment every bit of pain, guilt and shame clashed. Endless tears steamed down his face. His chanting, repetitive. Johnnie's head tilted to the side. His forehead crinkled. His eyebrows knitted close together as he tried to unravel the words. Anthony's voice became louder. Stronger. Clearer. Johnnie frowned and shook his head in disagreement. Peering beyond Johnnie's protesting motions Anthony's words defied all logic. His repetitious mumble consistent in pitch. Sitting up on the lounge he began to rock back and forth.

"I am the gatekeeper, I am the gatekeeper, I am the gatekeeper… it's my fault, it's all my fault, I am the gatekeeper."

With the sword clenched closely to his chest his face remained expressionless. His eyes stared. Johnnie glared. His jaw tensed, his head continued to shake.

Why was Anthony calling himself the gatekeeper?

CHAPTER FORTY TWO

Police cars sped through the narrow streets of Paddington. Lights flashing. Sirens blaring. Based on third party information a threat to lives was imminent. It was their responsibility to respond. Assistance was required. A call over the radio requested urgent back up. Detective Superintendent Beau Bailey was in nearby Rushcutters Bay and responded to the appeal. Four police cars were now en route.

Officers Murphy, Walden and Fergus would enter from the north. Officers Smith, Bunting and Bailey would approach from the south. The first priority would be in restricting access to the street. Reducing the threat was crucial. Details provided were limited. However a domestic violence situation could quickly turn into a hostage situation. Both circumstances had the potential to be highly volatile. Offenders were unpredictable. The involvement of drugs and weapons had not been suggested but could not be ruled out. Constant updates were broadcast. Probationary Constable Walden clung to his seat. His body propelled into the door of the squad car as they sped around the corners. His heart racing. His adrenaline pumping. He had never attended a domestic violence situation. Trying to contain his nerves he swallowed hard. A nervous lump met his dry gulp. He had left his water bottle at the station.

He thought of his family. They were proud he had chosen to follow in his father's footsteps. He wondered what they would think if they saw him now. Would they notice the fear he felt or would they see a hero in the making? His dad had retired with the rank of Senior Sergeant. He had received countless awards and certificates of recognition of his exemplary service and acts of bravery. Gripping his seat Walden prayed he would simply make it through the day. *Oh my god*, he thought, *what have I gotten myself into*. Surely there were other ways in which he could make his family proud. Safer ways. Strangling his seat belt he hung on for dear life. Beads of sweat decorated his forehead. He glanced towards the driver's seat looking at his superior. He was seemingly unaffected by nerves. His hands clasped the steering wheel like there was no tomorrow. Nothing was going to get in his way. There was no time for second guessing. Senior Constable Murphy was like a machine. Focused. Every ounce of his energy and knowledge committed.

A call came over the radio, Walden fumbled with the hand piece trying to provide an update on their location. All units were getting closer.

Glancing towards his young partner, Senior Constable Murphy could sense his concern. Apprehension was written all over his ghostly face. His teeth clenched, eyes wide and staring. He needed to reassure him all would be fine. Officers had to act with a clear and focused mind. There was no time for second-guessing. A pep talk was required. Reassurance was necessary. Officers relied on the backup from each other. It took only one failing officer for an operation to go to shit. He knew. He had seen it before.

"You'll be fine. You're a great officer. You have a proven record of success. Today is just another day. Listen and follow orders. You'll get through this. We will all get through this. We will all be fine."

Walden gave a half smile and nodded. Nothing could hide the fact he was scared witless. Murphy continued in a calm but somewhat authoritarian tone. He believed providing a brief summary of what could be expected would do no harm but help prepare his partner.

"Now remember all lights and sirens will be turned off when we are two streets away. Police cars will be parked two houses from the location and we will approach on foot with firearms and tasers drawn. Detective Superintendent Bailey is now in charge of the operation. Try to think of it like just another training exercise. I know you blitzed your training. I know you know your procedures. Tell me, what is the role of the officers first responding to the scene?" he asked.

"They must quickly assess the totality of the situation, secure the area, gauge the threat to victims and or to hostages or bystanders, and request additional units as appropriate," Walden snapped his reply.

"Correct, you certainly know your procedures," Murphy nodded and chuckled; he was confident his young partner understood procedures but all the practice in the world would never completely prepared anyone for the real thing.

"For situations like this I always keep three things in mind. Firstly, a successful outcome requires a good foundation. We have that. Secondly, basic police procedure dictates any crisis incident be contained using both inner and outer perimeters established and maintained by the police. We will do that. And finally, following orders will increase chances of rescuing victims, capturing assailants and will ensure everyone returns home safely to their loved ones. We will achieve this."

Walden sat nodding, his eyes flashed back and forth between his wise superior and their racing path. While nothing would completely prepare him for what was about to happen their brief exchange had quelled the intensity of his apprehension.

Murphy offered a reassuring smile. It had been a long time since he had experienced such fear, yet he could remember it as if it were yesterday. This would be the story Walden would talk about with his mates and family. This would be the operation he would remember for a lifetime. Officers always remembered their first major incidents.

CHAPTER FORTY THREE

Anthony's thoughts returned to the here and now. His life was in tatters but was it worth giving up?Looking around the room he cast his eyes towards the faded remains of paper chains hanging around the ceiling. He knew why they were there. But to understand where he was, he would have to go back long before he was even born. This ghostly house existed because of one evil person – Shirley Rumming. It was his mother-in-law Shirley Rumming and her secrets and lies, that had led him through the front door. She was a killer. She was a liar. She manipulated innocence and destroyed happiness. Her evilness extended beyond the grave. Her secrets had created friction in his relationships. His wife had died searching for the truth behind her mother's words. His family cursed from the moment they laid their hands on the book she had left; Pages Of Your Life – The Secret Life Of Shirley Rumming. The title sounded intriguing. Her words sucked you into a world of innocence. But the content revealed sinister actions. A life built of secrets, lies and deception. Shirley Rumming had poisoned the mind of her grandson, Ben. Her elaborate fantasies were woven into the minds of her unsuspecting victims. Little by little, like a spider in a web she sucked them into an inescapable turmoil. The secrets and lies from decades past seeped into the current day like a deadly virus. But the past had been and gone. Resurrecting it would not change his current situation. Dwelling over things was useless. He could not change the past, no-one could. The only thing he could control was the current moment. Current actions were what influenced the future. It was up to Anthony to draw a line in the sand and move forward. We all had demons, Anthony would not let Shirley Rumming be his.*Adapt to survive*. He thought, it was all about adapting to survive.

Johnnie's eyes were wide. His breathing heavy and ragged. His fidgeting constant. It was clear he was panicked. Staring he waited for instruction. Anthony looked towards the ceiling. He inhaled the musty air. Being inside the house was suffocating. He could not bear to look at the galoot. Johnnie was also responsible. Had he not interrupted their visit his son would still be alive. He was to blame. It was Johnnie who had stormed in. Johnnie had killed Mr. Benson. Johnnie had hacked up his body. Johnnie reinforced his son's delusions. He was to blame for it all. He had to pay. He couldn't get away with it. There was no way he would allow him get away with it. Glaring towards him Anthony's rage intensified. He wanted to know who the hell Johnnie was and how he had become so involved. But there was no time.

"Sit still and shut the fuck up, I need to think," he demanded.

Johnnie frowned, covered his ears and looked to the floor. His actions resembled those of a defeated oversized child. Hitting his hands against his thighs, anguish was written all over his face.

"Lord Benami is dead...I have failed...Lord Benami is dead, I have failed."

Sobbing, he began to beg Anthony for direction.

Anthony feared if he didn't act he would lose control. Jonathon Fox and Shirley Rumming would not destroy his future. Claire may have been Shirley's daughter but more than that, she had been his loving wife. Ben had been his lovable son. He had to protect his family. He didn't want anyone to find out about his son's involvement in the gruesome events. A child deserved his fathers protection. There was no denying Johnnie was one very disturbed individual. A madman. And now he would be his pawn of protection. Sitting up on the lounge Anthony clenched the side of his torso. The blood had stopped seeping. It was time to set his plan into motion. Leaning forward he calmly offered Johnnie the instruction he so desperately wanted to hear.

"Listen to me!"

Johnnie's head snapped up. His sobbing ceased and his eyes stared. He waited for his directive. Wiping the snot trail from beneath his nose with the back of his hand he sniffed and finally responded.

"Yes, my King!"

"I am proud of you…Queenie is proud of you…Lord Benami is proud of you…the gods are proud of you."

Johnnie smiled.

"I know you stabbed Lord Benami. You were compelled to kill him. He was infected by evil. The devil warriors had taken control of his body. If it wasn't for you killing him, we would all be dead."

Johnnie returned a puzzling smile, his head tilted to the side, "I killed Lord Benami?" he questioned.

"Yes! But I forgive you…it was the evil warriors, they made you do it."

Johnnie lowered his head and began to sob, "I am sorry, my King."

"Shhh! It's okay. I forgive you, in the name of the almighty Queen and with the power of the Gods I forgive you…but…you must swear your allegiance. You must swear your secrecy. If you break your vow of silence and your allegiance to Queenie the dragons warriors will attack."

Johnnie burst into tears, his body trembled and his head shook.

"No, no…not the dragons…please not the dragons!"

Anthony smiled, his response was pleasing. Leaning forward he urged Johnnie to come closer.

"Shh! Then listen to me and listen good, come closer…we don't have long…the dragon warriors are coming!"

The tables had turned. Johnnie no longer felt an outcast. Antony, King of the tracerteps appeared as his friend. It was crucial to please his new friend. King Antony's wish was his command.

Anthony knew his communication had to be positive, clear and extremely specific.

"I have been infected. The evil is contaminating. I can feel the evil from within. You must release it before it is too late."

"How?" Johnnie questioned, scrunching up his face.

"You must stab me so the evil can escape."

Johnnie's eyes widened.

"I can't stab you. You are King Antony," he whimpered.

"Yes you can!"

"No, no I cant!" he argued.

"Yes! You have to…you must. I order you!"

Johnnie cowered. He placed his hands over his ears. Squeezing his eyes closed he shook his head.

"No!" he began to sob.

"Do it! You parasite…do it or I will die and the dragons will drag you to hell!"

Johnnie opened his tear filled eyes. He peered across at Anthony. He could feel the pulse beating in his ears. He hated loud noises. He couldn't handle raised voices. He liked rules. Simple rules.

"What do you want me to do?" he questioned, having forgotten his instruction.

"You need to stab me…I have been infected…you must stab me so the evil can escape. Grab the sword. I will guide the blade. You must push it in. It has to be you, my powerful gatekeeper."

A smile returned to Johnnie's face. He was proud to be the mighty gatekeeper.

Anthony wiped the handle of the sword with the end of his shirt and handed it to Johnnie. Sweat poured down Anthony's brow. He struggled to his feet. He staggered towards the front door. To complete his plan he would need to stand otherwise evidence of the stabbing may be found on the lounge. He needed people to believe he had been attacked while trying to flee from a madman. He braced his body. He smeared blood from his right hand along the wall. It looked as if the smearing was created by someone who was trying to escape. He planted his left hand firmly against the wall. He pointed to the lower right side of his torso. Johnnie nervously watched on. He held the sword within his trembling hands. His shaking made Anthony hesitant. One wrong move and he could die. His life flashed before him. He swallowed hard. He questioned the sanity of his intention. He pointed to the right side of his torso. He instructed Johnnie to rest the tip of the sword next to his finger. Johnnie did as was ordered. Light reflected off the blade. The razor sharp tip pierced his skin. Johnnie stood frozen. Staring. Huffing and puffing. One wrong move and Anthony could be dead. Closing his eyes Anthony tried to recall the location of vital organs. Lungs up near the heart. Liver under the lungs and diaphragm, below the liver were his kidneys, large and small intestines. The stab entry point needed to look authentic while not putting his life in danger.

"Do it!" he screamed, "release the evil!"

Shocked by the force in Anthony's voice Johnnie jumped and pulled his hand back. He dropped the sword to the floor and began to sob. Anthony couldn't believe his eyes. How the hell could this be happening? Johnnie had killed. All he asked was for him to thrust the sword in and then straight back out. He didn't want him to slice and dice. He didn't need to twist and turn the blade. In and out. Thrust in, pull out.

"I am your King I order you to release the evil," Anthony demanded, nodding his head.

Johnnie stood shaking. Staring. Puffing and panting. He bent over and picked up the sword. He edged closer extending his hand. He pointed the tip against Anthony's torso. A small trickle of blood the size of a small teardrop marked the location. Anthony could feel the sharp blade; like dozens of tiny needles being pushed against his skin.

"You have to do it or I will die and you will be dragged into an evil abyss."

Johnnie stared. He began shaking his head. Anthony feared they were running out of time.

"On three…nice and steady, nice and smooth…I will count down from three and you must push the blade in then pull it straight out."

Johnnie nodded. He squeezed his hand firmly around the grip of the sword. Anthony looked. His hand guiding Johnnie's. He began to count down. It was too late to doubt his intention.

"Three, two, one!"

Johnnie thrust forward as hard as he could. The blade drove into Anthony. Johnnie pulled back, extracting the sharpened cold steel. The stabbing took seconds. Initially Anthony could feel no pain. It was more so a tugging feeling. He feared Johnnie had not completed what was so desperately required. Looking down he could see blood. A dull ache entered his side. Blood seeped to his shirt. A widening redness surrounded the slitted pathway to his pain. The gateway of fear unlocked. Throbbing began. Panic set in. Chilling pain invaded. Excruciating pain. His cold pain turned to red. Hot. Burning. Anthony became frantic. He screamed in agony. Johnnie jumped. The pain was intense. Anthony feared he would vomit and pass out. Blood continued to seep. He clutched his hand over his wound. He needed to control the bleeding. Closing his eyes he began to feel light headed. A prickly sensation covered his body. Stars flickered within his closed eyes. Had he made a bad decision? He applied pressure.

Regret.

Why the hell was he acting like a crazy person?

How the hell could he be so stupid? To jeopardise his own life, for what…

CHAPTER FORTY FOUR

Anthony had been sucked into insanity. He knew time was of the essence. Opening his eyes he needed to be sure Johnnie would do as he instructed. Leaning forward sweat dripped from his forehead. He spoke with a trembling voice.

"You have done good. I am proud. But you must guard our secret society. They will pressure you. You must remain loyal or the dragon warriors will attack and drag you into the abyss of hell."

Johnnie stood staring. He was petrified of the dragon warriors.

"I don't want them to take me," he sniffed.

"They won't take you away if you do as I say. You must tell them what you did. You must tell them you killed the evil that was inside Mr. Benson and Ben. You must tell them you stabbed me. It is your only chance. You must prove your allegiance to Queenie. What is your name?"

Johnnie stared at Anthony blankly and did not answer. Anthony was certain Johnnie's non compliance was threatening his very existence. It was vital for Johnnie to follow his instruction.

"I asked you a question. I expect an answer…what is your name?" he snapped.

Johnnie peered towards Anthony with mournful eyes.

"Johnnie."

"No, what's your powerful name?"

"Johnnie Fox… I am Jonathon Fox, son of Felicity Fox… grandson of William Bunbagel."

Anthony shook his head.

"No, no…who are you? What are you?"

Johnnie raised an eyebrow as if searching out his answer.

"Oh, I am the gatekeeper," he squealed.

"Yes, yes…but you are not just any ordinary gatekeeper. Who are you?"

"I am the gatekeeper, the powerful gatekeeper," Johnnie's voice became loud and determined.

"Say it again, mean what you say. Be proud of who you are," Anthony urged.

"I am the gatekeeper, the powerful gatekeeper!" he roared with enthusiasm.

"That's right and you killed Mr. Benson and Ben because they were evil. You stabbed me because of the evil inside of me. You will be a hero. Everyone will hear of you. Your face will be on the front cover of the newspaper. Jonathon Fox; the gatekeeper who killed because of evil."

Johnnie listened intently as he pictured the whole plan unfolding in his mind. He got excited and started fidgeting. He was going to be a hero. He would be a celebrity. Only famous people had their name and picture plastered on the front cover of major Sydney newspapers. Maybe the whole world would learn his name. He raised a double fist to victory.

"That's right now you've got it." Anthony smiled, nodding at his success. His plan was coming together. A few more details and all would be set. "Now, a hero requires announcing. I must announce you to the world."

"Yes, yes…will you tell them who I am? Will you

tell them what I did? I am the gatekeeper. I killed them because they were evil. I stabbed you because you had evil inside. Please… please can you tell them."

Anthony nodded. "I will. I will tell them. I will tell them how you hacked up Mr. Benson. I will tell them I feared an attack. I was locked inside a room. Tortured. I will tell them you slaughtered Ben. They will see my wounds. The world will know who you are and what you have done."

Johnnie sprung into the air cheering.

"Yes, yes, yes… I killed them, I killed them, yahoo I am a hero. I killed the evil."

"Then you must let me go so I can announce your powerful exit."

Johnnie nodded. He could barely contain his excitement.

Anthony stared towards him. Johnnie was definitely mad. He had the propensity to kill. There was no doubting he would kill again if given the opportunity. Johnnie did not understand the act of killing was wrong. All he required was an excuse, a reason.

CHAPTER FORTY FIVE

The four police cars parked strategically, two at each end of the street. Superintendent Beau Bailey spoke with Senior Constable Murphy over the radio while the other officers listened in. As the senior officer it was Bailey who would take charge of the operation. The need for a secure inner perimeter was obvious. However, creating an exclusion zone was the first priority. Limiting potential threat and containing the offender or offenders was vital. A crisis incident such as this required an emphasis on a well-controlled outer perimeter. Officers Fergus and Smith were directed to man these posts. Their role was to prevent a crowd from gathering. Crowds could be extremely dangerous. Made up of bystanders, the press, and possibly family members. It was important offenders were not be given an audience to "play to."

Detective Superintendent Bailey and Senior Constable Murphy drove their cars down the street and stopped two houses up from the reported address. This would assist in an element of surprise. Eyes peeled for any suspicious activity. Tensions high. Alert. All was quiet. They continued to scan for possible suspects. Anything could happen. Danger imminent. The street was locked down. Officers Walden and Bunting moved quickly from door to door advising residents to remain indoors and away from windows. The suspect or suspects were unknown, as was the presence of any drugs or weapons. Investigations had shown no history of domestic disputes at the reported address. But no one could predict the future.

With the door knock complete, police took up perimeter positions around the house. Detective Superintendent Bailey coordinated the positions and paths of all officers to ensure the house was completely encircled. Establishing no escape could be made via the right of the house, focus was placed on the front door and to the left of the property. The highly unstable nature of the incident made it imperative for them to be prepared to take the suspect or suspects into custody at a moment's notice. In fact the surrender phase represented the most critical stage. In some cases surrender could occur very rapidly. They all prayed for an incident free surrender.

Officers readied themselves. The residence was surrounded. There was no way anyone would escape unnoticed. All eyes were on the house. Firearms and tasers drawn. They waited a minute. Listening. Watching. No sign of life. No audible sounds. It was an especially trying and stressful juncture. They waited another minute. Probationary Constable Walden braced himself for the worst. *Maybe it is a hoax*, he thought. He took cover behind a parked car as instructed. He feared an attack was fast approaching. Things were too quiet. There was an eerie stillness. It was possible their presence had been detected. *This could be the calm before the storm*, he thought. He was convinced; he had seen movement in a front window. He cringed at the thought of being hit with flying bullets. Bullets that would tear through his flesh and possibly end his short life. During training he had heard how these situations had the propensity to turn deadly in a heartbeat. Walden felt as though his heart was in his throat. Glancing towards his superior he sought instruction. No training exercise had ever resulted in the extreme intensity. A thumbs up signal along with information further back up was on its way provided him with assurance. There would be safety in numbers. All was quiet. All was still. Besides the police the street was deserted. His nerves increased. They edged closer. Eyes scanning. Hands waved. Fingers pointed. A tactical plan was put into play.

In their new positions behind the cover of cars, near the fence line and in the bushes, they paused. Listening. Watching. No sounds heard. No movement visible. No lingering smells in the air. Time appeared to stand still. Something was about to change.

CHAPTER FORTY SIX

Time was of the essence. Anthony had heard distant sirens. They had appeared closer, louder. Now they were silent. The end was near. For all he knew they could be outside. He needed them to be outside. It was vital for him to flee into the arms of the law. They had to witness his panicked face. They had to see his battered and bloody body. To hear his panicked cries. To watch his stumbling body. They had to feel pity towards this distraught man who had escaped the clutches of a killer. If the street was vacant, his plan could fail.

One loose end remained. It was vital for Johnnie to keep quiet on certain things. Urging him to come closer and listen Anthony's tone became serious. His voice slightly louder than a whisper. His pain neared an unbearable level. He gasped as he spoke. The warmth of blood filled his palm.

"I am proud of you. I trust you. But you must promise never to reveal Lord Benami or the fact I amKing Antony of the Tracerteps." He paused as he studied Johnnie's face, "Queenie is proud, she watches from above as do the gods but we need you to promise. Slaying Mr. Benson and Benami proved your allegiance. But you can never reveal our parallel world. The survival of our existence depends on your ability to keep our secret society hidden. This is your final test. Silence brings rewards. Tell and you will die."

"I promise, I promise… your secrets are safe with me. I am the gatekeeper, the powerful gatekeeper."

Thrusting the sword into the air, Johnnie could hardly control his excitement. Everyone would soon know who he was.

"Tell them, go tell them," he screamed, "I am ready for the world. You have my promise. I will make you proud."

"I will tell them, I promise you… I will. Give me till the count of ten. Let me go first to announce your presence. When I have gone you must count down from ten and then run out for the whole world to see."

Anthony limped towards the front door. Johnnie giggled and bounced around with excitement. He waved the sword in the air. He swung it to his side making swishing noises. Anthony stopped. He looked back. He struggled to come to terms with his actions. It was one of the worst moments of his life. He had been betrayed by his son. He had killed his son. Now he was going to destroy someone who appeared to trust him. But what he could not forget was that this clumsy galoot was a killer. A killer who was largely responsible for his pain. Just because he now appeared to trust him did not excuse his actions. He needed to pay for what had happened. Anthony's actions had only been a reaction to the situation. His hand had been forced. He took a deep breath. *Here we go,* he thought.

He grabbed the door handle. He reefed it towards him. The door flung open. He dashed forward. Stumbling he struggled to pull the door shut behind him. He hurtled towards the stairs. Frantic. A trail of blood followed. He could see no one. But there was no turning back. Johnnie would not understand his return. In life it was never possible to go back.

Staggering down the stairs he clung to his chest.

Excruciating pain shot through his body. His mind a mass of confusion. Where the fuck where they? He advanced forward to the path. Droplets of blood marked his route. The sun shone in his eyes. A thunderous noise entered his ears.

"Stop Police, get on the ground and don't move."

Panic overrode his ability to understand. He kept floundering forward. Terrified. Oblivious of the firearms and tasers pointed in his direction.

"Stop Police, stop or we will shoot." This time he heard the words. Yet fear compelled him to keep moving. They didn't understand. They couldn't shoot him. He was the victim. He needed to get away. Halfway down the front path. His legs felt like jelly. The gate and safety was in his reach. Nothing else mattered. But would he make it?

A sudden jolt knocked him off his feet. Torturous pain shot through his torso. He hit the ground with a thud. Officer Walden was on top of him. Anthony screamed in agony. His hands were reefed behind his back. Cold steel wrapped around his wrists. Face down on the ground. He inhaled the fresh smell of grass. He could feel the dampness of the earth below. He scanned but could not see any movement inside the house. He burst into tears.

Inside Johnnie jumped up and down. Oblivious to the commotion outside. Chanting with excitement, "I am the gatekeeper, I am the gatekeeper." He imagined crowds cheering his name. He began to count down from ten, as instructed.

"10, 9, 8, 7, 6, 5, 4, 3, 2, 1"

Holding the sword upwards he screamed as loud as he could, "I am the gatekeeper!" He was beaming.The gods would be proud. He charged out the front door. He resembled a brave soldier stampeding into battle. Fearlessly following his leader's commands. Oblivious to the consequences of his actions.

His brouhaha caught police by surprise. They refocussed their attention. They spotted the sword. Anthony was safely restrained. He released a silent cheer. His prayers had been answered. Unable to erase the images of his son's pleading face he began to tremble. Uncontrollable wailing.

Johnnie raced forward. Sword high in the air. Determined to gain attention. Audacious. Driven. Crazy.

"I am the gatekeeper! I am the gatekeeper!" he howled. His vehement ranting echoed through the quiet street.

"Stop Police, stop or we will shoot."

Johnnie spotted the police. He froze. He cheered. He jumped up and down. He threw the sword to the ground. He punched a double fisted victory. He had been noticed. He would soon be famous.

"I am the gatekeeper, the powerful gatekeeper!" he yelled jumping up and down. Hands waving in the air as if he were greeting his fans.

"Get on the ground and don't move," a voice demanded.

Johnnie dropped to his knees. He began to chuckle. His hands continued to wave.

"Look at me, look at me… I am the gatekeeper, I killed the evil," he cheered.

Within seconds his face smashed into the path. Police swooped in and forced him to his stomach. His giant hands made it difficult for him to be handcuffed. His crazy ranting continued. All weapons were holstered. An ambulance was called for Anthony. Johnnie was taken into custody.

CHAPTER FORTY SEVEN

Police declared the initial crisis over. An ambulance arrived for Anthony and a police officer accompanied him to the hospital. He would be required to provide a statement as soon as practical. The lone suspect was taken into custody. He would undergo an extensive interview. He would be stripped, his bloodied clothes would be kept for evidence. His finger prints taken and DNA obtained. The crime scene was taped off. Additional officers were called to complete a sweep of the house and surrounding areas. Preserving and extracting evidence was crucial. Testimonial and physical evidence would establish key elements to the case. Their findings, nothing less than grim.

Officers were stunned. Probationary Constable Walden described it as, "A brutal blood bath." It was a scene he would never forget. No one expected to discover multiple victims.

Under the house they unearthed what appeared a mass grave. For the Major Crimes Squad and Forensic Officers their examinations were just beginning. A full investigation was essential. Great care was required to avoid disturbing or destroying vital evidence. Every crime scene was three dimensional. Every crime and crime scene was different. Nothing could be dismissed. No conclusion could be drawn. No assumptions made. Stains, marks, fingerprints, footprints, blood spatter, drag marks, hairs, fibres, all evidence required gathering. The scene was searched, examined, reviewed and analysed.

Evidence had to be accurate, investigations had to be methodical and detailed and above all unbiased.

The first body discovered was that of a male, possibly in his early to mid teens. Lividity had set in, making his face and hands a dark greyish-blue. Rigor mortis had not yet begun. Smaller limbs such as the neck, arms, shoulders and legs were flexible. This made his removal from the scene easier. Time of death was estimated within the hour and was consistent with information provided. The young male was identified as thirteen year old, Benjamin White.

Removing the first body officers were shocked by the discovery of additional remains. Initial inspection determined the dismembered body parts belonged to an elderly male. They had been scattered with no regard, like off cuts thrown to a butcher's floor. The elderly male was identified as seventy six year old, Charles Benson.

Blood from the first and second victims spread over yet another shocking discovery. Half buried, skeletal remains. Bones, teeth and hair. In total another two bodies.

It was news which shocked the neighbourhood.

All remains were removed and taken away for forensic investigation. Each body would tell a story. Close analysis would determine how and what inflicted wounds. Forensic investigations would conclusively determine the cause of each death.

Autopsy findings – Benjamin White had sustained defensive wounds to his fingers, hands and arms, indicating he had put up a significant struggle attempting to defend himself and get away. Lacerations and bruising determined he had not died without a fight. Dirt found under his nails indicated he had clawed at the ground.

Cause of death, a fatal stab wound to the chest. The symmetrical elliptical wound with both ends pointed and clean cut edges without any associated bruising indicated a knife blade with a double edge. Cardiac penetration proved lethal. Significant force also resulted in penetration of the bone. A small metal fragment found in the bone matched the sword surrendered by the suspect. Blood evidence indicated he had been murdered outside just behind the side gate that framed the backyard. His body had been dragged under the house and dumped into the hole.

Charles Benson had sustained defensive wounds to fingers, hands and arms. Wounds were clean cut indicating a sharp weapon. The cuts appeared frenzied, shallow, deep, long and short. Made by an attacker who was in a heightened state of excitement. Several fingers had been completely severed. Two fingers were discovered on the floor behind the front door of the house. His body had been dismembered. The hole under the house was the dump site. Investigations determined the attack to have taken place in the lounge area of the house. A pool of blood with matching DNA was located close to the internal stairs.

DNA evidence, the recovery of a sword, fingerprints, wound analysis and the suspect's chilling confession confirmed what investigators suspected. Jonathon Fox had murdered twice. Charles Benson was an unsuspecting victim killed in cold blood, simply to cover up his manic behaviour. Charles Benson had been in the wrong place at the wrong time. Benjamin White had known the killer. No logical motive was given for his murder other than they had had a disagreement. Jonathon was adamant in his belief that Benjamin deserved to die as he was evil.

A step by step account was provided by the killer, it mapped out in detail the horrific events.

DNA samples were gathered from the skeletal remains. Tests proved beyond any doubt the remains belonged to husband and wife, Reginald and Eleanor Rumming. The two had lived at the residence up until they vanished without a trace on Christmas Eve in 1939. It was a mind blowing find. What was more stupefying was the confession found at the scene. A hand written note, dated and signed by none other than William Bunbagel; grandfather to Jonathon Fox.

Felicity Fox's world came crashing down around her with one knock at the door. Her son was in police custody. He had been charged with one count of grievous bodily harm with intent to murder. Further charges were expected to be laid. These included two counts of murder. Distraught, she collapsed to the floor and burst into tears. It was a mothers worst nightmare. *How can this be happening?* She thought.

The revelations were devastating. Felicity's world was ripped apart. During her police interview she admitted to her son returning home earlier in the day. She broke down as she described his dishevelled state; how she had mistakenly shrugged off his haunting words and had tried to rationalise what appeared to be blood covering his body. She recalled Johnnie had said, "I did a bad thing." But how could any parent believe a bad thing would be so bad? He had described a castle, his words strikingly familiar to those she had heard from her father. When she was growing up her father had claimed he had buried bodies under a castle. She had justified his claims by reassuring herself he was simply trying to scare her. Overwhelmed by the unmasked reality she was sick. The interview was suspended. Resuming ten minutes later, she was shown a sealed evidence bag. This contained a hand written confession to two murders in 1939. Felicity was mortified. She acknowledged the writing could have belonged to her father. It was extremely similar. She had no doubt he may have been involved. The date on the letter was just before he had been sent to goal for the last time. Her suspicions were confirmed by forensic handwriting experts. The signature at the end of the confession was that of William Bunbagel.

Jonathon Fox remained composed as he delivered his chilling confession. He was a bloody mess, calm and content. He displayed no remorse as he spoke. When asked if he had murdered he replied, "Yes." When asked if he had planned to murder he replied, "No." When asked why he had murdered he replied, "I just lost it." He paused, staring towards the ceiling, his eyes vacant. He grinned.

"They deserved to die," he said in a haughty dismissive tone. He was unflinchingly brutal as he revealed his motives behind the murders while sipping on a cup of water.

"I did it for the good of all for I am the gatekeeper. Do with me what you wish. I killed them. They deserved to die. They were evil." His words defied moral logic. He took pleasure in the act of taking a life. He seemed to enjoy slowly revealing his secrets. His words limited. He appeared smug and accepting.

"That's all I am saying, do with me what you wish… I did it, I murdered them… That's all I am saying." He closed his eyes. He refused to say another word.

Anthony trembled with anger and grief. His story was painfully sad, tragic and horrific. His wounds reflected the nightmare he had survived. Detectives assured him they would do everything in their power to keep Jonathon Fox behind bars. A full confession had been provided. Anthony smiled, he thanked them for their support. He thanked the residents of Sydney for their outpouring of support. He released a statement requesting privacy so that he may grieve.

CHAPTER FORTY EIGHT

Recovery - A time of reflection. A solemn moment and the deepest thoughts from a person far beyond reproach. How is it that life can be so confusing? Why do things not go as we plan? Is happiness real? We are all born into innocence. So what can be said about the virtue of a child? In their early years they are impressionable sponges who absorb everything. They start as a blank, unblemished canvas. Exposed to the world they must adapt. Mindful of their surroundings they comply. Adults actively mould the attitudes of those children around them. Shared environments result in mutual views. They hear our secrets and they themselves learn how to be secretive. They discover our lies and they themselves master this treacherous behaviour. As they mature they acknowledge us as their teacher. Attitudes are their platform. Learned behaviour their building blocks. Our opinions, behaviour and attitudes are reflected within theirs.

Racism, bigotry, prejudice and hate - these are all learned behaviours.

Love, acceptance, open mindedness - these are all learned behaviours.

Rules and ramifications enforce acceptable actions. Without guidance a child may become lost. Ignore a child and they will be drawn towards whatever appears attractive, like a moth to light. Love shared. Lessons learned. Treachery creates indifference. When we get older and mature we realise the relevance of time, the importance of taking control of our lives. We realise time lost, can not be found. We can not undo the mistakes we have made. Ingrained views and beliefs become difficult to change.

We are all the architects of our own fate. While some people prefer to take a back seat and simply go with the flow others possess an internal drive. A drive that requires them to take charge of every situation. I am the latter of these two. From the very start my destiny was one of greatness. There was no way on earth I could just idly sit by and watch others destroy what was so clearly intended to be mine. My lessons had been varied. I had experienced both great happiness and misery. I had been taught we all have a place in life. I had been taught the best victim was a blind victim and the best attack was by surprise. I had also been taught to achieve forgiveness one must first reveal the truth. Life was all about living and learning. Some lessons were harder than others. We are all engineered by nature and nurture. Our actions persuaded and influenced by others. In life sacrifices were essential. Some sacrifices were made in order to protect. Events create memories. Not all memories were pleasant.

From a young age we hear of stories, fairytales, myths, legends, and fanciful creatures. In our innocence we close our eyes and believe we can see, touch, smell, hear and sense the truth in the words.

It is only as we mature that we differentiate between what is real and what is questionable. But then we must go back to the blank canvas. Is the sky really blue or it is blue because that is what we were told? Is there honestly no parallel universe? Who says there is? Who says there is not? And what about Darius, does he really exist? Is there really anything else beyond what we can see?

Is happiness just a word or will I find it one day?

Only time would tell. Confusion. A solemn moment to reflect on my deepest thoughts.

One thing I knew for certain was the secrets and lies of one person, even from years gone by have the ability to affect those in the future. We should all be careful of what we say. Secrets and lies will not remain hidden forever. There will always be a time when someone discovers where the secrets lie.

LEANNE WOOD

CHAPTER FORTY NINE

More recently I had been exposed to a new teaching. A belief regarding the Sacrament of Penance. I had listened in church as Father David described sin as a raging infection, a pus like bacteria that damaged the soul. Venial sins; such as impatience, unkind words and gossiping inflicted slight wounds. While mortal sins; grave acts that were committed with free will and the knowledge that the matter was grave had the ability to propel the sinner into an abyss of fire and fury. Without absolution, mortal sins could not be forgiven and the soul damns itself to the eternal abode of Satan and his angels of darkness. A place of velvet gloom, filled with pain and horror, where your soul is engulfed by fear and sadness, tortured by eternal unrest within the endless lakes of fire.

Father David's words instilled fear. I did not want to be cast aside or damned to hell for all eternity. The Sacrament of Penance represented a clearing of my conscience and involved three simple things. Contrition, I had to examine my conscience and be remorseful of my sins with a true purpose to amend my ways. The next step was to take confession, only when I confessed my sins would I be able to gain satisfaction; the penance and finally I would be given absolution.

Kneeling down behind the panelled wall with its olive green curtain the only thing that could be heard was my breath and I wondered what would happen next. Should I speak up or just wait? It had been years since I had experienced a confession. The last time I had attended church with any sense of regularity was when I was a child. Was the Priest near me or was I foolishly alone? Looking up I studied my surrounds. I was enclosed within a box like structure. It was somewhat dark inside with a musty smell of old timber. I wondered if it was like being encased within a coffin only this space was a tad bigger.

My studying and wondering thoughts ceased when I heard Father David clear his throat from the other side of the confessional. I could not see him and he could not see me.

"May God bless you that you may make a good confession. In the name of the Father and of the Son and of the Holy Spirit."

His voice was deep yet the projection of his words gentle. I wondered if those outside would hear our words. Making a sign of the cross as he spoke my nerves increased. I felt as though I should just flee. Would the repentance of my sins resolve my ever burdening visions? Would it put a halt to the voices? What would be achieved by telling another soul of my wrongdoings? Would Father David judge me? Would I be his number one topic of conversation? Would he take details of my confession to the authorities? A priest is bound by the seal of the confessional to never reveal details heard during reconciliation by a penitent. Would this apply even in those cases that involved murder?

"Forgive me father for I have sinned. I have not been to confession for years and these are my sins. I have wished evil on others, committed evil deeds and participated in unspeakable acts at least a dozen times. I have lied and committed perjury three times. I have crossed the path of evil and have been forced by this evil to take part in the murder of another person on one occasion. I have been overwhelmed by my greed for riches, doubted my faith, given up on hope more times than I can remember."

Bowing over all was silent and so I continued disclosing all those details I felt necessary in order to move on hindrance free. Once I began the words flew from my mouth like verbal diarrhoea. I wanted to make sure I included absolutely everything, no matter how big or small. If I included even the slightest of sins then maybe, just maybe Father David would believe my words were sincere.

"I have had at least twenty five impure thoughts and failed to attend Mass for many, many years. I have acted out of jealousy and wished ill on others countless times. For all of these sins and those which I can not recall I am genuinely sorry as I ask for forgiveness. I wish to be a better person, I promise to amend my ways and to live abalanced and virtuous life. I am truly sorry."

For a moment there was silence and I wondered if he would ever speak. Had my confession been too large, too telling? Maybe I should have held off on some detail but then it would not be possible to move forward. Father David coughed, then coughed again. Was he lost for words?

"You say you were responsible for murder," he paused. I sat silently nodding my head. He continued, "what was the context of your action? Was your act deliberate? Was it an accident? Did you act in self defence? God forgives all sin but you too must be able to forgive yourself."

Inhaling deeply, I feared if I gave too many details Father David would work out who I was.

"I did not mean to kill. I thought I was going to be killed. I knew I was going to be killed. He told me.

He said; I am going to kill you. It was kill or be killed. He forced my hand and for that I have great regret." Breaking down I began to sob, it was the first time I had disclosed these details. As the words left my lips I could feel a weight lift from my shoulders.

Father David cleared his throat.

"When we sin we have failed. We are conscious of this failure. It is like when we cut ourselves. We bleed. We bandage. Our wound heals. But our wound leaves a scar. We are conscious of this scar. Our scar reminds us of the cut we once suffered; the pain we experienced. Although we may not notice our scar every day, we never forget. It is the healing process that takes time. God forgives all sin, but we still need the gift of healing. I do believe you are truly sorry for your actions. I can hear the pain within your voice; you have struggled with this detail. And now you have opened your heart to the Lord and you must show your repentance. To do this you must help out in the Matt Talbot soup kitchen in Sydney for the next month. Although I would encourage you to speak with the authorities. I cannot make this a condition of the absolution. However speaking with the authorities will assist in your search for peace. Without peace you may never heal; the wounds from your actions will eat away at you and weigh on you. As I said, God forgives all sin but we still need the gift of healing."

Nodding my head I said nothing, believing I had said enough already. I had been kneeling down for what felt like an eternity. I had disclosed my most guarded secrets and at last it seemed as though he would speak the words I longed to hear. He would grant me absolution. I would stand tall as I left the church. I would walk proud, unburdened of my wrongdoings. I would happily complete my penance as a sign of inner conversion.

"God, the Father of mercies through the death and resurrection of his Son has reconciled the world to himself and sent the Holy Spirit among us for the forgiveness of sins. Through the ministry of the Church may God give you pardon and peace, and I absolve you from your sins in the name of the Father, and of the Son and of the Holy Spirit. Give thanks to the Lord, for he is good. His mercy endures for ever. The Lord has freed you from your sins. Go in peace to love and serve the Lord."

"Amen," I cheered.

Jumping to my feet I grabbed the door handle and thrust it open. Inhaling the cool fresh air I dared not to look back as I made my hasty exit.

CHAPTER FIFTY

Walking out of the church I sighed with relief. It was over, it was all over. At home Rebecca would welcome me with open arms. She and I had grown close over recent times. She had offered more support than I could have ever wished for. Rebecca believed in the church and all it represented. She understood the importance of forgiveness. Her kind heart and forgiving nature were traits I could only wish to develop over time. Extending her hand of friendship and generosity when I was most vulnerable had been my saving grace. Taking me under her wing and offering words of wisdom had provided hope. I knew going to confession would bring a smile to her face. I wanted Rebecca to be happy.

An overwhelming calm pervaded my body. An inner peace. Standing still I inhaled the freshness of the air. My lungs expanding as my eyes closed. My back straightened as my arms stretched up towards the heaven above. Opening my eyes I was welcomed by bright red hands streaking across the sky. It was a sign. I was sure it was a sign. Tomorrow would be the dawn of a brand new day, a new life.

It was time to head home.

Strolling along the pathway one lone little voice spoke, "I have a castle, it holds much more than just a secret garden." The voice reminded me that some family secrets were worth keeping.

I smiled.